# THE FACTS

## BEHIND THE DISAPPEARANCE of B.W. LANE

## By L. WARREN BRYANT

*Fiction wanders down a path through a forest of reality.*

*Many of the characters and incidents in these pages are the product of the author's imagination; however, there are many references to circumstances, events and people which are quite real. The reader can sort through "the facts."*

*They said, "You can't prove anything."*
*He said, "I don't have to... it's fiction."*

Copyright © 2013 L. Warren Bryant
FORTUNE * WELLS AND ASSOCIATES
All rights reserved.

ISBN: 0988863405
EAN-13: 9780988863408

Library of Congress Control Number: 2013930661
CreateSpace Independent Publishing Platform, North Charleston, SC

# CHAPTER ONE

Was this happening or was it a nightmare?

Through eerie shadows of the early morning, the stillness had a tranquil effect on the soldiers as they watched the village across the clearing—that is, until the silence was broken by a stern voice that crackled from a radio that was strapped to the young man's camouflage vest.

"Wolf, do you have the target?"

There was no response.

"Wolf…China Seven. Do you read? Have you acquired the target?"

"Sir, I have the target, but there's no enemy."

"Fire the goddamn missile, Wolf, or by God, I'll come over there and fire it myself!"

Silence was the only answer.

The stern whisper continued, "Did you hear me? You either fire the son of a bitch at them or fire it at me!"

\* \* \*

The first week of January should be a great time for starting new projects. After all, each New Year has a life of its own. For some people, its pages full of new goals; for others, the New Year only provides an opportunity to fail a New Year's resolution.

No one keeps resolutions anyway. It's a ruse. At least this was the opinion of Grant Harris as he left his two-bedroom apartment in Houston's West Village and headed toward the Southwest Freeway.

It wasn't a great day. To begin with, it was colder and wetter than it was supposed to be in the sunny coastal bend of Texas, and everyone knows bad weather can hamper one's ability to keep New Year's resolutions, particularly if they're difficult ones.

What was all this negativity about? His football team had gotten their butts kicked hard enough to knock them out of the playoffs, and if this defeat wasn't enough to start the year on the wrong foot, he had received a call to come into the office early to meet with Internal Affairs about a "significant" interagency request.

Grant sat at the entrance ramp to US 59 and waited for the traffic to pass. *FBI personnel should be exempt from traffic jams*, he thought. *Maybe they should pass a law… Hold it. No more laws. We've got too many as it is. Calm down. No point being in a hurry. I may not get there at all.*

He smiled, remembering his New Year's resolution—to slow down and relax.

*Right? Slow down and relax. In this job? Can't.*

His last few months had been a nightmare at fast pace, but slow down and relax is what he needed to do—right now.

Slow down, be calm; a tough resolution to keep when you're driving into downtown Houston. Slowing down or stopping is very easy, but being calm and relaxed during the process is not.

Grant finally begged his way onto the entrance ramp. Traffic during rush hour, particularly on US 59, had a way of being unforgiving. It seemed he always ended up in the wrong lane, and just when the traffic was either stopped or barely moving was when he had to meet with Internal Affairs.

*Oh, well*, he thought. *Don't worry. It'll probably be a discussion about something that'll never matter to anyone anyway.*

Grant reflected on many subjects and combed his mustache with his forefinger as he watched the traffic creep along.

*Internal Affairs. Those people just make work for themselves. But an "interagency" request is better than an "internal" problem. Probably should have taken another route, Westheimer. It has a hundred lights, but at least it moves.*

The FBI offices were located in the dead center of the worst traffic congestion in the state of Texas. Somehow the government had a way of committing those blunders. The GSA couldn't even pick a reasonable site for an office. *Nothing I can do about it now,* he thought.

Then there was the matter of his New Year's resolution.

As the circus of automobiles finally started a slow crawl down the freeway, he reflected on the traffic problems again. *Maybe they create the situation themselves,* he thought. *The government employs too many people. This is the reason for all this traffic.*

Grant decided to suggest this to Internal Affairs; maybe they could fix the problem by getting rid of some people. He chuckled to himself. A GS15 shouldn't be thinking this way.

Anyway, today's meeting might create an occasion to see Delaney— Special Agent Eve Delaney, the prize of Internal Affairs. Maybe she would handle the case herself. Now, there would be a possibility for the New Year.

Grant considered the bright side. His cholesterol was normal, and he wasn't more than a couple of pounds overweight. He still worked out two or three times a week, when he wasn't in some other FBI office scoring political points or at a training seminar explaining "clue-arrangement strategies in crime solving" to new recruits.

Thankfully, he didn't have much to do with politics anymore, simply because he wasn't as good at playing the game as he once was. His last three promotions were strictly due to merit: no orchestrated effort, no political games. "No politics" was how he liked it.

*Exit downtown, and then I'm home,* he thought. *Home? What? The office is home?*

Grant thought, this time aloud, "I need a vacation."

Unfortunately he had to wait a while. This year's vacation wouldn't be until June. He'd have the kids for two weeks, and they could all go on a trip to the mountains. Jacob and Laura were barely teenagers but the perfect age for a great trip this year. They could do some hiking, fly-fishing, and have a good time camping. The kids were looking forward to it, and so was he.

Why did he have to start out the New Year with 'interagency' business? Interagency requests just led to politics, and he didn't feel political.

Grant had been an agent with the FBI since he had graduated from law school almost twenty-five years before. Now, as the assistant bureau chief, or assistant SAC (Special Agent in Charge), he had plenty of stroke but his true value as an agent was his supernatural ability to see and interpret circumstances that led to solving crimes. He could project the direction of an investigation, intuitively know the players, and many times conclude the answer before anyone else knew the question.

Nothing of importance escaped his attention. He listened to what was said and how it was heard. Words were so important because small things make big pictures. Ideas from conversations, books, songs, poems—they all formulate thought, and hence, motivation, and the "why" becomes critical. Someone once commented that, when playing the board game Clue, Grant could ask everyone just one question and then tell you that Colonel Mustard had done it with a candlestick in the library before anyone could sort their cards. If you know anything about the game, this would require reviewing a lot of possibilities and cutting to the chase.

Now look at him. He was starting to get burned out. He had been elected "Most likely to…" in his senior class, but he couldn't remember 'most likely' for what.

'Most likely' to be stalled in traffic on a Houston freeway. 'Most likely' to become upset and break his New Year's resolution…

With a small sigh, he rescued himself from his negative thinking. *Relax,* he told himself.

Thankfully, the traffic yielded to his positive attitude. Finally he turned the last corner and arrived at the building. As he turned into the private parking entrance, he watched as the automatic gate arm pointed to his office three floors above.

Perfect. He had successfully completed the mission, again…just as he did nearly every day. He looked at his watch. Of course, today's drive had taken two minutes longer than his normal commute, but the traffic had been a nine on the scale.

*Look at the bright side,* he told himself. *The gate arm functioned properly today. It may be a good year yet, and my resolution is still intact.*

Grant exited the elevator on the third floor, said hello to the guard at the information counter, walked to a steel door, and punched in his security code. The door opened, and he walked past the receptionist and toward a large room with many official-looking cubicles.

"Good morning, Georgia." He winked as he passed the middle-aged secretary.

She smiled. "Watch yourself, Chief Harris. Sexual harassment, you know."

Grant smiled back and continued down the aisle. "You'd *better* smile when you say that, or you won't get a raise."

The Justice Department had received an overabundance of ridiculous cases involving sexual harassment claims, to a point where those that were serious couldn't receive the needed attention. Of course, all the cases used FBI investigation files, and it generated an increased workload for everyone. Far too many lawyers were trying to hop aboard the money train.

As Grant opened his office door at the end of the aisle, the intercom buzzed.

"Special Agent Delaney telephoned." It was Georgia's voice. "She's running about fifteen minutes late. The traffic's bad coming in on the Southwest Freeway."

*It is Delaney*, Grant thought. *The interagency request should be more interesting. Much better.*

He smiled to himself and responded, "I came in on the Southwest Freeway, and I was on time. Have you noticed traffic is only a factor for people in Internal Affairs?"

They both laughed lightly, then Georgia asked, "Do you want some coffee?"

Grant responded to the intercom as he headed back toward the door, "I'll bring you one."

After the brief distraction from the routine of the first Monday morning after the holiday, Grant returned to his office and looked through the briefs on the front page of the *Wall Street Journal*. Typical crimes, business, foreign affairs, no White House scandals to report. *It's the nineties,* he thought. *Anything goes in Washington.*

A certain diversion, however, continued as his thoughts refocused on Special Agent Evangeline J. Delaney.

Evangeline Delaney was a staffer, the department head for Internal Affairs, and an extremely attractive woman in her late thirties. She looked just like her name—like an 'angel'—and her written name, Evangeline

Justine Delaney, looked as pretty as she did. She had medium-length brunette hair with enough of a dark-red essence to confirm her Irish heritage, along with blue-green eyes that Grant was sure could glow like Kryptonite through a lead door.

In general, no one was fond of Internal Affairs types or auditors, but Delaney was more tolerated than others. She was intelligent, committed, aggressive, and fair. Actually, she was a case of her own. She presented herself as so totally capable that she was almost intimidating.

It was probably her eyes. Call it intuition, or whatever, but she could read people—and she wasn't timid or shy with her knowledge. When she thought the time was right, she'd be very direct and use whatever information she had. People who knew her well called her Eve or by her nickname, Evee.

Grant admired her from a distance and even had thought about asking her out on a date at some point, but he dismissed the thought. Such an action might interfere with FBI business. 'Interference' was the same excuse he used for all the women he thought about asking out.

Did she intimidate him? No.

The true problem was a big question that remained unanswered in many of Grant's current relationships—whether she would say yes, or whether he could handle the answer if it was no. It could have been this uncertainty, or maybe he hadn't fully recovered from his divorce.

A year should have been long enough for him to get past the marriage, but he had been off the market for almost twenty years. Grant even questioned if he knew how to behave on a date.

He took a moment to try to evaluate his feelings.

*What is it about Delaney that causes so much emotion to build inside me?* He wondered. *Is it recognition of my own loneliness? Can I admit it?*

He wanted to be lost in those beautiful eyes. There was something about her mood and manner, not just her beauty that drew him into an unexplained alliance with her.

Grant reflected on the first time he had seriously noticed Eve at the previous year's Fourth of July party. He was standing in the office mezzanine thinking somberly about his divorce when she had approached him. He was listening to a song from a KLOL oldies program that was playing on the Muzak system. It had caught his attention, and evidently Eve had noticed. The song, Tom Springfield's "The Carnival Is Over," was performed by The Seekers.

Eve walked up to Grant while the song played. *Like a drum my heart was beating, and your kiss was sweet as wine, but the joys of love are fleeting for Pierrot and Columbine… Now the harbor lights are calling, this will be our last goodbye… Though the carnival is over, I will love you till I die…*

He thought about how he felt looking into her eyes, but he hesitated. He couldn't allow anything to get started; his divorce had only been final for a few months. How would it look for him to be dating so soon?

Eve spoke. "Is the carnival over?"

Grant smiled. "Never went there, but looking at you makes me want to go."

Staring intently at him, she said, "Not like Pierrot and Columbine." She hesitated. "Do you know who they are?"

"No, I don't."

Before she had a chance to respond, another agent, Jeff Heard, interrupted them, and the conversation was awkwardly halted.

Eve said, "Maybe someday we'll have a chance to talk about it."

Although nothing had transpired since their chance encounter, Grant cherished his thoughts of the brief conversation and reviewed them often.

*Is it all right?* He wondered. *Would it be OK for a boss to go out with a subordinate? Would it cause problems? Could I be accused of sexual harassment just for asking? What would people say? Which article is it that stipulates you have to be at the same level before you can even talk to somebody?*

Grant dwelled on these thoughts for another moment then threw his attention back to the *Journal*.

\* \* \*

Grant's office was a mixture of the symbols of early US government service and a fifteen-year history of fatherhood. Pictures of his two kids, at every age, appeared on his desk and in every open space. A pastel drawing of a beautiful orange-and red-sunrise, titled *Fire in the Sky*, decorated the wall across from his desk, and a brass statue of an eagle flew up from the credenza below. He liked the way he felt when he looked at the sunrise piece, and he also liked the title.

A quick view of the office might have established him as an attorney, the identification coming from the stacks of legal-size file folders that seemed to grow from every inch of his large desk and the floor surrounding it. Grant liked to leave all his active work where he could see it. His mind dealt with all of his cases at once, like a computer database, and if he needed to see a file, he didn't want to take the time to pull it out of some drawer. Filing cabinets were for when he was through with a file, which didn't happen until the case was solved.

He retrieved another cup of coffee and sat down at his desk. *Which agency needs help this time? Since it's the first of the year*, he projected to himself, *it's going to be Treasury, probably Customs or the IRS.*

He hated those requests.

*Or maybe it'll be something more interesting, like the State Department. Maybe it'll have to do with some investigation that will lead to Hawaii, and I can handle the case myself.*

For an uncomfortable moment, he regressed, remembering his wedding…and his honeymoon trip to Maui.

*Stop the press!* He thought. *Don't print the 'failed marriage' story. That's a bad idea, a personal game of nostalgia. No more time on the past. No looking back.*

Reversed thinking was negative energy—time wasted. Grant knew what had gone wrong with his marriage. He opposed surrendering his entire life to the pursuit of Junior Service League favors and never-ending social schedules, but he wasn't sorry for the experience. It was time to just bag it and leave it. Fortunately he did have the kids and some good memories.

A couple of minutes departed from the clock, and the buzzer sounded again.

"Agent Delaney is coming in to see you, and she has someone with her."

"Thank you."

In a beat, Eve Delaney walked through the open door and introduced her guest.

"This is Agent Jackson, CIA, Grant, and they need our assistance."

CIA. That answered Grant's first question. However, this particular agency, in itself, opened a myriad of other questions. When the CIA needed anyone's assistance, it was usually a severe problem. Grant knew the drill. The CIA created more problems than they ever corrected, and Central Intelligence carried an attitude that proclaimed they didn't need any help from anyone.

When Grant first had decided on government law enforcement early in his career, he had a chance to go the CIA route but chose not to. Anyone working for the CIA had to be able to "act without question and kill without a reason." Grant couldn't do that—with a reason, yes, but it had to be a damn good reason.

As Grant stood up and offered his hand, he studied Jackson. The agent was unassuming: short of six feet and not very big. He appeared too rugged-looking to be wearing that impeccably tailored suit and fifty dollar tie. After acknowledging Delaney, they seated themselves. Grant leaned forward and looked directly at the man, who carried a typical CIA emotionless gaze. "What do you have, Jackson?"

Having been down this road before, he knew the FBI wasn't going to get all the facts, because CIA operatives didn't work that way. As a group—and in all circumstances he had ever witnessed—they held every piece of information on a need-to-know basis. In short, they wouldn't tell you squat.

Jackson spoke in a low, steady voice, more like a tape recording than in a conversational tone. "We've lost an item, and we need your help finding it."

*An item?* Grant thought. *I know what 'an item' is.*

He stared at Jackson, then at Eve Delaney, then back at Jackson. "Are we talking about a person-type item, Agent Jackson?"

Grant knew the answer. He just wanted to ask the question. After all, this guy was in his office and needed his assistance.

"His name is Benjamin Wells Lane, and he disappeared last Friday. He was a one-time operative back in the sixties, and he's been under class-three surveillance since 1969."

*Oh, wow!* Grant thought. *This guy has been tracked off and on for almost thirty years?* Grant was very controlled in response. "That's a long time, Jackson. Why were you watching him? What'd he do?"

Grant paused, read Jackson's constraint, and saw the jerk was preparing to evade the answer and stall. He waited for the perfect timing.

When Jackson started to respond, Grant joined him, and together they repeated in unison, "Need to know."

Grant shook his head. "That's the trouble with you guys. You ask for our help, but you won't give us any information."

Jackson maintained his perfect imitation of a wax dummy. Grant glanced over and smiled at Delaney, shook his head, then shot arrows from his eyes back at Jackson.

"What do you want me to do with him when I find him?"

Jackson replied very matter-of-factly, "Just tell us where he is, and we'll take care of it from there."

Grant remarked facetiously, "Yeah, I'll bet you'll take care of it. You're dreaming. You guys can't do anything in-country. You understand that, right? You shouldn't even be watching him. He's got rights, you know."

Grant and Delaney looked at each other and traded disgusting smirks. It was apparent Eve didn't think any more highly of the other agency than he did, and Jackson's behavior was textbook CIA.

Jackson placed a folder on Grant's desk. "This file contains everything you need to know about him. After you read it, if you think there's anything else you need to know, call me, and I'll get another release approved through channels. I can tell you it has to do with information of a very sensitive nature."

"Yeah, it's all sensitive…isn't it, Jackson?"

"We need to have Lane back in, and we need him in now. I can't stress this enough. Timing is critical. We need to know whether anything has happened to him, and we need to find him before anybody else does." Although Grant was puzzled and short of information on many fronts, one question immediately stood out. "What do you mean, 'before anyone else does'? Who the hell else is after him?"

Back to his wax-dummy routine, Jackson responded, "That information wasn't in my briefing."

"You've had him in your sights for twenty-five or thirty years, and you haven't used him for anything. He disappears, and you want him back in? It doesn't sound to me like he was ever 'in.' "

This rock wasn't going to roll, and Grant knew it, so he called it like a line judge, without hesitation and precisely as he saw the answer. "You want to make sure he doesn't embarrass your department by talking about something you guys did in sixty-nine."

Jackson was silent.

"What makes you think the other guys don't have him now? You're going to have to tell me who they are."

The CIA was in the corner with this comment, and Jackson apparently knew it. It was time for the CIA agent to retreat. "Mr. Harris, I don't have all the information myself, and all I'm authorized to give you is in this file. I haven't even read all of it."

He motioned to the file as if it would confirm his story. Of course, it didn't matter to Grant. He knew the meeting was over. Match point.

Delaney and Grant stood up at exactly the same time, and Grant smiled at her as he extended his parting comment to Jackson. "You get that next release approved so you can tell me who else is involved in this thing. I'll be in touch."

After the two departed down the aisle, Grant sat down and looked at the sunrise on the office wall.

*Fire in the Sky…*

He looked back at the file. It wasn't very thick and was probably a tutorial in redaction.

Clearly it was just some CIA information about a guy who had done something, or knew something, back in 1969, something that had followed him like a nightmare for a few decades.

Maybe he could get Delaney to work with him on this case. Those penetrating eyes—maybe she could see straight through the cover of this file and tell him what had happened to the guy.

More than likely, he would have to find out what the CIA didn't want him or anyone else to know. What happened in 1969? And why the rush? What was so critical about the timing? Why was all of this so urgent? Who else was involved?

The worst thing about this situation wasn't the secrecy, nor was it the hindered involvement. Grant could get past the roadblocks, but he knew the downside. If the CIA wanted B.W. Lane badly enough to ask for FBI assistance, they were desperate. Although they couldn't operate in the United States, they could covertly deal with their own. More than that, if the FBI was going to find this guy Lane, Grant and his staff had better be quick. The CIA would be continuing its search, and if Lane was still around, he wouldn't have much time.

Grant stopped and stared at the picture on the wall again, *Fire in the Sky*. Yes. He liked this kind of adventure and recollected others from his past.

This situation was similar to another case he remembered. It involved a Cuban businessman shortly after the Bay of Pigs fiasco. Grant was a student at the time, and too young to remember it clearly now, but he did study some of the old FBI files, the ones that contained unsolved crimes. In this particular case, the Bureau was sure the CIA, or one of its other clandestine undercover units, had eliminated a man because he had threatened to expose their screw-up. They were bad and made an example of anyone who snitched on them. The CIA shot the man so many times that they had to use dental records to prove who he was, and the case remained an unsolved mystery—unsolved to the uninformed, but a few people can see beyond what others let pass as obvious.

The sunrise on the wall and the brass eagle flying toward it kept Grant's attention.

*How much do you suppose the contracts are paying?* He asked himself. *What does Lane know, and how much is his silence worth? How did this man stay out of the CIA's way for so long?*

Something in this file would have to spark an answer. Some facts had to be hidden in the pages, facts that should provide some answers about the disappearance of Benjamin Wells Lane.

# CHAPTER TWO

After three hours or so with the CIA file, Grant retreated through the noise and busy-ness of the outer office and ended up in the men's room. He splashed some water on his face and gazed into the mirror.

*Mirror, mirror on the wall...*

Never mind. He wasn't the fairest, never was.

For a moment he felt sorry for himself. After all, he was middle-aged, divorced, single, and alone. What a shame for the guy who once won a contest for looking the most like Magnum, P.I. He was just over six feet tall, with dark hair, handsome—more or less—and a thick mustache. Although he might have borne a slight resemblance to Tom Selleck, he didn't feel like *Magnum* today. This case was peculiar to start with and becoming more complicated by the minute, and his intuition told him he was behind the door. As he gazed at his reflection, questions grew from his confusion.

*If the CIA wants him and they didn't get him, who did? They say he disappeared. Is he lost to them or to everyone? After almost thirty years, why do they want him all of a sudden? Why is this so urgent, and who else wants him and why?*

Grant sprinted a ten-second hundred back to his office. He buzzed the intercom to call Georgia, who appeared almost immediately.

She was an excellent staff assistant and liked to be prompt, prepared, and professional. Georgia was also very fond of Grant, as were all the people on the third floor. It might have been his pleasant demeanor, or his rustic smile, or simply his way with people. He always found time to be friendly, and he paid attention to everyone and almost every detail.

Grant, however, had cast his typical mood and manner aside today as he appeared in one of his trancelike stupors. When deep in thought, he just stared at the painting or the eagle. Such was the case today.

After a prolonged silence, he said, "Georgia, this guy seemed to be an ordinary businessman. He owned a couple of apparently successful businesses, an insurance agency and an Internet service. According to the information in the file, he paid his taxes, went to church, and probably helped little old ladies cross the street. If the CIA has their story straight, he did something in sixty-eight or nine. Now they're hunting for him, and they want him desperately. At least according to the CIA's account, Lane has disappeared without a trace, and we need to find him…and also find out if someone else is after him."

Grant paused for a moment then continued. "Let's suppose he wasn't kidnapped. No foul play. Then he just took off. What would cause that?" He paused again. "I wasn't very good at being married, so answer a question for me." He paused for affect. "What would it take for a guy to just pack it and leave his family? How do you go through twenty-something years of marriage and then…?"

He stopped talking for a moment as he stared at the papers that covered his desk. For Grant, this behavior was common. He would talk to himself, ask himself questions, and interrupt himself constantly, while Georgia listened and took notes. She actually enjoyed the process. He'd assess the clues; she'd watch; and eventually he'd turn them into answers.

At the moment she was listening as a student to the teacher.

"He was married twice," Grant said, "once at the age of twenty to a woman named Bobbie. He had a daughter with her. He divorced eight years later, remarried after two, and is still with his second wife, Veronica. He has two teenage kids who are a little older than mine."

His strained expression showed feelings regarding the kids.

"Then blip! Gone. Off the radar screen. It's got to have something to do with whatever happened almost thirty years ago." Grant thought, *somebody's got to know something.*

Georgia looked puzzled as he continued to talk to himself while staring at the file folder.

"In the CIA file, there's no record of military service or problems with the law. We know Lane had a current passport." He hesitated. "Why don't you see what Washington has on him? Here's his address in McAllen, Texas." With a bit of humor, he added, "If the information isn't in one of those files Clinton lost at the White House."

Georgia recognized it wasn't actually a joke and knew instinctively not to comment.

"Call Hector Perez in Brownsville and tell him I'm coming down there; I haven't seen him in a while. Also see if a missing person has been reported to the police or to our office in McAllen. I can't remember who's heading up that office now."

Georgia continued to take notes, and Grant stopped talking for a moment, collecting his thoughts, then pressed on. "Find me someone who's familiar with computers and the Internet…a specialist. I know it's new technology, but since this guy Lane owned an Internet service, maybe we can find some clue out there on the ole' info super-highway. I mean one of our people, not an interagency loner, and one who knows it very well, not just a little. Get me the guy with the highest IQ out of all those whiz kids out there, and schedule a meeting with my team for two o'clock.

"I'll need our plane or a reservation to McAllen at the earliest time they can get me there tomorrow morning, and tell Perez or whoever runs the McAllen branch to pick me up. I need some fresh tapes for my recorder and a reservation for a rental car, just in case. What else?"

He must have realized how harsh and commanding it all sounded, so he finished with a big smile. "Thanks, Georgia."

As she prepared to exit, Grant's eye eased back to the sunrise pastel of the fire in the sky. He thought again about the CIA and their manner of handling problems, missing 'items' and such. A disturbed look clouded his face.

"Remember the movie *Three Days of the Condor?* Well, that may be all the time Mr. Lane is going to have."

In the remaining hour before the scheduled meeting, Georgia managed to get Lane's file updates from D.C.

A quick look from the master sleuth rendered no verdict—nothing in the passport inquiries, nothing of note in the Treasury application for an insurance bond; Treasury investigators handled those things, and he knew they were very thorough.

He did find that Lane had been audited twice by the IRS with no corrections. What…an honest man?

The only strange thing was the lack of information in any of the files before 1981—just a Social Security number. Grant thought about it briefly. Back in the 1960s, there were usually draft notices or draft-assigned lottery numbers, and there had to be a background check if the CIA had used him for anything—unless they hadn't used an FBI investigation and had done something on the covert side. Some of the operatives never had a file, and to the same point, some never had a name.

*Sometimes what you don't find is as important as what you do,* he thought. *Was this a clue?* In this case, 'no information' might prove to be 'a lot.'

Grant hadn't uncovered any significant evidence for the meeting with his team. Even so, he needed to inform them of the new case and get updates for all the other cases which were pending.

Since Senior Chief SAC William 'Will' Masters was out of the office for a month, Grant was handling all the administrative duties as well as his own work. He didn't care much for the management detail, but in the next year or so when Masters retired, he would be taking on the responsibility; so he tended to it faithfully, though with as much delegation as possible.

The only other new case since the holiday break involved five pints of blood that mysteriously appeared at the emergency room of the M.D. Anderson Cancer Hospital. Since there was no identification or consignee, the hospital immediately questioned the find. Although standard blood labels had been applied, the identifying inscriptions had been removed. Without indication of a shipper, and thinking the shipment might have been interstate, the hospital notified the FBI for assistance in tracking the source.

The team meeting concluded without event, and Grant informed his staff about his plan to leave town on the new 'interagency assist.' In the midst of the usual duties that consumed his time in the afternoon, the new mystery seemed to call from a distance. CIA smoke or something more? The FBI hadn't received any notification of missing persons, and the local FBI offices would be following up with local law enforcement before Grant arrived in McAllen in the morning.

He wondered about the actual circumstances surrounding Lane's disappearance. Those thoughts grew into a myriad of questions through the afternoon, the night, and the early-morning hours. Grant's thoughts seemed to zero in on the *absence* of facts. He was like a hound on the scent.

* * *

On the plane the next morning, he looked at his watch so often that he thought it stopped. Maybe it would be a good thing for Lane if time did stop. It would give the FBI an opportunity to gather some of the information the CIA was evidently hiding from them, and it would give Grant time to catch up.

He began to think about the case as if it were something personal. He deliberated about those people and their 'items.' The CIA had lost 'an item.' *Hell, they spend too much time reading comic books and watching themselves on television*, he thought.

The clandestine nature of the CIA's activity tended to make its agents weird; in fact he felt assured that 'weird' was a job prerequisite.

The plane landed, and Grant was greeted by Special Agent Hector Perez and Special Agent Cliff Bartow of McAllen, Texas. After cordial greetings and a short walk to the parking lot, they were on the way to McAllen Police Department.

Perez and Bartow related a conversation they'd had with Detective Mitchell Rice which informed them about the preliminary information that had been uncovered regarding Mr. Lane. Lane's wife, Veronica, had notified the police the preceding Friday evening, when her husband hadn't returned from work. The police explained they couldn't handle missing-persons requests until twenty-four hours had passed, but she convinced Rice that her husband wasn't one of those types who would fail to come home.

Lane had spoken with Veronica by phone and mentioned stopping by his Internet business on his way home. According to employees, he had been at that location and left around six fifteen p.m.

His Chevrolet suburban had been found in the H.E. Butt grocery store parking lot on North Tenth Street the following morning. It was unlocked, and the keys were on the floorboard. There were no signs of foul play, and the parking-lot security guard, who was on duty the previous evening, had not witnessed anything unusual.

Veronica Lane had been in touch with Detective Rice and, at last contact, hadn't received a call from her husband or anyone demanding anything. Although she thought he had been kidnapped, Lane's disappearance was still being handled by the PD as simply a missing-persons case.

Certain family members including Lane's brother had been with the Lanes over the weekend, and through Rice's exchanges, all felt the family was doing well given the circumstances. The children, ages fifteen and seventeen, were shaken by their father's disappearance and had been spending time at their grandmother's home, since they were on winter break from school. Although Lane's wife was in mild shock, she seemed to recover somewhat after the weekend.

None of this surprised Grant. He felt Lane's disappearance was more than likely related to the CIA's interest from the past. Where those people were involved no one else ought to be. There was never a seemingly good—or final—outcome in their schemes, and it gave a new definition to the word *lingering.*

*They intimidate you,* he thought, *and I'm sure Lane was intimidated, since he was under class-three surveillance for twenty-some years.*

In other words, Lane knew that the CIA knew where he was, and the CIA knew that he knew—McAllen, Texas, seven miles from the Mexican border.

A great place for a standoff.

Grant, Perez, and Bartow arrived at the police department and went directly to a meeting with Detective Rice. Grant started the discussion by offering his complete cooperation with Detective Rice's investigation.

Then Rice told Grant what he had both feared and expected. Two government people, with intelligence credentials, tried to ask Lane's employees some questions regarding his businesses and his family.

Grant sighed. "What did they learn?"

"Nothing. The office managers at both businesses wouldn't let them in and told them to talk to me." He continued, "I wouldn't tell them anything. First, I don't know anything. Second, I don't know who they are, and they wouldn't tell me on the phone. By the way, Mr. Harris, what's your interest?"

Grant spelled it out as honestly as he could. "We're handling this as a kidnapping case, which puts it in federal jurisdiction. Between us—and this needs to be kept at the highest level of secrecy, your eyes only and no more—Lane did some work for the government a long time ago, and we think that connection has something to do with his disappearance." Deepening the communication channel, Grant continued, "I'll need to know about any and all contacts those government people make around Lane's employees and family, and we need to find out who they are. Can you help me with that?"

Rice acknowledged that he would handle the assignment.

Grant went on, "Hector, you and Bartow make visits to the businesses and find out about the contacts with law enforcement, or anyone else for that matter. See how easy it'll be to get cooperation from the staff, and look for general information. I'm going to make a personal call on Mrs. Lane. I'll ask Detective Rice for a ride and an introduction."

Bartow was partial to Mexican food, so they all agreed to meet at Rosita's restaurant on Farm to Market Road 495—to the natives, Pecan Street—at noon for a review.

As Grant walked to the car with Rice, he spoke quietly to himself. "This is like playing soccer in the dark."

"What was that?" Rice asked.

Grant repeated, "This is like playing soccer in the dark. You can't see the ball. You just hear a bunch of guys shuffling around."

Rice thought about the comment and smiled. It was certain they couldn't see anything, at least not yet.

\* \* \*

After a brief and cordial introduction, Mrs. Lane and Grant retreated to the living room of B.W. Lane's castle.

An older home in a nice, established neighborhood, the house had restored hardwood floors and beautiful and immaculate landscaping. Grant liked the presentation; his eyes were drawn to the baby grand piano and the interesting mixture of antique and casual furniture. There was a blend of decorative iron and wicker and a zebra-print rug. Everything tied perfectly together. It was both interesting and inviting. Every piece of the décor seemed to have a story.

He wasn't sure whether it was a European flavor or simply an artistic touch of someone with talent, but the room definitely wasn't cold and sterile, as his ex-wife had favored.

After the brief regression, he focused his attention on Mrs. Lane. Veronica Lane was a mid-forties mother and housewife with a pleasant smile and demeanor. After having two children, she maintained an acceptable figure; auburn hair framed her light-blue eyes. As Grant looked around the room, he suddenly recognized a feeling. He was on hallowed ground.

He was in the middle of someone's space, and he knew instinctively that something was very, very wrong. Something was missing. Something had caused this peace to be interrupted. Lane wasn't here, but his footprint was. This was his domain, what he had created for himself. Yet it felt empty. Empty of what? What had happened? Did someone flip a switch, and Lane lost it? What did he suddenly discover? Was it something so startling that "it broke down his desires like a light through a prism"?

Grant remembered the verse from his favorite old First National Band album. He likened the verse to his failed marriage and to other things that break apart—"into yellows and blues and a tune that he could not have sung." Something was broken here. Was it personal, corporate, or both? Grant wasn't sure, but if it was a CIA tune, he knew no one could sing it.

"Mrs. Lane…"

"You can call me Veronica."

"OK, Veronica. I'm going to need your help to find your husband. I need to know everything you can tell me about him and you, the kids, the business, and as much as you know about his life before you…any details you think might be important, little things he said about his past, even if they didn't make sense."

"Do you think he was kidnapped?" she asked.

"It's a possibility, but since you haven't been contacted for money, let's hope not."

"Well, I think he's all right. He's a survivor. We've been married for twenty years, and I'm sure I'd know if he was dead." After a thoughtful pause, she added, "He was careful."

Grant followed up. "How was he careful?"

With confidence, Veronica responded, "It's like…like when we would go to a restaurant or a party, he counted people and remarked if something looked out of place. He always positioned himself with his back to a wall. Ben didn't like anyone standing behind him. He had to see the entrance of the room. He was careful. Maybe it was paranoia, but I never thought he was crazy."

"That strikes me as unusual. Did you ever ask where that behavior originated?"

"No, but I can tell you he didn't like surprises. He was always in control. He wouldn't let me give him a surprise party or anything. He wanted to know as much as possible about what to expect all the time."

"Did he ever tell you why?"

"He was poetic about it. He said he had to keep his life simple because his dreams were complex…and they were more important than most of his memories."

There had to be a clue in there somewhere.

What dreams? Good ones or bad ones? Happily married husbands and wives share everything with their spouses. At least this is what you're supposed to do. Grant admitted to himself that nothing is as it appears to be. Reflecting on his own marriage, he realized it had been more of a life of silent desperation.

"Anything else you can tell me?" he asked.

Veronica paused and continued thoughtfully, "He was intuitive. Smart. I mean, very smart…like a fox."

Grant continued to look around the room as he absorbed her comments. "Mrs. Lane, if we follow your hypothesis and your husband is OK, he's going to need some money to get by. Did he carry much with him?"

"Not more than a couple of hundred dollars, but he had checks and credit cards."

Grant thought about the credit cards for a moment and reasoned Lane probably knew enough not to use them, as the CIA could monitor them for location, date, and time. Veronica did say he was smart like a fox.

Grant was onto a feeling. "If he wasn't going to use any credit cards that could be tracked, he might have needed another way to get cash."

Veronica looked up, surprised. "He did have some cash here. He called it his 'running money.' It was his safety valve if the government ever closed the banks. It was for running the house, if it ever happened."

Grant had a different idea about what 'running money' was, but the "why" wouldn't have mattered, and the money was either there or it wasn't.

"Do you know where he kept it?"

Veronica stood up and headed toward the hall that led to the bedroom. "I'll be right back."

She returned almost immediately, appearing almost happily alarmed. "It's not there!"

Grant smiled to himself. "Mrs. Lane, I think you're right. For now your husband is OK."

He paused to let her relax with the moment.

"If he's hiding," he told her, "it may be to protect you and your children, but there must be something he's running from. Do you have any idea what?"

She thought for a moment then responded slowly. "Not anything he ever talked about, but now that this is happening, I have to say I'm not surprised."

"Has he given you clues over the years? Anything about government service. Military service?"

Veronica sat back as she gazed at a bronze casting of a Native American on horseback, holding a lance over his fallen enemy. The bronze said "Counting Coup" and that meant keeping score. As she stared at the piece, it seemed to transmit understanding, and she began to speak as if she were reciting from the tenth chapter of *The Biography of Benjamin Lane*.

"One time he told me he had worked on a top-secret project, and because of it, he had a military deferment." She smiled to herself. "After *Top Gun* came out, if someone asked him about it, he'd use Tom Cruise's line, 'I could tell you, but then I'd have to kill you.' Then he'd change the subject. He didn't want to talk about it, about any of his past. He said he didn't remember anything, and he refused to talk about it. He didn't have any friends from the time before, no pictures, almost no life. He just wanted to look forward, not back."

Grant considered her remarks. "You didn't find that curious?"

"Yes, but I was afraid to talk about it. No one ever brought it up, not even his family."

"How about his health?"

Veronica looked down for a moment, as if putting together the pieces of an aged puzzle. "Good and bad. He was never sick. His general health was excellent. He didn't catch colds or viruses or the flu, but he had shoulder surgery, and knee surgery twice…and a fusion in his neck. He had reasons for those, like old injuries or a job injury. But he was still athletic enough to play golf and do things with the kids."

Veronica handed Grant a photo of the family in a snow skiing setting. Lane was dressed more like a homeless vagrant than a skier. Blue jeans and some type of Indian-looking leg-gaiters. It was hard to tell his exact appearance with the stocking hat and goggles, but he either had a light beard or he failed to shave for a couple of days. Grant appraised the information, Lane wasn't long on fashion but he had long skis. Grant knew long skis made you ski faster, so Lane was either somewhat proficient or somewhat reckless.

Veronica hesitated. "Why? What do you know that you're not telling me?"

Grant considered a response. "If it's all right, I'm going to delay answering that question until I see you later."

Veronica appeared frustrated. "This isn't acceptable, Mr. Harris. It's not acceptable for you to know something and not tell me. I know something's going on here. If my husband wasn't kidnapped, why is the FBI involved?"

This was an excellent question, and Grant knew she deserved the answer. She had to deal with questioning kids as well as a missing husband. She felt angry and abandoned, and it wasn't her fault. In fact, in might not be Lane's fault either.

Grant hesitated, then said, "I need to get some more information before it'll make any sense. We're trying to keep something from happening."

"Well, you're too late. Something already has happened."

He became more understanding. "I know I owe you a complete explanation, and I'll give you one as soon as I have it. Please forgive me. I'll tell you everything—at least everything I know—this afternoon after I get back from another meeting. I need a few more answers myself, then we'll talk."

He knew she had to know about the CIA. He just wanted to have a better understanding of the extent of government involvement before he offered the information. After all, it was still top secret and of a "highly sensitive nature," as the CIA mouthpiece, Jackson, had stated.

After requesting and receiving a portrait photo of Lane, Grant excused himself but left the telephone number for the FBI office in case Veronica came up with any other information. She promised to give it some thought, but Grant wasn't expecting to get much more.

This was classic. Lane had been living with the knowledge of something, and he suspected eventually those intelligence thugs would take him out. He had learned or seen something, the manifestation of which made him think the time was *now*.

Yes, something had led the guy to the edge. Lane believed his number was up, so he left in a hell of a hurry. But what was the reason behind the disappearance of Benjamin Lane?

# CHAPTER THREE

Detective Rice returned to transport Grant to the meeting at 'Rosita's briefing room.' Grant had gathered some information from his conversation with Veronica Lane, and he was now in position for a more direct attack on the facts—call it a "lock-on target." All he needed to enhance his focus would be the information Perez and Bartow should have harvested from the business fields.

The four took seats in a private area of the restaurant. McAllen, only seven miles from Reynosa, Mexico, was a haven for authentic Mexican food. Grant looked at the menu then reviewed the table: fresh tortilla chips, queso dip, and salsa. He read the house specials on the board: fajita tacos, beef skirt in a flour tortilla, and enchiladas.

It all sounded great. Maybe he should just move down here. McAllen didn't have traffic, not like Houston anyway. He wouldn't have to worry about the route—Westheimer or 59—and South Padre Island was only an hour down the road. Perhaps living here, he would be able to keep his New Year's resolution.

*Slow down,* he thought. *Relax. How about it? Is it possible?*

Hesitantly, he answered his own mental question. Moving here was unrealistic, but maybe he would come back to McAllen for a visit sometime. He had spotted a sign for Pepe's by the River, which looked very interesting—the river being the Rio Grande. Maybe he could find the courage to ask Delaney to join him, and they could stare across the river at Mexico.

*Stop it! Focus. Keep Delaney out of this*, he thought with a wry smile. *Get with the program! Lane's clock is ticking.*

Grant explained to the others about the missing 'running money,' deducing that Lane was likely responsible for his own disappearance.

Although there was some relief that he may not have been kidnapped, the ultimate question remained, "Why?"

Grant wasn't surprised by the information his associates had gathered. The other Feds, of questionable association, had made both rounds the day before. It was strange that they hadn't given their names or allowed anyone a good look at their badges—not long enough to get the information anyway. According to witness accounts, the agents looked around, as if casing each office, and then excused themselves when questioned.

Why did the CIA want the FBI on this case in the first place? As Bartow confirmed to Rice, the CIA didn't have any policing authority in the United States. Lane's employees weren't required to give these people any information, and evidently they hadn't.

But the pursuers, whoever they were, had at least a one-day head start, and Grant really had the answer to his own question. This charade was intended to make sure the FBI had enough background information so that a covert activity could be covered up if something went amiss. In other words, it was a smokescreen. Get the FBI involved so the CIA could make something happen. *When it goes down, the FBI becomes the alibi*, Grant thought, *because we "knew all along."*

A bad ending for the CIA would occur if they failed to get Lane before some other entity did. Who could it be? Another intelligence group? The CIA after their own guy? International even? But the game had already started, and Grant had enough confidence in himself to believe he had a chance to find Lane first. He didn't care if the CIA had a thirty-year head start.

Business was apparently good at the insurance agency and the Internet service, according to Perez. Lane was an effective manager, and his employees liked and respected him. No one could think of any reason for his unexpected disappearance. As one might imagine, none of the employees had any idea about Lane's enemies, past or present.

Although the staff was courteous, no one was overly talkative, and they appeared almost a hindrance to direct questions from the inquiry. Perez had requested permission for him and Bartow to search Lane's office at the insurance business, but the office manager had refused. Lane did not maintain an office at the Internet service.

The office manager at the insurance agency suggested that if Veronica Lane approved they could look through her husband's office for more information. Knowing this, Grant was confident he could handle the problem after a talk with Veronica. He planned to do that a little later in the day.

For some reason, more intuitive than factual, Grant thought about electronic communication and how Lane might have tried to get answers. One thing was becoming apparent—in some way Lane had made a contact that had set these events in motion. Whatever was communicated had caused his life to change abruptly, and whatever contact had been made, it was private enough to escape everyone else's attention. But how had the communication been made? Through text or with a person? No one around him seemed to have any clue about his contacts or the timing of his disappearance; schedules were rather random on the Friday at the end of a holiday week. Lane was simply there, and then he wasn't.

The fajita tacos arrived just in time to relieve the pressure that was building in Grant's head. The group halted their discussion, and Grant used the time to review his thoughts.

He had completed one day on the Lane case, and it seemed like a month, but for now he had kept his New Year's resolution. Through the innumerable thoughts cluttering his mind, he pieced together distant images. He hoped his intuition could successfully find a path through the unfolding mystery.

Lunch completed, Grant outlined the strategy with his troops. The FBI should expect the CIA web of deceit to be woven tighter than the wicker basket on the table. He decided to focus their attention on the covert perimeter of the details. Lane was running from something. What was it? Someone had to know.

Grant instructed Bartow to call his office and have internal security check all phones, modems, and cables. The spies were probably stalking the FBI network in order to mirror, if not get ahead of, his investigation. Bartow and Perez would continue to chase down the other Feds, and Rice would take Grant to pick up his own set of wheels.

It was important to contact Veronica and discuss the possibility of searching her husband's office at the insurance company. If time allowed, he also wanted to talk to Lane's children to find out if they had any thoughts that might magnify an otherwise insignificant clue. *In a case like this, nothing was insignificant, and kids always know more than adults think they do.*

* * *

While he waited on the delivery of his auto, Grant made a call to Georgia to see if the wheels were still on the Houston wagon. When she excused herself to organize the information, Grant studied Lane's photo. He was just an average looking guy with unremarkable facial features and light brown hair. If anything set him apart from average, it was the intensity in his face. Although his countenance was kind, his gaze seemed to reveal a deep understanding and his expression was something between a smirk and a smile. Grant summarized that Lane's face had the same look as Hawkeye Pierce when Trapper John told a joke that wasn't funny.

The wheels were still on the wagon, and Georgia had located the computer whiz kid that Grant had requested, Special Agent Anne Shelly from the Dallas office.

With the contact, Delaney had worked out Shelly's temporary transfer to the Houston office. She was being transported to McAllen on the FBI jet with an ETA of four fifteen p.m. To make things even more interesting, Internal Affairs had decided to get involved in the investigation. Delaney was coming with Shelly.

So Internal Affairs Special Agent Delaney—Eve— was coming. Grant hesitated. This was stretching the scope of Internal Affairs. He didn't dwell on her position, though; she made her own schedule. Relaxing a bit, he thought Eve might be good addition to the team if they ended up in some conflict with Langley. She seemed to know about the inner workings of every department and their 'internal' rules.

Then his attention turned to social thoughts. Honestly, he wanted a chance to be with Eve again, and he hadn't orchestrated the encounter. He thought about the special feeling he had when her name was mentioned, the feeling that tended to shove loneliness aside. It was quite a change for him. This was a new year, a new case, and circumstances were taking an interesting turn.

*Maybe it's time to get a life.* He wondered if Eve had any idea about his feelings. *Can those eyes see through me?*

Smiling to himself, he refocused on the case. Computer whiz Special Agent Anne Shelly—how good was she? The Internet was unknown territory to everyone except the military and educational communities, but the new commercial application was forming.

Considering Lane's position at the cutting edge of the technology, there could be an enormous amount of data in his computer. Since Grant needed clues and some creative help finding them, he appreciated having the ability to call on experts. This might be critical to the case, because his work had to be done quickly. There had to be some suggestion of Lane's imminent departure in some of his correspondence—either in what he read or what he wrote. A change this drastic in a person's life could not have happened undetected, or at least without some notice or warning. Grant had to find that clue.

Hopefully, Veronica could supply something more in the way of detail and also allow the FBI access to everything in Lane's office. She could also direct the Internet-service office manager to aid in the search.

As the details of the case increased, Grant thought about the complexities—like Delaney's choice to join the investigation. *Of course, everyone knows IA operates outside the norm,* he thought. *It's the nature of the beast. But is Eve involved because this involves CIA interagency communication or because I wished it? If people wish hard enough, desires can become realities.*

Grant sought to make his longing more legitimate, but to him it was just a 'mind thing.' Maybe Eve could help with a different interpretation of the facts. Whether or not his feelings were legitimate, he admitted he wanted to be with her, to have a chance to look in her eyes, get the answer to her question about the carnival, about Pierrot and Columbine, and to revisit leftovers from the incomplete conversation on the mezzanine.

\* \* \*

Veronica Lane was glad to see Grant return, and soon they were conversing about the interviews with her husband's business associates earlier in the day. Nothing about the businesses set off any red flags for Grant, and the companies were apparently well managed in Lane's absence. It was an ideal situation for the plot of a movie—disappearance, intrigue, and suspicion—but no one had surfaced to collect the insurance…and there was no butler.

As the conversation continued, Grant felt, whether from worry or thoughts of desertion, that Veronica was becoming weary from the ordeal. She voiced her concern about the children, particularly her daughter, and her own vivid fears about the situation itself and the ensuing feeling of abandonment.

Veronica held the FBI to its promise of telling her the information they knew and she did not. Grant brought up the subject of the CIA. "You said your husband never told you anything about his military or government service except his secret project."

"That's right."

"Well, in the late sixties he worked for a secret unit of the CIA. It could have been almost anything during that time. I need your help to look through his office and see whether we can find anything—old notes, diaries—that can help us identify what he knew. Something has to lead us to what he might have been involved in and tell us where he might have gone. We need names or places, any kind of clue."

"I can't believe he hid this from me…" Veronica paused, "but honestly, I guess I can believe it. I just didn't want to know." Redirecting, she asked, "So you think someone is after him?"

"Looking for him, yes, but I don't know why."

"Are they going to hurt him?"

"Could be, but I don't think so. They've had plenty of opportunities in the last twenty-five or thirty years. On the surface, none of this really makes sense, but they could do something drastic if they feel threatened by something your husband might say or do. Since we don't know what this is all about, we have to find him first. Then we can protect him."

Veronica was very quiet for a moment and composed herself. "Let's see what you can find out. I'll go to the office with you."

Grant had been on the case for four hours and ten minutes plus a day, and he was confident he would fix on the trail before the day was out.

Veronica excused herself for a moment to prepare to leave and, after seeing Grant eyeing her son's room from the foyer door, allowed him to go in and look around. The young man's room was a cross between busy and interesting.

Wade Lane was seventeen and a high school honor student. As Grant looked at the shelves covered with trophies, he felt a hole in his relationship with his own son, Jacob. Here were Pinewood Derby racers; trophies for football, soccer, tennis, golf, archery, and scholastic achievement; and a library full of John Grisham novels; and there, on top of the stereo, was the grand prize—an Eagle Scout award. Grant himself was an Eagle, and he knew the commitment required to become one.

He felt a sense of guilt about the lack of time he was able to spend with his son. If possible, he decided it would be good to talk to Wade when he and Veronica returned.

After she rejoined him, they left for the short drive to the office.

\* \* \*

The investigation of Lane's office didn't deliver much useful information. It contained typical business applications for account information, journals, computer literature, network processing information, accounting software instruction manuals, and the like. His private files seemed in order, at least as far as Veronica was concerned.

The major questions were about Lane's computer. Most of its programming was independent of the network system, and it was the sole computer in the insurance agency that was tied to the Internet. None of the other employees had any knowledge of personal information in his computer files. The insurance systems were administered from the provider, HiLite, which was Lane's new business interest.

Grant flipped to the previous week in Lane's personal calendar. There wasn't much there.

*Finch: lunch.*

Veronica explained that Gerald Finch was a banker. They went to lunch every so often.

*Dr. Sanchez: checkup.*

This was the Lane family physician, and he had periodic physicals.
*Haircut: Mary.*

Mary was Mrs. Lane's hairdresser as well, so this was nothing unusual.

As Grant riffled through the credenza, he spied a thick leather-bound notebook. He retrieved it for a closer look.

Veronica watched him with interest.

"That's a screenplay he wrote before we met," she said. "He wrote some songs but couldn't sell them, so he put them in there. I never paid any attention to it…" She seemed put off with the subject. "…because it was before my time."

"Interesting. A songwriter, eh? He must be a romantic."

It seemed uncomfortable for Veronica to talk about her relationship with her husband openly and freely. Although Grant sensed a truth in her responses, it was becoming apparent that she didn't know much, if anything, about his past, and she wasn't comfortable going any further into a discussion of his previous relationships.

"I guess you could say that," she said, "but I'd say idealistic and impractical. I liked it when we met. He was understanding and natural. After a while it seemed somewhat unrealistic. He said songwriters have to go deep into feelings, because they have to get something said in three minutes or less." She hesitated then added, "Really, I can't relate to that. I never could."

Grant followed her train of thought. "Anything specific you could relate to?"

Veronica sat quietly, composing a response. "I remember one song. 'You remind me of a little bird, wounded by a smiling hunter… You're afraid to land and afraid to stay.' He sang it, and that's the way I felt at the time."

"Then you did relate to something, eh?"

Veronica reflected silently but didn't respond. Grant sensed he was treading on emotional ground, so he changed the subject. For a moment he thought of himself as a shrink.

"What else about him?"

Veronica paused in thought then said, "His favorite movie was *The Man of La Mancha*. His favorite food was filet mignon, and…"

She stopped in the middle of the sentence, apparently realizing this wasn't the line of questioning Grant was pursuing, but she didn't seem to care. He had asked for it, and she was tired.

Actually, Grant appreciated the detour. Any information might be important. The truth is always in the details, and he was trying to analyze this guy. Behavior is important, and the reason for it is paramount.

Although many people didn't see or remember *The Man of La Mancha*, Grant liked it.

It stars Peter O'Toole and Sophia Loren; James Coco plays Sancho Panza. "To dream the impossible dream." It's a story about crazy men who chase evil foes, enemies who disguise themselves as windmills. Most people remember something about the men chasing windmills, if nothing else.

Grant didn't make an outright admission, but he was beginning to associate with Lane. They seemed to have something in common. From what he had heard so far, they shared likes and dislikes, favoring the same types of music and movies. Maybe it was because they were both raised in the sixties. Lane wrote songs, and Grant liked to listen to them, explore the words and get into what the writer was thinking.

Now he would need to watch *The Man of La Mancha* again, this time for specific content, to expand his interpretation of Lane's wavelength. *People act the way they believe, and decisions are a direct result of those beliefs.* The origin makes almost everything a clue—and sometimes a fact.

"To dream the impossible dream… Fight the unbeatable foe… Run where the brave dare not go." Clues to Lane's character, if nothing else. From where did his behavior originate? There was a lot of depth in this information.

Veronica gave the FBI permission to take her husband's computer and allow Special Agent Shelly to explore data in the program files. Knowing Grant's interest from his questions, she offered to let him take the screenplay, *All for a Song*. Maybe he could learn more about Lane from clues on those pages as well.

As they exited the insurance office en route to the Internet office, Grant glanced at his watch. Perez and Bartow should be picking up Agents Shelly and Delaney in the next few minutes. Lodging had been arranged at the old, unique, Spanish-style hotel Casa de Palmas, and the FBI had reserved a conference room there to use as an office. If the schedule was maintained, they would all meet there between five thirty and six.

The best news Grant received in the last twenty-four hours was that Rob Garza was the executive vice president and chief operations officer for Lane's Internet company.

As he walked in, Rob came forward and held out his hand. "Hey, Grant. It's been a while."

Old friends were reunited. They both smiled, and Grant shook his head. Not realizing the two had known each other for a long time, Veronica was taken by surprise and appeared understandably puzzled.

Grant responded, "Rob, why didn't you tell Perez and Bartow who you are?"

"Oh, they would have told you sooner or later, and I didn't want to spoil the surprise." Rob realized Veronica was left out of the conversation, so he interjected, "Sorry, Veronica. Grant and I have known each other since the Cold War." It sounded like a long time ago, but ten years wasn't that long.

Grant couldn't get over the surprise. Rob had served in computer and electronics technical support for the FBI on a contract basis for more than fifteen years. The two had worked together on bank fraud, a couple of search investigations, a cellular phone scam, and so on. Rob was a middle-aged man on a lanky six foot frame and looked like a computer geek from a generation ago. What little hair he had left was salt and pepper colored and it matched his light scruffy beard. He looked like he might have wandered off of a mountaintop in Tibet about the time Steve Jobs was born, and he spoke foreign languages: languages like Basic, Fortran and Cobol. He was a team player, but only if it was a small team, and his friendship with Grant sustained one major dynamic: trust.

"I knew you were still in south Texas," Grant said, "and the rumor was that you were working at a new Internet business. I just didn't put it together that it would be this one."

"This is the best one. I gotta bloom where I'm planted." Rob turned to Veronica. "Have you heard anything from Ben?"

She shook her head.

"What do you know, Rob?" Grant asked

"They didn't get him. He's just getting out of somebody's way."

"Why?"

"I don't know, but somebody's after him."

"What makes you say that?"

"Grant, I know when things don't add up. You know I've been on the edge of your business, and I understand what goes on in the government underworld. Ben was concerned about something for a while. He didn't tell anyone about any kind of problem, but last week someone hacked our system, and whoever it was cleared out some of his e-mail. I don't know what they wanted, but I'm trying to find out."

"How are you looking?"

It was evident Rob knew exactly what he was doing.

"Our systems administrator is going through the logs to see what newsgroups Ben was corresponding in. When I find them, I may be able to retrace some postings and see who he was corresponding with and about what. I may not be able to locate it all, but if I find a name and a subject, it'll be a start."

Grant had unlimited confidence in Rob, and he knew to let him have as much rope as he needed. "Did he ever talk to you about the military?" Grant asked.

"No, but he was familiar with the military in some way or another. He knew about aircraft, helicopters, ordnance, and weapons, but he never talked about his own involvement. Is there something you want to tell me?"

"Need to know."

"Oh, no. Not those guys. I didn't want to know that. What the hell do you suppose he was doing with them?"

Rob had top-secret clearance with the FBI, so Grant filled him in on the story, at least as much as he knew. Then he mentioned the CIA guys who were hanging around the day before, but Rob disagreed about their identity.

"Those guys weren't CIA, Grant. When they saw me coming to the front of the office, they took off. I didn't talk to them, but I saw them from a distance. They looked more like those spooky defense intelligence guys who used to run around the barracks hunting for spies."

Grant argued, "Then why would Central send their man, Jackson, to get my assistance in the first place?"

"Maybe just to throw you off track. Maybe the CIA doesn't know the real story. You know that the covert military is the absolute worst about their secrets…and covering their asses." Rob stopped himself. "Sorry, Veronica."

She remained silent but nodded and took the opportunity to excuse herself from the conversation.

When she crossed the hall toward the computer support area, Grant continued, "It's interesting that you would say they're from another branch, because I've had our people in Houston monitoring the CIA office for activity, to see if they're tailing us, and they haven't found any evidence of it. I'm surprised they're not in on this, but someone is." He thought for a moment and asked, "How long have you known Lane?"

"Ben and I have been friends for about five or six years. I set up the systems at the insurance company and started to get him computer literate. Actually, because of my involvement with the government, I saw the commercial side of the Internet as having a great future, so I decided to embark on this new venture. I used Ben's money and started the company a couple of years ago. I'm the reason he's in the Internet business."

"Do you know him well enough to tell me what's going to happen next?"

Rob thought for a moment, then laid out his assessment. "I can guess. First he's going to contact someone and tell the family he's OK and give a hint of some kind, but he won't do it in a conventional way with a phone call or visit. He knows more of what's going on here than we do, and he won't put Veronica or the kids in any danger."

"What ideas do you have?"

"Something on the Internet. He's got a laptop with a cellular modem, but he'll have to be careful, since he already knows we were hacked. It probably won't be e-mail. More than likely he'll use a Usenet posting or a webpage. I'm watching for any funny activity on the server."

Grant looked at his watch. "I'm going to meet with our support staff, who should be coming in about now. We'll be at Casa de Palmas. Here's the number. We'll have one of our computer people there, and I want you to be in contact with her. Her name's Anne Shelly. Use her in any way you can. I thought I'd start by letting her take a quick search through the correspondence on Lane's office computer."

"OK. I don't think you'll find anything in there, though. I imagine he was being careful, but go ahead and give it a try. Let me know if you find anything, and I'll buy coffee in the morning."

"Deal."

The two said goodbye, and Grant left to take Veronica home.

On the way, he sat in silence until she said, "I should have asked Ben more questions."

"You shouldn't look at it that way. Asking him questions might have made it harder. I'm sure it's what Rob suggested—a way to protect you and the kids."

Grant looked over at Veronica and saw she wanted to believe it. A hard four days had been thrown at her, and continuing to be strong in this situation was even harder. Somehow he knew she would reach a new height and survive. She appeared to be that kind of a tough person, spirited and a survivor. She'd change with the experience, but who knew how.

As Grant drove, his mind quickly relived his last day-and-a-half. This case was like a six-coupon ride at the state fair; it took all of a person's energy, and it was a very quick ride.

Still, Delaney was joining him on the case, and he'd be with her soon. He wondered how it would feel when he saw her again and what he could tell her about B.W. Lane.

# CHAPTER FOUR

The FBI plane landed on time. When Grant reached the hotel, his associates had already checked in and were waiting in the conference room.

The room, measuring about twelve by twenty feet, had been transformed into a mini federal office. Briefcases and papers covered the conference table, and Delaney, sitting in a chair at a small table, was on the phone to Houston. Agent Perez had returned to Brownsville and left a message to let him know if he was needed for anything else.

Bartow and Shelly were discussing something about the modem configurations as she worked on her laptop computer. Rob had made contact and spoken with her about a temporary Internet connection so her access would be activated when she completed the configuration.

Grant liked the hotel arrangement, where he operated his organization more like a war room. People could have privacy in their rooms if they needed it, and he was free to work all the time, if he wanted to. Although he generally used the FBI's local offices, he had been accused of turning all the other employees into workaholics, because he tended to work nearly 24/7. Beyond those given reasons, he wanted freedom to move quickly without protocol of the office. He had a feeling this thing would be over soon anyway, and he didn't want to make a career out of this one case.

Agent Shelly was introduced, and Grant was pleased with the way she presented herself. She was a short woman in her mid-twenties with medium-length light-brown hair, almost blonde, and round light-framed glasses that bore a Bill Gates look. When Grant first saw her, he thought she had a permanent smile on her face, but later he realized it was a demeanor of contentment. It was evident she was happy with who she was which is a quality usually reserved for those with more age and experience. Her pleasant mood and manner were accompanied by a very positive personality and anyone could tell she had abundant self-confidence. Grant was sure that if she was in a group for longer than ten minutes, she wouldn't need a nametag. Everyone would know she's Shelly.

After the introductions, she returned to her keyboard, while Bartow retrieved Lane's computer from the bellman's cart and set it on the table. He plugged in the monitor and keyboard and strung the cord and telephone line to the wall plugs.

Grant went over to greet Agent Delaney, who had completed her conversation with the Houston office.

"Hi, Eve. How was your flight?"

She smiled. "A little bumpy, but we ended up in the right place."

"Glad you came. Any special reason why?"

Eve replied, in detail, "Well, the plane would have been out of route if I had gone back to Houston. Anyway, there's nothing significant going on at my office, so I wanted to keep an eye on the CIA, see McAllen for a day or two, and…watch you work. You know Internal Affairs people like to get in the way occasionally so we can uphold our bad reputations."

They laughed, and he focused on her eyes. In the back of his mind, Grant wondered if Terri Hatcher had a sister; he also wondered if beautiful people admit to their own good fortune. Eve returned the gaze without hesitation, and he blinked first. She smiled, and Grant had that special feeling.

"Well, I'm glad you're here," he said. "This has been a busy day, and it's not over yet. In fact, when we get this computer up and running, it could be starting all over again."

Eve interjected facetiously, "Well, you know I love a nine-to-five."

Eve reported that Veronica Lane had called the FBI office with the telephone number for Lane's older daughter, Julie, in Fort Worth. She decided that Julie would be the only person who might answer some of the questions regarding Lane and her mother during the earlier years, the time before Veronica had entered the picture.

Grant explained the situation to Eve and then called Julie at her home number.

After a brief introduction, Grant explained his need for clues to Julie's father's past. She was pleasant and cooperative while being somewhat hesitant about giving too much information. Perhaps she was a little baffled by the whole matter, since she was born in 1968, which was the period of Grant's interest. She had an attitude of "What can I possibly know?"

Although the conversation was slow to develop, it involved Lane and other people with whom he might have maintained contact through the years. Julie explained that her mother had died of cancer a few years earlier, but she didn't relate any facts about her father's work history or any work-related occurrences. Her mother had suffered from severe depression and some sort of mental disorder, but Julie stopped short of blaming the problems on anything that her father might have been involved with—particularly anything of a military nature.

Julie said she had heard the name of his old employer, Skyland Technologies, and did have a recollection of it being a weapons-type business. However, she didn't think her father maintained any contact with old coworkers.

The only person she thought might know any more about the situation and the time was her grandfather, John Hearn, who had been involved in the military-aerospace industry at the same time. Hearn was acquainted with Lane's employers at Skyland, and he probably had been instrumental in helping his son-in-law obtain employment with the company.

When asked about Lane's relationship with his father-in-law after the divorce of her parents, Julie said that Lane and his father-in-law continued to be friends, and still are. She further related that they spoke often on the phone and Lane maintained a great deal of admiration and respect for Hearn.

After warming up slightly through this part of the conversation, Julie told Grant an interesting story her father had repeated on numerous occasions. It had to do with the high degree of respect he held for her grandfather and one of the reasons why.

In the early days of Lane's involvement in the government military crowd, Hearn was chief of subcontract quality control for Bell Helicopter, which was the primary supplier for helicopters used during the Vietnam War. In this position, he held the number-two QC stamp, which was the only stamp that could approve or disapprove—in other words, scrap—critical parts for the helicopters.

At some time during the conflict, a shipment of rotor assemblies had been received—parts that showed small hairline fractures in the pin assemblies. In difficult maneuvers that might overstress the component, the tiny fissure could cause the rotor to fail. Hearn scrapped the parts, and a situation developed between him and some other management people, who claimed the deficiency was not overly dangerous or severe.

As the critical nature of the disagreement became the priority, a meeting was called to make a final disposition regarding the parts. After all the facts were gathered and everyone's testimony heard, it was decided to let some of the rotors continue through processing to be included in an urgent shipment of choppers that were needed under severe time constraints.

The situation intensified, and in front of the senior management of the company, John Hearn reached into his pocket. They all knew, because of government regulations, that the 2QC stamp had to be affixed to the paperwork on the rotor assemblies or the parts could not be used. They watched in dismay as Hearn lit his cigarette lighter and melted the stamp beyond recognition. He was later fired for insubordination.

Although Hearn's career in the industry was briefly interrupted, his reputation remained unblemished. He went to work for a company that created preformed explosive charges for the oil-field drilling industry, and later, the military.

B.W. liked to tell the story, because he respected his father-in-law for having done the right thing, beyond whatever punishment would follow, and the story had a happy ending.

Hearn and two other men ended up buying the company's ordnance division. After his partners were killed in a research accident at the plant sometime later, Hearn moved the plant to Arkansas where it was still active. Together with its missile and bomb ordnance, another one of the of the company's product lines was a small explosive capsule used to inflate automobile airbags—SRS, or supplemental restraint systems.

After this education, Grant tried to get a little more personal about Julie's feelings for her father. Was there anything she knew about him that might give the FBI any other clues for their search?

Julie said she believed her father is driven more by "what is right" than "what is easy."

Grant asked, "What makes you say that?"

"Well, he spent a lot of time making sure everything turned out OK for people, even if it meant he didn't get what he wanted. He tried to do what was right. That's what gets me about this situation. He wouldn't have left without a good reason, Mr. Harris. He wouldn't just leave the kids."

The conversation concluded with the promise that Grant would keep her informed, and likewise Julie would let him know if she remembered anything else that might seem important.

Eve and Grant discussed his conversation, and then Eve gave him an updated summary from Houston. In the exchange, Grant reviewed the day's activities—the fact that Lane was apparently on the run, and the important role of Lane's computer, if Rob was right about the news-group communications.

Since Eve had been included in the conversation with CIA's Agent Jackson the day before, she already knew the dark side of Lane's background and only needed the current update. Grant further acquainted her with the information he had learned about Lane, his wife, his family, and the other intelligence operatives who were on the scene.

"Tonight, I get to read a screenplay called *All for a Song*. Lane wrote it in the seventies. It might tell me more about who we're hunting."

Eve responded, "Behavior analysis? Grant, you'd better be careful getting into his head. You might end up on a 'lesser-traveled road.' I mean, like wearing funky clothes, reading tea leaves, and then disappearing yourself."

They laughed.

"And then I'd have to write you up," she said.

"You'd do that? You'd write me up?"

She looked directly at Grant, smiled beautifully, and replied, "Damn straight, Harris…in a heartbeat!"

In the moment, Grant recognized his ease with the conversation. He liked being who he was and where he was, and it wasn't only because of his position. It was Eve. In her company he felt something, and he wasn't afraid of the feeling. For some reason, his attitude improved when Eve was there. She was confidently at ease, positive, and unreserved.

His thoughts compounded. She was good support. Maybe it was the timing of her entry. She appeared at a time when Grant sought answers to important questions. *Why does life seem more significant now? Why is my world being turned right side up after being so upside down?*

Evidently, life had a different meaning this day—a day that had permitted his presence in someone else's space and his recognition of the feeling. There was a story behind every item he saw. What was going on?

He realized nothing had changed during the day, except his own attitude. He was looking at things differently, and there was an absence of the loneliness that had been his only recent companion.

He recollected the uncertainty of his thoughts while visiting Wade Lane's room in the home, which allowed his trespass, along with the feeling when he knew something was wrong.

What was wrong? Why did it happen?

Grant awoke from his trance to the view of Eve's inquisitive eyes. He had gone from humorous to serious within his own thoughts. He made a hasty retreat to lucidity.

"I'm going back to the Lanes' in a while to talk to their son," he said. "Would you like to join me?

Eve was pleased to be included in the plan. She was in Internal Affairs, but she was still an FBI agent and welcomed being treated like one. Somewhere in the back of her mind, she harbored a notion of being transferred out of IA and into some kind of fieldwork. It was more exciting. Like Grant, she too was an explorer, pursuing some far-removed thought or dream. She was searching for something, something that might add both hope and adventure to her tomorrows.

By this time, the day had surrendered to the night, but work was continuing in 'Little Houston,' which Anne Shelly had named the office. After all, she was a temporary transfer to Houston, wasn't she? Never mind that she was sitting on the Mexican border in McAllen, Texas.

Earlier, Grant had dismissed Bartow for the evening. Delaney's attention was on the monitor as she looked over Shelly's shoulder, watching her search through the correspondence file of Lane's computer. Grant was thumbing through the screenplay, not ready to read it but glancing curiously.

*All for a Song.* It was the story of the extremes to which a person might go in order to reach a dream. *Written by a former CIA operative?* Grant thought. *I doubt it.*

The phone buzzed.

It was Veronica Lane informing Grant that her son had returned and telling him to come over whenever he wished. Grant told her that Agent Delaney would be accompanying him and suggested she and Veronica might visit while he spoke with Wade. Privately, he thought about taking Delaney to dinner after the interview, but he didn't plan to discuss it until the time was right.

* * *

When the two arrived at the Lanes' home, they were warmly greeted. The atmosphere wasn't quite upbeat, but the mood had improved from earlier in the day. Grant could not exact a reason.

Wade was a big boy for seventeen, more than six feet tall and muscular. Grant commented that he looked as if he had been lifting weights, and the boy confirmed it, relating his exercise to sports. As Eve and Veronica began to talk, Grant and Wade excused themselves to his room and to conversation concerning the boy's Eagle Scout award.

Grant broke the ice. "What did you like most about your scouting activities?"

"Being outdoors, camping, wilderness survival. That was Dad's favorite part."

Wade stopped talking for a moment, picked up a handmade arrow which rested on his shelf, examined it, and replaced it in its berth.

"We built wigwams and thatch huts, made traps. We made camp without a lot of supplies, roughing it."

"Where did your dad get his training?"

"I don't know. Scouts, I guess. Maybe from his great-grandfather. He was a Cherokee. Dad liked to think he was a Cherokee, but he was only about a quarter." Wade smiled. "He said it was his best quarter."

After a few more questions regarding the young man's scouting background, Grant decided Wade was sharp for his age, but he wasn't offering much in the matter of specific information.

Grant chose to be more direct. "Right now we think your dad has disappeared on purpose. Can you think of anything he might be running from?"

Wade took immediate offense. "What makes you think he's running from anything?"

Grant realized perhaps he had phrased the question improperly, so he paused to redirect the conversation.

During Grant's silence, Wade said, "Mom said you think someone was after him. Maybe he decided to make it harder for them to find him."

"I suppose that's a good way to put it…make it harder for them. If your dad wanted to contact you, how do you think he would do it?"

"Through the Internet. Hard to bug it."

"Where would you look?"

"Not the usual places…like e-mail…in case we get hacked again."

Wade knew about the hacking incident at the insurance company, and through the conversation Grant discovered Wade worked for Rob at the Internet service. It wasn't difficult to determine the young man was light years ahead of Grant's computer knowledge.

Grant asked Wade if he'd like to go to Little Houston to work with Agent Shelly for a while. Although Wade appreciated the invitation, he decided to postpone the discussion until the following day.

Veronica and Eve were still talking when Wade and Grant entered the living room.

Eve spoke first. "Your mother says you play the piano. Will you play a song for us?"

Wade smiled sheepishly and sat at the piano bench.

"Play 'The Balada,' " Veronica coached. As an aside to Eve and Grant, she added, " 'The Balada Para Adelina.' His dad's favorite."

Grant was impressed by everything he saw and heard from Wade, but this took the cake. The song was quite difficult, but the football player performed it with grace and enthusiasm. It was beautiful.

The questions hammered into Grant's thoughts. *How is this kid so together if his dad is some CIA spook? Why isn't Lane home with his family? What was so important in the scheme of mysterious government bullshit to pull this guy away from his family? Why are the Jacksons of the world chasing him?*

After the song, Grant said, "Mrs. Lane, Wade, from what I can see, you have a very wonderful family. I also see, from your pictures, that you have a ballerina here as well. I'm sure she'll be equally as interesting and charming as the two of you."

As they prepared to leave, Eve assured Veronica, "Don't worry. We'll find your husband. We won't stop until we do."

* * *

As they drove away from the house and turned onto Tenth Street, there was a poignant silence in the cool night air. Eve had been in town only three-and-a-half hours, but she already felt the intensity of the day. As they watched the lights drift across the car windows, neither wanted to break the silence.

Finally Grant said, "There's a saying a friend gave me a long time ago. It was graffiti, in a Tasmanian youth hostel. It said, 'I didn't come this way to realize dreams that are hundreds of years old. I came because it was a road that might have an end.' " He paused, remembering. " 'I know now that I must make my way back someday, taking with me a particle of the night's silence and the day's honesty."

Eve stared out the window as she composed a response.

Almost mesmerized, she said, "Grant, say it again."

She turned her head and smiled at him with those Evee eyes that could see through a lead door and into his soul.

Grant repeated the saying, then asked, "If someone finds out I'm occasionally…idealistic, will it pose a risk for me at the bureau?"

"I'd say 'romantic' rather than idealistic, but it's not a problem for me." Eve responded, returning her gaze to the window. She pondered out loud, "Making my way back someday… the night's silence, the day's honesty… That's beautiful." After a pause, she continued, "If you ever find your way back someday, maybe I can go with you."

Grant was stunned. She shared his understanding.

In the silence, she said, "When I look at people like Jackson, I get the creeps. His thing about losing an 'item.' You know, well… We just spent some pretty valuable time with the family of Jackson's 'item.' I can't believe this is happening." She held her hand up, with her fingers marking a short distance. "But you and I are this close to understanding what's happening here. I can feel it."

Grant wished he shared the same confidence. Her candid response found him unprepared to respond, but he was glad to have brought the saying into their dialogue. He was also relieved to be able to talk freely about his deeper thoughts. Eve, however, wouldn't let him look into her eyes —not at that moment—as she continued to stare into the escaping lights.

Neither agent had an answer for the mood, but something was happening, and they were sharing it. Assistant SAC Grant Harris and Special Agent Evangeline Delaney were being brought together by 'a something' that kept others apart: the disappearance of a guy named Lane.

# CHAPTER FIVE

A thoughtful silence pervaded the return to Little Houston as the two agents pondered the first of their shared journeys. Eve wondered whether she had displayed too much emotion, while Grant questioned his newly experienced freedom to share.

As they walked to the second-floor mezzanine and toward the conference room, Grant seized the moment. Using the excuse that Bartow had suggested a good restaurant, he asked Eve to join him for dinner. They agreed to talk to Shelly before finalizing their plan.

Agent Shelly, now becoming the 'Super Hacker of Casa de Palmas,' was where they had left her, glued to Lane's computer and maneuvering around the program files. She was a sight, sitting on her right leg, her shoes across the floor under the table, and Coke cans in three places. The vest she had been wearing was draped on the chair behind her. She scarcely looked up as they entered.

"How are you doing, Shelly?" Eve asked.

The young agent continued to stun the keyboard as she responded. "Cool. I've been through about half of his correspondence, and I have an idea where to look now. I found a second e-mail program. It was independent of the Internet browser, and it doesn't appear to have been damaged in the hack. Unfortunately there's not anything worth mentioning yet."

She continued to tap away at the keys. Grant watched her movements and didn't think he had ever seen anyone type so quickly. As he studied the screen over her shoulder, it appeared she was typing faster than he could read.

"The only problem is that it's password protected, so I'm working on breaking in to have a look." She looked up and smiled. "Anybody want a Coke?"

Eve declined the offer, and Grant looked back at her. "It may be a long night," he said. "Do you want to try Bartow's suggestion or eat here?"

Although he was speaking to both women, Shelly responded. "You all can do whatever, but I ordered pizza. I decided to stay after this a while, because I think I'm onto it."

Grant looked at Eve again. "Well? We can talk about the screenplay over dinner."

Special Agent Evangeline Justine Delaney, Director of Internal Affairs, Houston Regional Office, Federal Bureau of Investigation, hesitated.

*Dinner? Is this correct behavior?* She thought. *If not, why am I questioning it?*

Smiling in recognition of the big deal she was making over this simple gesture, Eve responded, "Sure, Magnum, P.I. We can solve the case over dinner."

Those eyes were back on him as he picked up *All for a Song*, and they walked out the door, leaving the enthusiastic and efficient Anne Shelly to her computer devices.

\* \* \*

McAllen was a small city of about one hundred thousand people, and when someone was in the middle of it, he wasn't far from anything. The restaurant, suggested by Agent Bartow as one of the finest, was at least a nine, even if you included the local country club. The Santa Fe Steakhouse, which was not far from the old hotel, the airport, or La Plaza Mall, owned a reputation that brought visitors from all over the area to eat finely prepared steaks and drink Texas-style margaritas. Since it was almost nine on a Tuesday night, Grant thought it might be slow, but good restaurants never are.

They were told of a brief wait and then seated in the cantina. Everyone in Texas knew that a cantina, on the border, together with a beautiful woman and a margarita, made for a perfect evening. The only thing lacking was good conversation.

Grant smiled and held his glass toward hers. "Cheers!"

As their glasses, and eyes gently touched, Eve said, "Cheers."

Returning the smile, she sipped the drink and glanced at Lane's screenplay, as if inviting the words to leap out and lead the conversation so she wouldn't have to. Honestly, in the moment, she didn't really want to talk about the screenplay. A part of her wanted to remove the emotions she felt, while her strongest desire was surrender.

As the song "Fernando" played from the speakers, and as the candlelight in the cantina reflected a beacon from her gorgeous eyes, she decided it would be all right if Grant knew about her feelings.

"I've been waiting for this for months," she said. "I hoped sometime you would invite me to dinner." Thinking the comment might be too direct, she added, "The word around the office is that you were torn up by your divorce."

Grant grinned sheepishly. "I didn't know Internal Affairs has been watching me that closely."

Eve laughed. "You know Internal Affairs people. We have to know everything about everybody." She hesitated a moment then followed on a more serious note. "What would you say if I told you, personally, just me asking…that I want to know how you're doing?"

"I'd be flattered to know you cared." Grant continued very directly, "It would make me feel better to talk about things, because my divorce isn't the problem. I'm over that. I've just had trouble adjusting to being single again."

Although Eve remained attentive, she refrained from speaking. Her eyes asked him to continue, and he did.

"I guess I've been afraid to have a close relationship with anyone. Getting out of that marriage was like a hat-trick. I never meant to let Leslie down. It was just… I couldn't live the lifestyle. It wasn't right for me. Everything was too planned out. It's like I never had any options."

Finally Grant found himself being honest about the failure. He remembered a few lines from an old David Soul song and repeated them. " 'So from the wall he lived behind… He took the bricks that were the greenest with moss and cut them out with a mason's crook… Gave a green-sided brick to each friend…and his wall was gone.' "

Responding, Eve imagined, "No walls. I like that."

Grant looked into her eyes and completed the thought. "I'm usually not this open. I guess I just gave you a brick."

Eve's eyes responded sincerely before she answered. "Thank you, Grant. I'll guard it…carefully."

Pausing, while smiling magically, she looked into her margarita, swirled her swizzle stick, and considered how deeply from her emotions she should speak on their first date. She knew it was a date, and Grant would have gladly admitted it.

"How about Evangeline Justine Delaney?" he asked.

"Oh, her?" Eve answered in the third person. "She was married very young, and it lasted about forty-five minutes." She laughed at the thought then became more serious. "She married a nice little rich kid she had known all her life—their parents were good friends—and it was just supposed to be that way. It didn't work out, though. They were too different."

Eve attended to the lime wedge in her margarita. "She wanted to be truly loved and cared for, but he just wanted another notch on his gun. He got the notch, and she got an education. At least she realized it before staying in it too long."

"Tell me about being 'truly loved and cared for.'"

Eve didn't respond but looked intently into his eyes. Then she gazed distantly to the side before she turned back to him and finally broke the silence.

"Let's not go there yet," she said.

Although she didn't answer the question, Grant respected the response. It was reward enough to be in the same little space with her on the same planet, and he could wait to revisit the question some other time. For the moment he was released to look into her eyes and spend some time there without someone at the office starting rumors.

Then he thought, *who cares? Let them start the rumors.*

Eve decided it was Grant's turn to answer some questions. "Tell me about you."

"What about me?"

"Well…how about your first love?"

"Oh, I don't know."

"Yes, you do. Don't say 'I don't know.' Say 'I won't tell.'" Eve had that way of being direct.

"You're right. It's just different to be talking to you this way."

"You don't have to…"

"It's OK. I like it," Grant admitted. "It's just different. For some reason, talking this openly…seems risky."

"Just think of it like you're giving me another one of your bricks."

Grant smiled. "First love. High school sweetheart. Our parents thought we were too young, so they kept us apart when we went to college. They didn't want us to be too serious too soon."

"Makes sense."

"So I broke up with her."

"And?"

"And I guess I shouldn't have, because I had a feeling for her that I never had since." He stopped in thought. "But you can't go back. Things like that can never be the same."

"Are you sure?"

"Remember the song 'MacArthur Park'? 'Someone left the cake out in the rain… I don't think that I can take it, 'cause it took so long to bake it, and I'll never have that recipe again'…"

Eve glanced at her margarita then looked back at him. "Maybe you should look for another recipe."

Grant smiled. "Know anyone who can help me?"

She returned a tight-lipped smile. "I might."

In the somewhat uncomfortable silence of her stirring, Grant decided to change the subject. This had gone deep enough for now. The screenplay needed attention. He explained the plot. It was about a jingle writer for an advertising agency who was getting a divorce and decided that if his whole world was going to be upside down, he would become a songwriter. Writing songs was what the jingle writer always wanted to do, so he made a demo tape with a friend of his named Wichita Johnson, and they took it to Nashville.

"They didn't do well because they were outsiders."

Grant flipped over to the page where he had left his bookmark. "He wrote a pretty good song, though. It said…" He found the place and read from the manuscript. "Good words. 'I know city livin' ain't the finest. It's unfortunate I have to stay… The prison in my mind is more apparent, 'cause I'd rather be in Malibu, watching the morning waves…

" 'All I see are city streets and sidewalks, where I used to see the flowers and the trees… I saw a kid on a skateboard, chasing waves down Forty-Seventh Street… Was it city livin' or was it me?' "

He started to lay down the book when Eve stopped him. "On a skateboard… Waves on Forty-Seventh Street… I like it, Grant. Keep going."

He relocated his place on the page and continued. "'The acrylics and the oils remain unopened. It's hard to paint a picture I can't see… The prison in my mind keeps closing in, 'cause I'd rather paint a picture of the mountains or the sea…

" 'And all I see are city streets and sidewalks where I used to see the flowers and the trees… I saw an artist in the park paint a mountain where there wasn't one… Was it city livin' or was it me?' "

Grant smiled at Eve then continued. "That's kind of tough. 'Prisons in my mind.' I lived in one of those, you know."

Eve listened, and he looked back at the book.

" 'Finally, I answered both those questions, and the thoughts of the mountains still remain… I escaped from the prison and looked around me. Though slightly masked, the beauty was the same…

" 'Now I look past city streets and sidewalks, and I focus on the flowers and the trees… The writer joined the artist and the kid on Forty-Seventh Street. It wasn't city livin'… It was me.' " Grant looked up from the screenplay. "It's hard to find the flowers and the trees," he said. "I've felt that way since I've been in Houston."

"It's all in your attitude, right? 'Paint a mountain where there isn't one…' Your CIA guy is a romantic."

Grant didn't believe the CIA had any employees with normal emotions and repeated a comment from their earlier conversation. "Delaney, you're the romantic."

She looked at him with those beaming eyes. "Do you think it'll pose a problem for me?"

"Not with me."

"What about Lane? I wonder if it's posing a problem for him."

Grant laid down the notebook as the maître d' interrupted, letting them know their table was ready.

On the short excursion through the restaurant to a table near the back wall of the main room, Grant studied his beautiful companion.

She glided down the aisle with stunning grace, and the beauty was deeper than her appearance. It also lay in her personality and in her always knowing the right thing to say, at the right time. He hoped the evening would continue to cooperate with his desire to know her better.

Grant held her chair, and in a heartbeat they were seated, eyes joined across a candle and a rose.

During their casual dinner discussion, Eve talked about her family back in Philadelphia, where she was raised. She had lived in an Irish neighborhood and attended a Catholic school a block from her home. She laughed as she talked about playing tricks on the sisters and getting away with it, and the time she had gotten drunk with a couple of her girlfriends on Annie Green Springs Apple Wine.

Eve had a fun and creative childhood and had fancied herself whatever she wanted to be. She was a movie actress one day and the President of the United States the next. She would change her name to match the day of the week; for instance, one day she would be Evee Tuesday and the next she would be Evangeline Wednesday. She always liked Sundays the best—E. Justine Sunday.

They laughed, and Grant felt himself falling for Evee Tuesday—and he was looking forward to Wednesday.

As their plates emptied, so did the restaurant. After they'd completed the second hour, it was evident the only way the evening could have been better was if it had lasted forever.

Evee Tuesday had captured Grant Magnum's heart, and as they walked out, he touched her hand. She hesitated briefly then slipped her hand into his.

Slowly, as they walked across the parking lot, she said, "This may be…uh, complicated."

Grant walked on, purposefully. "For me it's worth it."

With the passing ribbons of light, the contemplative silence ruled their ride back to the hotel, where each knew they would sleep alone. Eve would retire with her thoughts of the evening, and tomorrow's tomorrow, and Grant with his thoughts of Eve…adrift within the mysterious fog which surrounded the disappearance of B.W. Lane.

# CHAPTER SIX

At eleven fifteen p.m., back in Little Houston, the 'Casa de Palmas whiz kid' was doing her thing and was in the middle of being proud of herself when Eve and Grant walked in.

"I got into the e-mail program and found a folder called 'Poems.' I found Rudyard Kipling's 'If.' Listen to this. 'If you can keep your head when all those about you are losing theirs and blaming it on you, if you can read this poem and learn the clues it holds for you, you may recover a page to see. Where evil looks, it'll never be.' It rhymes, but that last line definitely isn't Kipling. What do you think?"

Grant positioned himself behind Shelly so he could see the message. "What do *you* think?"

"It's got to be about the Web. If he put up a page, we need to find the URL, and it's not going to be where evil finds it. So…OK then. We'll look where evil…does not look?"

Shelly went on to explain about the resource locator or URL being the address that was directed through the server and that it would have its own identity.

"It would be like http://www.hilite.net/~ after the forward slash, and the tilde there would be a name after it, which could be anything—or it could have its own domain, like www.domain."

"Would Rob be able to give us any help?"

"Sure. If he gave me root access, I could find out what's been put on the server in the last few weeks."

Grant called Rob immediately and found he was still at the office. However, Rob said no to Shelly getting root access, even if his wife was being held for ransom. He did agree to comb the file for any new webpage postings going back a couple of weeks. He said he'd give them a call back if he found anything. It hadn't been very long since Lane's disappearance, so there probably wouldn't be more than three or four hundred new postings.

Shelly asked aloud, "I wonder why he's so stingy with root access?"

Grant responded, "He's been around this business for a long time. He doesn't trust anyone."

Then she talked to herself. "Wrong attitude, Rob. I'll either find it without you or hack your server. I'll play it any way you want."

To start with, Shelly had a clue—"You may recover a page to see. Where evil looks, it'll never be." Since Lane wanted the clue to be found, he wouldn't have hidden it very deep in the system, so Shelly decided to investigate all the directed outbound links for the local participants on the HiLite homepage. Although Grant didn't understand it, she explained what she was going to do while she waited for Rob.

Eve said goodnight and retired to her room.

Grant picked up the screenplay and thumbed through it, as if measuring the time it would take to finish reading it. Then he decided to do so in the comfort of his room. He excused himself to Shelly and retired as well.

* * *

After getting comfortable in his room, Grant stacked up the bed pillows and lay down to read. He moved through the part where Bryan, the songwriter, left Kansas City, thinking he could better forge his songwriting career in Los Angeles. He wanted a singer named Abbey Fleming, a Linda Ronstadt type, to hear his songs, and he was sure she would like them.

There was a fun part where Bryan found a dog in a roadside park. He named the mutt E99, because it had a dog tag that read, "Vaccinated E-50499," and he shortened it. The most interesting thing about E99 was that the dog would nod or shake its head—yes or no—when Bryan talked to it. If he made the slightest head movement, either positively or negatively, the dog followed his lead. It was really a great part—the dog using its head to agree with everything he said. The two vagabonds found their way to California, but Bryan didn't have any luck selling his songs there either. Grant decided everybody needed a friend like E99, someone to agree with them all the time. Lane was a clever guy.

Another song caught his attention, and he marked it to show to Eve the next day. It contained the line that Veronica Lane had recited earlier in the day, about the little bird that was afraid to stay.

Grant reread it then continued to the final verse.

> *You told me your fears and dreams... We laughed at tomorrow's magic... Today is here, and tomorrow will never be... You touched my heart so softly, as your lips kissed mine so gently... For a moment you belonged to me...*

*How about those lines? That's hot!* Grant thought. *It's no wonder Veronica didn't want to get involved in Lane's conversations about his past.* This was getting a little more complicated, and the clues were mounting up.

> *I saw your smiling tears and I knew, and because I understand, I cried for you... Because we're all the same, I cried for you.*

" 'Because we're all the same,' " Grant spoke aloud. "Yeah, I guess in a lot of ways we are."

He continued to analyze his thoughts. This guy wasn't capable of doing CIA bullshit—unless he had made one hell of a change between whatever he had done in 1969 and when he had written these songs.

The plot deepened, and later in the story, Bryan befriended a grandmotherly-type lady at a roadside diner near Malibu. He ended up staying with her, helping at the diner and singing there in the evenings. During his stay he found an old guitar case with some handwritten music in it. He started to play the song, but the old guitar strings broke, so he put the instrument away. However, he kept the song, finished it, and referred to it later in the story.

When Bryan had exhausted all his leads and more or less given up on his songwriting career, the old lady, Dee, came to the rescue.

She said, "Bryan, I never told you about my husband, but I'm going to tell you about him now. He always said, 'You don't lose if you never quit.' He never sold his songs neither, Bryan, and when he knew his life was over, he looked in the mirror and said, 'Dee, I figured it out. The victory wasn't a prize. The victory was the journey.'"

Lane got that one right. The victory was the journey. Grant wondered why he never sold the movie.

The ending was touching, when Bryan sang the song he had found in the old guitar case. It was the one written by Dee's husband, but she had never heard it.

> *We were sitting alone… She was the princess, and I was the frog… I'll never forget the kiss that she gave me, because I turned into a king in a moment with her… Thank God for memories… It was a Sunday, and we were laughing and that's when I told her I hoped she'd remember… forevermore.*

Grant was almost mesmerized as he continued to play a behavior-analysis role he wasn't trained to do. He felt himself needing to take this to the finish.

> *By now she's sitting alone… The princess is queen, and the frog has gone… The days, the seasons, and the years they go by… like a two-minute ending on a ten-second song…*

This song and scene were like the summation of a life—maybe two, maybe more.

> *Thank God for memories, because on some Friday, when this song is over, she may remember the time I told her… Memories last forever… forevermore.*

The old lady remembered 'the time he told her'. Some things did last forever.

Grant remembered thinking that death and taxes were the only things that lasted forever, but Lane was right—memories did too. The guy he was chasing had a lot of experience in *living* and *loving,* and there was a lot in this story about not giving up—as well as the value of memories. These were facts, and Lane was full of clues.

*To dream the impossible dream,* Grant thought. *We're all the same. Memories last forever.* He summarized what he knew about Lane. *Is this the same guy who worked for the CIA? Couldn't be. What the hell happened in sixty-nine? I have to find him.*

Somewhere, between the confusion of what had happened before Lane had written the screenplay and conflicting thoughts of having Eve in his arms, Grant fell asleep.

* * *

At Little Houston, however, Shelly and the computer worked through the night. Her combination of intelligence, creativity and persistence won out, and the phone in Grant's hotel room rang.

In a stupor, he fumbled for the phone and answered instinctively, "Harris."

"Mr. Harris, I found it."

He sat up and looked at his watch; it was just after four thirty a.m. He rubbed his eyes as he tried to make his brain catch up with the time. "Found what?"

"The page Lane posted. It was in a hidden file behind a church homepage."

"Behind what?"

"A church homepage. 'Where evil looks, it'll never be.' There was a webpage for Saint John's Church on the HiLite server, and I found it in the Internet directory, so I played with some URLs and finally made it work on *'tilde-If.'* I wouldn't have bothered you this early, but I thought you'd want to know. It's a letter to someone named Doc, and it tells quite a story. I think this is what you're after."

"I'll be right there. Do you have any coffee?"

"No. I have some Cokes, though."

"Thanks anyway."

Grant called room service and ordered coffee for Little Houston. He pulled on his pants, went to the sink, splashed water on his face, and headed for the small office.

He wanted to see what Shelly had uncovered so he would have time to consider it before he met with Rob.

Back at the conference room, Shelly took off her glasses, smiled to herself, and gave a small yawn. This had been rewarding so far. What was next on the plate? What now, since the game had picked up speed?

In the matter of two more swigs on the Coke, Grant was back in Little Houston. He walked over to Shelly and the computer, and started to read the page. It was a letter without a date, just the salutation "Dear Doc."

Grant stopped for a minute. Veronica Lane had mentioned her husband's brother flying down from west Texas to be with the family on the weekend, a day after Lane's disappearance.

"Doc could be his brother," Grant suggested and continued reading.

> *I wanted you to have this in case something happened. I don't understand what's going on, but it has to do with something I did a long time ago. Not very many people knew, but I was in Vietnam in 1969. I wasn't there long, so it was easy to keep it secret.*
>
> *The mission tested one of our missiles with little capsule explosives in the warhead. It was top secret. No one had names, just code names, just a secret group for one mission. You may remember the time I went to Fort Hood - that was part of it. I had a chance to be a patriot, and I took it.*

Grant looked at Shelly. "Anne, you're great. This information might put us on the fast track."

She was glued on Grant. "Keep reading. It gets better."

> *John told me it was twelve guys. The training was three days at a time, about two months, and the mission lasted about ten days. That's all he'd tell me. Bobbie knew a little, but she didn't know where I was or for what. It was handled like I was out of town on business.*
>
> *When I got back, they told Bobbie and John that my head wound caused amnesia. I don't think so, but I was confused. I think they drugged me or gave me shock treatments, because everything was a blur. I couldn't remember anything, it was all blank. Even friends and their names. Nothing. I didn't remember you. I don't know if you remember how crazy I was or not.*

*Since I didn't see the family much around the time Julie came along, my condition didn't pose a threat. Bobbie helped me remember the parts of my life that I needed to know, and I tried to figure out the rest. I couldn't get past the nightmares. So I tried to forget about it, drink a lot of scotch and forget about it.*

*Long story short, I still can't shake the thoughts. I remember a village and a helicopter and a few things. Everything is fuzzy, like a dream. John kept saying things would come back, but they didn't.*

*When I worked at First American in Kansas City, I decided to try to find out about it. I called Jim Gates at Skyland. He didn't return my call, and the next day a guy showed up at the bank. It wasn't Gates, but I guess he called them. Can you believe it? Eight years and three job changes, five hundred miles away?*

*He sat in my office and asked me about Bobbie and Julie. He said they were checking on my mental condition! Hell, it was this son of a bitch and his friends who drove me crazy! He said he knew I was having marital difficulties and wondered if I was going to be all right. I couldn't believe it, after eight years, from one phone call.*

Grant stopped for a moment. "This is a classic intelligence tactic. They keep intimidating you until you think you're crazy. It sounds more like the Defense Intelligence Agency than the CIA, or something like that. We'll have to check into that. Defense Security Division would be the worst." He went back to the screen.

*I don't know what hole these guys crawled out of, but it made me think even harder. I don't remember what we did, but it must have been bad. The guy gave me a card with an 800 number, in case I needed to talk someone. I took that to mean I wasn't supposed to talk to anyone but them, so I took the hint.*

*You remember coming to Kansas City after Bobbie and I separated? I was real screwed up, and I was afraid they'd think I called you to come, but I didn't hear from them again until South Padre Island.*

"Anne, it sounds like our friend, Lane, might have done more than one disappearing act," Grant said.

*I wrote the Department of Defense to see what they had on me, and guess what? I don't think they know I exist. But the same guy came to the island a couple of days later, just to say hello and let me know they knew where I was. They knew I had talked to Defense, and they didn't want me to talk to anybody. They explained that again, real loud. The guy was really pissed.*

Grant stopped again and looked at Shelly. "Why do you suppose this guy Lane is still walking around? Most of the time, these creeps make people have accidents. Damn, they've taken out a lot of people for a hell of a lot less."

As he started to read again, the phone rang. Shelly answered.

It was Rob. "I found the link," he said.

Shelly smiled. "Me too." She mouthed "Rob" to Grant.

"How did you find it?" Rob asked.

"Well, turkey, since you wouldn't give me root access, I used my brain, which is what they taught me in school."

"Wise Guy University?" Rob teased her. "OK, one for you. If you ever give up the easy life of government service, come see me. Is Grant there?"

"Sure. Hold on."

She handed the phone to Grant. The two confirmed their plans to meet for coffee at the Country Omelet on Tenth Street at six a.m. and untangle what information was possible from Lane's letter. After Grant finished talking, he returned to the computer and Lane's letter.

*I stayed out of their way for years, until I found Usenet. It gave me a chance to snoop anonymously. A vet buddy of mine told me to check out an airfield at the Quang Tri beacon near Song Thach Han because I remembered the name. I found it, and it had been used by Special Forces for airlift to the DMZ.*

*I have vague memories of helicopters, and falling. That's all, except faces kept talking about what I remembered, and I felt like I slept a month. John joked that they gave me a frontal lobotomy, and I'm wondering if there's such a thing as a partial. Anyway, I want to forget, but I can't...and I think I'm losing it.*

Grant murmured, "Maybe you did."

*I posted to a newsgroup, alt.war.vietnam, about anyone remembering anything about a missile test in '69 around Quang Tri. I got a garbled response. It was jumbled or encrypted to the point where I couldn't read it. It said "King Arthur," and it was signed "Bret" without a return address. I saved it.*

Shelly went back to the other computer and started typing away. "What are you doing?" Grant asked.

"I'm going to locate the newsgroup and see what kind of activity it has. Then I'm going to try to find the 'Bret' file in Lane's computer and see if we can find the message."

Grant returned to the letter.

*The next day our server got hacked, and my e-mail was trashed. Everything's gone, so I'm sure someone was watching the newsgroup or me. I think I'll get another visit real soon, and I don't think they'll be very nice. I don't think they like me anymore. They sure don't like me snooping around.*

*I'm not going to mail this to you; it'll be too easy to trace. I'm posting it so somebody smart will find it... I figure if you get it, they're on our side. Love ya. —Lone Wolf*

Grant combed his mustache with his finger as he sat assimilating the information.

Lone Wolf. One quarter or so Cherokee...

The room was silent except for the slight sound of Shelly's touch while her fingers danced across the computer keyboard as she scanned articles in the now important Vietnam newsgroup.

Grant printed three copies of the letter and brief-cased a disk. He made a joke about the fact that computer people never sleep. Shelly laughed and kept searching.

It was going on five twenty a.m., and he was meeting Rob at six, so he excused himself and went to his room for a quick shower.

He wondered if Eve was dreaming about him. They'd had a wonderful dinner. Time would tell. Maybe next he could get a response to the question about what it means to be "truly loved and cared for," and he could share the rest of Lane's story. But at this time, his thoughts were jumbled between the case and Eve.

Lane had led him onto a trail that revealed an intense history of surveillance, yet the illusive question still remained—"Why?" This fellow didn't fit the CIA profile. Who has the kind of resources it takes to track someone for decades? Now Grant and his team had joined the chase, and he was becoming totally invested, almost obsessed with finding the answers.

Among the many queries, Grant questioned whether his romantic desires would interfere with his tracking down Lone Wolf Lane.

# CHAPTER SEVEN

As Grant was leaving the hotel en route to the Country Omelet for coffee with Rob, the early-morning light snuck around the winter-looking clouds like a game of hide-and-seek. It duplicated the picture in his office—a 'ten' sunrise was on the way, *Fire in the Sky.*

*What's the old saying?* He thought. *"Red sky in the morning is a sailor's warning..."*

Grant wondered if today's sunrise was a warning.

Although he hadn't slept long, the time he'd spent resting was enough to refuel, and he was ready to go. After ordering coffee and an English muffin, he and Rob discussed the letter. They reiterated it line by line, but Rob didn't have anything new for Grant's analysis, and he didn't think Lane's letter needed to be overly interpreted.

In a humorous way, Rob noted that Lane was as straight as a trombone player's arm on a low note. He had nothing to hide and evidently skipped town thinking the hack was related to his past encounters. He was probably right.

Grant dropped a piece of ice into his coffee and stirred it. "We need to find out which agency is after him. Then we can focus on why." After a pause, Grant continued, "We ought to get this. This is decades we're talking about. Think about it, Rob. These guys were after him, and nobody close to him knew it? How did this guy keep that kind of a secret for so long?"

"You know as well as I do. He never broke silence."

Grant shook his head questioningly. "Well, he got close a couple of times, and I guess he broke it now."

Rob nodded slowly. "That'd be a damn good reason to want to disappear, don't you think?"

Grant drank from his coffee cup then responded, "Actually, he didn't roll over, because he still doesn't know what this is about. Unfortunately, neither do we."

Rob seemed particularly serious. "Ben's too close to something, so they're going to bring him in or shut him up."

"Well, they'll have a hell of a time finding him. The guy has lived through about thirty years without anyone knowing anything about this. He took the 'top-secret' part seriously. Most people can't keep a secret until a party's over, at least not normal people."

"Guess you have to assume Ben isn't normal, at least in that regard." Rob adjusted himself in his seat. "He's reserved, quiet…a loner."

"Lone Wolf. I guess we can agree that his disappearance has something to do with the Department of Defense, or military intelligence, and his participation in some covert mission."

"That's my guess."

"If we get the timing right, because of his daughter Julie's age, the mission must have taken place shortly after the start of the Tet Offensive, and if the letter is true, Lane doesn't remember much about the mission at all."

Grant summarized. "The letter sounds pretty confusing, and any effort he made to find out about it was appearing to become detrimental to his health."

After reading the letter again, they planned an afternoon meeting then left the restaurant for their respective destinations. Rob went home to get some sleep, and Grant returned to Little Houston.

* * *

The office was quiet when Grant returned. He assumed Shelly had gone to her room, since she had been awake all night. With a slight yawn, he checked the coffee and was pleased to discover it was mildly warm. He poured a cup and, in the silence of the early morning, sorted his thoughts as he gazed through the conference room window at the palm trees and lush undergrowth beyond.

He asked himself, *what do you know, Grant? What are the facts?*

With lingering thoughts about the intelligence community and questions regarding why Lane hadn't been eliminated, he took the pen out of his shirt pocket and wrote on a post-note pad, "VIETNAM MISSION" in neat capital letters. Thoughtfully, he pulled the slip from the top of the pad and placed it on the wall next to the small desk that held Lane's computer.

After sitting back and looking at it, he repeated his task and wrote, "VACUUMED FILE." As he affixed it to the wall beneath the first note, he changed his mind and placed it to the side.

Then he wrote "INTERNAL AFFAIRS," and placed the slip carefully over the outside column above the note that read, "VACUUMED FILE."

Continuing as if writing an outline for a thesis, Grant looked back through the letter that contained Lane's communiqué.

He wrote "SKYLAND" and posted the note on the wall in the "MISSION" grouping.

During his continuing deliberation, he poured another cup of coffee. After sipping a little, he placed the pad down and called room service. After a brief conversation on behalf of Little Houston, he had negotiated unlimited hot coffee and Cokes for the day. For now they would be delivering pan dulce, a mixture of Mexican sweetbread pastries and doughnuts.

Grant was the FBI Assistant Special Agent in Charge, and he knew how to take care of his people. He also selfishly thought he might score some points with Shelly and Eve when they returned. He might need some special favors if the investigation heated up, and he needed to move as fast as Lane needed him to.

He sipped again, from the almost cold coffee, and continued his posting exercise.

"JIM GATES" was aligned under "SKYLAND" and "MISSION." Grant paused and stared at the wall as if arranging the items in his mind.

*Could Miss Scarlet be in the kitchen?* He thought. *If so, who has the candlestick? Why did they use a civilian technician as an operative on a military test mission?*

He wrote, "WHY CIVILIAN?" and placed it sideways across "SKYLAND" and "JIM GATES."

After some almost-tortured thought, and with a slight scowl, he wrote "CIA" and "DOD" on individual notes then placed them under "INTERNAL AFFAIRS." Eve could deal with those.

After reading the letter again, Grant wrote "KING ARTHUR" and affixed the note under the "MISSION" grouping. Then he wrote "BRET," which he placed off to the side next to "KING ARTHUR."

This was shaping up like a chess game. The pieces were maneuvering into play, but it hadn't progressed far enough for him to develop a strategy. It would help if he knew the opponent, but Grant thought he'd eventually learn who the enemy was from the moves that were being made.

The minute hand on the clock finally moved back to the top. Grant decided to call Big Houston at eight to see what Georgia had to tell him about the big picture.

As he prepared to pick up the phone, the door opened, and in walked Eve Delaney. He had never seen anything as beautiful as she looked this particular morning, the morning with a fire in the sky. Her dark hair glistened as it reflected the light.

*Is she always this radiant?* He wondered. Grant decided she was, but he had never allowed himself to notice.

She smiled with a naturalness that made him feel like a teenager. "Good morning, Grant. Sleep well?"

He smiled as he thought about how to make his heart slow down. "Sure, maybe not long enough. Want some coffee?"

Eve took the coffee and looked at the etchings that had newly appeared on the wall—courtesy of her friend, artist Harris.

"Before you tell me about those," she said, pointing at the notes, "did you finish reading the screenplay?"

"I got through it, read most of it, and skimmed through the rest. It's pretty good. Would have made a decent movie."

He thought about how the plot eventually turned into a love story, but he kept that to himself.

"There were more songs in there you'd probably like."

Maybe they could talk about it later, about how 'Thoughts are not a good cold-night companion, but memories hold me, until I hold you again…'

The songs—riding a merry-go-round and taking a romantic walk on the beach—all yielded interesting opportunities for discussion; he knew Eve would like the ending of the screenplay.

"Any clues in there, or just these here?" she asked, looking again at the notes.

Grant thought for a moment. "I'll tell you one thing, Eve. Something's off with this. He wasn't one of them."

Eve walked closer to the postings and pointed to "INTERNAL AFFAIRS."

"What are you getting me into?" Obviously, she wanted to know, and noticeably, she was pleased to be included in whatever exercises Grant had in mind. Even so, she tried not to act overly enthusiastic.

He went on to explain where Anne had found the letter that Lane had left for his brother, and the world to find, and then reported on his meeting with Rob.

Grant then summarized the current position. He would need Eve's help—first to notify Jackson and put him on the spot to secure the additional information about who else was involved. The FBI had to find out who they were dealing with. If the approach didn't work, at least the communication would let Jackson's people know the FBI had sufficient information to conclude that Washington was somehow involved, either directly or indirectly, in Lane's disappearance.

Another major item for consideration was how to get Central Intelligence to disclose its involvement with either the Defense Intelligence Agency, the Department of Defense, or the DSD, the Defense Security Division. This had to be accomplished without any department finding out that the 'Little Houston' team had uncovered knowledge about their covert action in Vietnam. This was probably the encounter they were trying desperately to cover up. The action, likely taking place sometime after the Tet Offensive, must have been the source of their distress.

While explaining the information to Eve, Grant became very serious. He looked firmly into her gorgeous eyes, hoping she would see through his. "From now on, this may be getting more dangerous," he told her.

"Why?"

"Eve, think about it. They're already here. We know that, and they know we're after them, and they're hard after this guy. It must be big, maybe critical, because I talked to Houston, and our file—the FBI file— had to have been cleaned out."

"I saw your 'VACUUMED' comment there, on my side."

"Yes, when we looked at our file on Monday, we expected there to be some information, but there wasn't much. All the info we're using now came from CIA. Lane was on a top-secret project in sixty-nine, so we would've run a complete file on him, or he wouldn't have received security clearance. He received top-secret clearance, so we ran a 'complete,' and there's nothing important in his file before nineteen eighty-two."

Eve looked serious. "They've had somebody on the inside."

"And if we figure this out, Lane is going to be more than just an embarrassment to the CIA. He can get a lot of people in a lot of…stuff. Did I ever tell you why I didn't go with Intelligence?"

"Because you had some?"

Grant responded seriously. "Because you have to be able to take orders and not question them. That's what *they* do. Thinking is not an option."

He didn't say "kill without a reason," but without being overly dramatic, he thought he had made the point just as well.

Eve looked into his eyes and recognized his concern for her well-being. Acting as if she didn't know how to respond to the feeling, she hesitated for a moment and realized how much of her life had passed since she had risked being this close to someone—close enough to really care.

After the brief eye contact, they returned to the subject. Eve discussed the possibilities for locating the file thief. Information could be tracked through the file references and logs to see who had accessed the Lane file and when. This could help in locating the culprit, but what about the information that had escaped down the river?

After further thought, Eve showed her expertise, and the reason she had achieved her department-director status at such a young age, by telling Grant something he didn't know. Back in 1972, before the new computer filing systems were installed, all the files were stored on microfiche. It might be possible to retrieve the missing information from the micro files that were stored away. She would have to research it, because she knew they were date-separated in a number of different locations.

The day was beginning to take shape, and just as Grant felt almost comfortable enough to ask Eve out again, Shelly appeared at the door. She walked in carrying a Coke, and everyone exchanged good-morning pleasantries.

"What's with the yellow wallpaper?" she asked.

Eve looked up from the list she was compiling. "Grant's making this a puzzle so we can put it together."

"Sounds like fun. Count me in. By the way, Mr. Harris, I had some more luck this morning after you left for breakfast."

"What did you find?"

"It's what I expected. Most of the Internet communication on Lane's computer was through the Netscape browser, but I found two other browsers, Chameleon and Internet Explorer. Chameleon's cache didn't show much activity, but the Explorer browser did have some data in a number of areas."

"And...?"

"I traced the cache history and found postings for 'alt.war.vietnam.' It was easier than I thought."

"Keep going."

"I found something posted last Thursday, the day before Lane's last connection. It suggested that he go to a chat room and leave an e-mail address for Bret. I went to the chat location, but no one was logged on. I thought I'd try again later today."

"Good work, Anne. Thanks."

Grant sat down and picked up the phone to call Big Houston; Eve did the same using the other phone. He spoke to Georgia and two other agents, but nothing noteworthy was revealed.

The jury-tampering case and an extortion attempt were being handled, and there still wasn't much on the blood that had appeared at the hospital. A blood specialist at M.D. Anderson had run tests and discovered that all five pints had been from the same donor. The only other information gleaned was that there was an unusually low corpuscle count in the samples. Grant's team traced the delivery to a local express-delivery company, but they hadn't found the source yet.

After receiving this information, Grant told Georgia what he needed to accomplish as soon as possible.

"I need all the information we can find on Skyland Technologies in Fort Worth, anything related to government missile contracts during or before sixty-nine…and follow up on Jim Gates' involvement with Skyland. Also, call David Lasorta and see if he can help with locating some information on defense projects or missions out of Quang Tri, Vietnam, in sixty-nine. Almost everything related to that time should be declassified by now, so maybe he can find a lead or two. The only code name I have for this would have something to do with 'King Arthur.' I don't know if it'll do him any good, but tell him anyway."

At the same time, Eve was talking to her office on the fourth floor. Her assistant, Darrell McCullock, was listening on the opposite end of the line and taking notes.

"The file we have on Benjamin Wells Lane doesn't have much information before eighty-two," she said. "He received top-secret security clearance for a government project sometime after sixty-eight. A copy of the original file is in Grant Harris's office, so get it and start a search on the logs to see who accessed it and when.

"Then find out which storage unit has the sixty-five to seventy microfiche copies of the files. We'll need to re-create the file to see what someone didn't want us to know. It's very important, Darrell, that we find out if the file has left the Bureau or if this work was done within our own organization."

As Eve continued, Grant paused in thought during his one-sided conversation with Georgia. This was exciting, but he felt like time was running short. Then, as usual, he asked Georgia questions she didn't have time to answer.

"What was so important about this project that made it necessary to use a civilian on a military test mission? Georgia, when you talk to Lasorta, ask him that question. Tell him this guy doesn't fit the profile. He's not one of them. There's something very unusual about the nature of this. Also, check military installation hospitals that were receiving stations for Vietnam casualties during the Tet Offensive. That should do it for now. I'll talk to you in an hour. Thanks."

Eve had completed her call and listened as Grant completed his. She asked, "Why would they use civilians on those kinds of missions?"

Grant thought for a moment before he answered. "Covert military operations use mercenaries when they don't want to be held accountable. The whole setup is for 'plausible deniability.' If anything goes wrong, they disavow any knowledge. Sometimes they use technical support people to fill in, just like we do—like Rob. Since Lane was probably some type of ordnance guy, we probably need to work under that assumption."

He stopped in the tracks of his thoughts. Suddenly a realization came to him, something he had felt all along—'ordnance advisor.'

He spoke to the others as if he was awakening from a trance. "Wait a minute. It wasn't a test mission. You don't go halfway around the world to test something. Why do you call it a test mission if it's not a test mission?"

He was talking to himself and Eve while Agent Shelly was tickling her keyboard yet still paying attention.

"Maybe they didn't want the civilian to know what they were doing," Shelly suggested.

Grant responded, "Good answer, but what were they doing?"

All three looked at one another for a moment, but no one had an answer.

Grant asked Shelly, "Woman, don't you ever sleep?"

She laughed lightly. "Only when I'm dead tired, and that's not often…at least not when I get excited."

Eve came back to the subject. "If you're right about this being military intelligence, what were they doing?"

"I think intelligence had to be working with someone else because they couldn't prepare for this type of mission; but whoever it is and whatever it's about, our catching up with them is getting critical. They might have outside professionals on it by now."

Shelly continued to tap the keyboard as she explored the newsgroup alt.war.vietnam.

Grant decided it would be a good idea to give Detective Rice a heads-up on the investigation and to pay a visit to Veronica Lane to discuss the letter Shelly had found. Eve phoned and set up a time with Veronica around nine thirty a.m., and Rice agreed to meet them as soon as they could get to the PD.

As Grant and Eve headed out the door, he glanced at the wall with the yellow sticky notes. He wished there was more information, but this would be a good day for gaining some more.

There was a *Fire in the Sky,* and he and Eve were on the same team, against the 'now-posted' facts about Benjamin Lane.

# CHAPTER EIGHT

The meeting with Detective Rice started less than fifteen minutes later. Grant had an assortment of information to present, although he had been in McAllen for less than twenty-four hours.

He gave Rice some of the information in the letter, but refrained from showing it, or from talking about the military involvement which might have remained classified. It was apparent that Lane's disappearance had been of his own choosing, and although it was still police business, as a missing-persons case, there seemed to be no foul play, at least not yet. Grant held a lingering opinion, however, that danger was imminent.

Rice explained his follow-up. He hadn't been able to determine any further contacts made by the intelligence officers and decided they must have disappeared from the scene. This came as no surprise to Grant, because Rob had pegged the guys as DOD or DIA, and they didn't seem to know what they were doing anyway. They were just a bunch of clowns hunting for a circus.

They could have been making their presence known in order to make the FBI think it had competition in finding Lane, but Grant didn't think so. He decided they were tagging along in order to move in and take Lane out quickly, after the FBI had his location. One thing was for certain as far as Grant was concerned—they hadn't left the scene. Maybe they were hiding in a sewer somewhere, with a tape recorder, but they were still there.

It was apparent Detective Rice was pleased to have received the heads-up from the main source, and Grant knew he could continue to receive whatever cooperation was needed as long as they remained in McAllen. The meeting concluded at a little after nine. Eve and Grant left with the promise to communicate again later in the day.

As they drove to Lane's home, Grant related his suspicions that the intelligence Feds hadn't left McAllen, nor did he think they would. He also confirmed Rob's recollection that they weren't CIA but other intelligence people—DSD, DIA, or military intelligence.

Although Eve knew Rob Garza's name and reputation as a technical advisor to the Bureau, she had never met him. She decided to withhold judgment regarding his credibility as a sleuth, or savant, until she had more information. This kind of skepticism was normal for Internal Affairs people; they questioned everything.

Grant made a mental note to have Eve check with Houston to see if they had made contact with Jackson yet, since he was the CIA humanoid who had started this. They needed to keep the pressure on him to find out who else was investigating Lane's disappearance. He began to wonder whether the CIA knew anything about this mission, or if they were out of the loop as well. Only forty-eight hours had passed, and the information was compounding. How dark could this be?

The agents arrived at Lane's house to find Veronica at home with both of her children. This was the first time either had met the Lane's youngest child, Alyce. She was a beautiful young teenager with an outgoing personality. During the first few minutes of conversation, the agents could tell she had a natural comfort around people. Eve was impressed by her success in the arts—ballet, drama, and chorus—and decided these activities must have given her maturity beyond her years.

Eve and Alyce were immediately drawn to each other, kindred spirits or some such thing. Grant thought about Eve's attraction to the young lady and hoped she would feel the same for his daughter, Laura.

After the introductory conversation, Grant handed Veronica a copy of the letter Agent Shelly had retrieved from the Internet and then explained how she had located it through a trail Lane had left in his computer. Lane wanted it to be found by the right people.

Wade read silently at his mother's side as Alyce looked on. Stillness ruled for the four or five minutes as the letter to "Doc" made its impression.

Finally Veronica said, "It's to his brother, but this doesn't surprise me. Somehow I had a feeling there was something that he didn't tell me. Now, I think nobody knew." Having the information almost seemed to irritate her. Maybe it was too much to assimilate, and she didn't want to know any more. Even so, she continued, "But why are they after him? What did he do?"

"Evidently he knows something they don't want him to tell," Grant offered. "To complicate matters, I'm still trying to find out who 'they' are." There wasn't much left to say, but after an uncomfortable moment of silence, he added, "We're going back to the office at the hotel. If you think of anything else, please call us."

* * *

Harris and Delaney departed for Little Houston.

Eve remarked, "The family doesn't seem to be as worried as they were yesterday."

Grant agreed. As they continued through the thought process, a natural flow developed between them. Colonel Mustard was heading for the parlor—but still in search of the weapon.

"If you follow it a step further, if you were Lane, and you didn't know exactly who they were or why they won't tell you anything, but you're sure they won't leave you alone..."

"I would try to find out," Eve responded. "And when I try, I get burned...three times at least."

"So what do you do?"

They both answered in unison, "Get the FBI to find out."

This had to be it! Lane had set up his own little sting operation so he could get someone to find out who was after him and what this was all about. Hell, he didn't know or have the resources to find out. He didn't understand the protocols, the nuances. He was just a civilian who had gotten caught in a bad place...*a real bad place.*

Grant laughed to himself. "Veronica said he was smart *like a fox.*"

"Or a *wolf,*" Eve murmured, recollecting the signature on the page.

If a sting was the case, what would be the next move? Grant had to assume Lane would know they would find his trail eventually and conclude he was leading them to something. Would he simply try to contact them?

Grant sped up a little to get back to the hotel office and see what information was being caught in the 'Big Houston' trap. Instinctively he knew that this was coming down.

* * *

It was scarcely ten a.m. Eve and Grant caught Shelly catnapping at the keyboard. Her internal sleep system had finally overridden the amount of caffeine in the case of Cokes she had consumed over the past twenty-four hours.

Grant gently roused her and told her to go to her room and get some sleep. In the somewhat agile stupor of the moment, she did manage to show the chief and Eve the "Bret" file she had found.

It read, "kingarthur.dir.missiondiamondstrike1. Starfinderdrop.blu-eretriever.recovery.nojoy.topsecret.hide."The postscript was "bret."

Maybe Lane hadn't seen the entire message, but he must have understood Bret's message to hide, because hide was what he did—and, of course, he solicitously left this message as a part of the trail.

Before Shelly retired to her room, Grant asked her about tracking the message to find out where it had originated. She said it was possible, but when she tried a trace route on the message, it had come out of an ISP in Oklahoma on a port-25 link, which meant, since it was an open line, anyone with some expertise could have used it to hide their address.

With a promise to be awake by noon, Shelly departed to her room.

Eve picked up the "Bret" message, which the printer had coughed out, and read it again.

"So does this mean 'King Arthur' was the mission director?"

She and Grant agreed, for the present, that this was the case. "Diamondstrike 1" was probably the name of the mission. Grant added that they couldn't leave out the "1," because the number may mean there was more than one Diamondstrike mission.

Eve wrote on the sticky notes and placed them on the facts wall. Under "KING ARTHUR" and "BRET," she placed "DIAMONDSTRIKE 1," "STARFINDER," and "BLUE RETRIEVER." She affixed "TOP SECRET" and "NO JOY" below the other notes.

Eve and Grant discussed other possible meanings for "hide," which also appeared in the "Bret" message, but they couldn't conclude anything, other than the fact that Bret was warning Lane that someone was getting close. "No joy" could have referred to the mission failure or a missile failure. Both agents were convinced the mission wasn't a test, as Lane had suggested, so failure might have been an embarrassment to "King Arthur" or whoever was responsible for the mission.

The phone rang. It was David Lasorta, the FBI special agent in charge of learning everything no one else could possibly find out. If there were such a thing as a covert FBI operation, Lasorta would be in the middle of it. It was like having a mercenary on your side.

Georgia had charged Lasorta with finding whatever he could about the Vietnam information Grant had requested.

"Hey, Grant. Sounds like you have a good one going now, back in my time."

"Yeah. Should be a perfect case for a scrounger like you…just about as old as we are, but for some reason it didn't go away for this civilian, Benjamin Lane."

"Well, I'm on it, and here's what I have so far. This is declassified information. Anything further will have to go through some channels. Skyland Technologies in Fort Worth had development contracts throughout the sixties and seventies as a major supplier for GSA and the Department of Defense. Probably should make a note of that since General Services spends a lot of money that isn't theirs." Lasorta continued. "There's nothing unusual about anything I found, except they had a reputation for taking care of the brass, if you know what I mean. They had beautiful secretaries who worked late and so on. Use your imagination, Grant, now that you're single. Heh…heh!"

"Enough wisecracks," Grant told him. "Listen, I just got a new clue. How about the name Diamondstrike?"

"Yeah, I might be able to help you with that one. The Diamondhead missile was one of the ordnance weapons under research and development at Skyland in the mid-to-late sixties. I saw some pictures of it. It was a funny-looking thing, about as big as a bazooka, and had a diamond-shaped nose that was bigger than the body. It was fired by a portable ground launcher, which was comparable to a grenade launcher but a little larger—almost like a great big RPG."

"Was it ever manufactured?"

"Let's see… Variations of the missile were, but Diamondhead was actually an introductory order for test-only deployment of a new delivery system for chemical agents. That's what made it unique. One of the Diamondhead missiles involved a low-level burst of numerous small-explosive canisters that could impact a well-defined area. Supposedly this was to allow for isolated targeting in heavily populated areas."

"I get it, just kill a *few* people and hold down the collateral damage."

"Right. Diamondstrike could have been a mission using the Diamondhead missile. What do you think?"

"Small canisters? Lane called them capsules in his letter. We're closing in on something here. Tell me more."

"The explosives technology was the forerunner of auto-airbag canisters," Lasorta said.

Something clicked for Grant. "Wait a minute… airbag capsules?"

"Yes, the small explosive pellets."

"Damn! Hearn knows something about this."

"Who's Hearn?"

"Lane's ex-father-in-law. He makes those SRS explosives now, and I'll bet he knew something then. I'll track that one myself. What else do you have?"

"The test runs on the missile and its delivery system were inconclusive," Lasorta said. "Jim Gates was part-owner of the company. He's clean. Security clearances and everything else checks out. There's no other information. The program was canceled in sixty-nine. Here's an interesting thing I was able to get from my source. The missile had a very complicated loading mechanism, and the intricate nature of the loading process was the reason for the project's cancellation. This might be the answer to your question, 'Why a civilian?' Lane did some drafting on the warhead. Maybe it was complicated, and maybe he was one of the people who knew how to load it."

"Did you find out anything about a mission?"

"Nothing we can hang our hat on, but I did receive a couple of leads to chase. Now that we've got some names, I'll see where it goes. I can tell you it looks more like military involvement and less of a direct relation to Defense at this point. Of course, you know where that goes... sideways."

"Anything on 'King Arthur'?"

"None of my name traces came up with anything on that," Lasorta said, "but that doesn't mean anything. We'll keep looking. By the way, Lane left Skyland in sixty-nine."

"Is that about it?"

"Yes, except my contact said to watch your 'six.' This isn't something they want to have investigated. It's deep cover."

"Well, we'll be the judge of what gets investigated. Are you sure that's all your source knows?"

"I think so, but I'll tell him what you said, Grant. Just be careful."

As the conversation concluded, Lasorta promised to keep Grant apprised of new developments. Grant was pleased to have received so much information in such a short time.

He summarized the other end of the conversation for Eve, and the pieces seemed to fit with the letter Shelly had found.

Grant posted "DIAMONHEAD" and "CHEMICAL WEAPONS" under the "MISSION" side of the facts wall. Then he wrote "HEARN" and "EXPLOSIVE CAPSULES" and placed those names to the side.

Eve was slow to remark, "Chemical weapons. It makes you proud to be an American."

Grant responded, "Got to keep up. Everyone else is doing it." He continued distantly, "But what do you tell your children?"

Eve gazed out the window. "We tell them what you said, 'Everyone else is doing it.' " It was obvious neither one liked the answer, but neither had a solution.

After a moment of silence, she said, "Maybe that's what happened, the reason they wanted Lane to forget. Maybe they really did a job on his head. I mean, like shock treatments or drugs. Maybe they got him involved, and it turned out he didn't want to do it. Maybe he disagreed with what they were doing. I wouldn't do it."

"It's certainly a possibility. Lane didn't think he had amnesia, and he still had trace memories of what happened."

Eve glanced back to the notes on the wall. "It sounds like he was torn between wanting to remember and wanting to forget."

For a moment Grant was silent. He thought about the other clues from Lane, specifically regarding *The Man of La Mancha*. After all, it was Lane's favorite movie. Grant remembered the line "Fight the unbeatable foe" from the song "The Impossible Dream."

"Don Quixote said, 'Some men's delusions are very real.' " He looked deeply into Eve's eyes. "Lane must have decided that if it was important for them to keep him under surveillance, it must have been something significant, but I still can't understand why they didn't kill him. I mean, it's a damn good thing for him that they didn't, but I don't understand it."

Grant seemed alert to something. He pulled out his notepad and flipped through it. Then he retrieved the phone number for John Hearn and dialed it. Eve looked over his shoulder, and he showed her the name of the party he was calling.

In the conversation that followed, Grant introduced himself and told Hearn of his discussion with Julie. He related a short version of their conversation, as well as her suggestion that Hearn might have some input into the happenings of 1968 and '69.

Although cordial, Hearn was elusive. "Guess you can try," he said.

"What do you remember about sixty-eight and sixty-nine?"

"C-R-S…"

"Pardon me? What's that?"

"Can't remember shit."

"Were you acquainted with Skyland Technologies?"

"Yeah."

"Were you acquainted with the Diamondhead missile program?"

"Can't say."

"Why not?"

"You know it's classified."

"Not any more. What about those little explosive canisters or capsules? I understand your company manufactures them now."

"Yes, something like that."

The voice on the other end of the phone was mostly silent, voicing only answers to Grant's direct questions.

"Mr. Hearn, can't you tell me anything that will help me find out what this is about? I need to find Lane, and I'm beginning to think I need to find him in a hurry. Anything about the missile, the payload? Was it a chemical weapon?"

Grant allowed Hearn the time to consider the question and the urgency of a reply.

"Mr. Hearn, I'm talking 'urgent' here."

Finally Hearn spoke. "I never told you this…"

"I understand."

"The Diamondhead was designed for a low-level burst of small darts in a limited area. The darts were propelled by small explosive charges. Do you think that makes much sense for a weapon of mass destruction?"

"Well, no."

"How many people are you going to take out with that type of weapon?"

"I don't know. Not many."

"Then maybe the payload was different."

"Like what?"

"Come on, Harris. Figure it out. They were planting something in a small area. Maybe they didn't want to kill a lot of people in a hurry." Hearn let the knowledge settle into the conversation. "Let's say they intended to plant a seed and let it grow."

Grant thought about this. He looked at the facts wall and back at Eve. He was getting a strange feeling, and he asked the next question in a very serious tone. "Biological?"

"I don't know that at all…and you never heard it from me, but that's where I'd be looking."

"What kind of biological weapons were they using?"

"That's all I can give you."

"Do you know where Lane is?"

"No. I doubt if he'd risk calling me. Don't worry. He'll probably find you before you find him."

"Why didn't they take him out?"

"He had something they wanted," Hearn said, "but I don't know what. I hope you find out. I'd be interested in that one myself. Ben came back a mess, but he did come back, so he must have had something on 'em."

The conversation ended, and Hearn asked Grant to call him again if he came closer to Lane, but not to call if he didn't. In short, Grant thought Hearn was concerned, but not overly so, about the dangers his ex-son-in-law might be facing.

Grant was silent as he placed the phone in its cradle. Eve watched him as he struggled with the questions. He leaned back in his chair and looked at the ceiling, then at Eve, then back at the posted facts on the conference room wall.

Eve sat in silence and watched him dwell in the rhythm of his thoughts. She couldn't help thinking how much he looked like Magnum, P.I. She smiled to herself. Even in the seriousness of the moment, Evangeline Justine Wednesday was glad she had made the decision to come to McAllen.

For a moment she fantasized about being in Grant's embrace, and then questioned her desire. *Is it infatuation*, she wondered, *or am I falling for him?*

As her self-analysis continued, it became apparent that she had strong feelings for him. She was glad she hadn't returned to Houston. She needed more time—time with Grant, time to get a few more of his bricks—but for her, the emotions involved with this case were complicating what should be simple to understand.

Grant sat up in his chair and returned to reality. His comment invaded the room like the clash of a symbol. "Hearn thinks they were biological weapons."

The room harbored a stunned silence as he continued. "It's one of two things. Lane has something they need, and they can't take him out." He paused while juggling between his own alternatives. "Or he's planning on telling a secret. I see some pretty heavy politics here, and I'm thinking Lane's just a pawn in their game. Maybe he was working for Defense and something happened. Something made the CIA get involved, and now he's in the middle of it. He could be playing both sides. What could that be? There's just not enough information, and he either knows or doesn't know…but he knows or doesn't know *what*?" Grant chided himself aloud. "Now that sounded brilliant, didn't it, Harris?"

They both chuckled over Grant's remark, and Eve made the move to call her office. It was time to find out the details Big Houston Internal Affairs had uncovered regarding the FBI file.

Darrell McCullock answered and said he had retrieved the file from Grant's office. The log listing from security was forthcoming in the next twenty minutes or so, and the 1965-through-1970 microfiche files were in a limestone cavern in Kansas City, Missouri.

Eve knew about the caverns in Kansas City. She had spent three months there when she was starting FBI legal training. Many people, even those living in Kansas City, didn't know the caverns existed. In an interesting location in the middle of town, they were accessed from a road on the side of a hilltop not far from Crown Center, the hotel-convention center and shopping complex south of downtown. The caves were a great place for storage and for certain businesses, such as sound studios, which required silence. A road led through the caves and offered access to many commercial enterprises. The caverns were ideal for file storage because they maintained a constant temperature of sixty-eight degrees.

McCullock gave Eve the name and number of the Internal Affairs agent in Kansas City to contact for access to the files.

"Another thing, Ms. Delaney," McCullock added. "I haven't been able to contact Agent Jackson to question him. Langley says he's out of the country."

"Out of the country?"

"Yes, and they won't tell me when he'll return."

"Who's his supervisor? Did they say?"

Knowing his boss was becoming irritated with the findings, McCullock told her, "They said they'd report your interest to his Bureau chief and get back to you."

"Right! I'm sure they will!" Eve stopped to recover her temporary loss of composure. "Good job, Darrell. Just call them every two hours until someone gives you an answer. And why don't you see what you can find out about Agent Jackson? Check our files."

"What about Jackson?" Grant asked.

"Out of the loop. Out of the country. What do you think?"

"Strange. I don't think that's good news."

Eve completed her conversation and made a few notes on her legal pad. When it appeared she had finished, Grant interrupted her thoughts.

"What are you thinking about, Miss Evangeline Wednesday?"

She smiled at hearing one of her many names spoken by someone whose affection she was beginning to cherish. She answered, "Kansas City. I love that city. It's where the microfiche files are. I was wondering if I should go up there and get them."

It was obvious Grant didn't want her to go. "Surely they can handle a simple request to copy one file between those dates in sixty-five and seventy."

He thought, *what am I doing? I'm coming on too strong.* Backing off the comment, he joked, "They'll get the info to us before you can get to the airport."

Eve smiled. She knew Grant wanted her to stay, and she was happy to comply with that wish. She really didn't want to go.

"Darrell gave them the information," she said, "so I guess we'll find out."

In the ensuing silence, Eve and Grant made affectionate eye contact and maintained it. Alone together in a historic Spanish hotel near the Mexican border, they were in search of a foundation for their relationship amid the complicated circumstances that encompassed them. Time was racing away in Little Houston, but there were now more facts on the wall to steer them in the direction of B.W. Lane.

# CHAPTER NINE

In the late morning of the team's third day on the case, the Little Houston office of the FBI exuded a more accommodating feeling as Grant and Eve reviewed the facts.

She leaned forward toward Grant. "How much do you want to bet Lane is in contact with his family?" She was very confident in her summation. "Do you think we should just ask them…or order a wiretap?"

Grant agreed. "Why don't you have our people check it out? We may want to see if anyone else has already tapped them. Call Bartow and have him check the lines at the house and the businesses."

It was close to eleven a.m. when the phone rang. Its signal interrupted the discussion, but it was an important call from Hector Perez in the Brownsville office.

"Good morning, Grant. How's the hunt?"

Grant briefly explained the information contained in Lane's letter and then redirected the conversation, "What do you have?"

Perez became excited. "Well…this makes more sense. About ten minutes ago, we received a call, anonymous, and the man said, 'Tell Ashell,' and he spelled it out, 'A-s-h-e-l-l,' 'to be at two-zero-six, seven-one, one-five-five, six-two at twelve-zero-two p.m.' That was all he said, and then he hung up."

After placing the phone on the speaker, Grant asked Perez to repeat the information. Eve wrote as he dictated the message.

Grant responded, "That's it. Shelly made contact with someone on the chat channel, and she didn't know it. But why did he call Brownsville? How did he know where the inquiries were coming from?"

They went on to discuss the voice characteristics or any other evidence that Perez might have gleaned from the call. There wasn't much.

He said it was a muted male voice with no distinguishing accent. The man spoke once, deliberately and slowly. He could have been military, or at least educated, because he said, "two-zero-six" instead of "two-oh-six," as many people do. This was all Perez could offer.

It was interesting though, that the man would call the Brownsville office to get hold of "Ashell." This deserved closer consideration. How did the caller know Anne Shelly was even with the FBI or that Brownsville knew anything about it? Brownsville is fifty miles from McAllen. Was someone covering a trail, or was someone afraid the FBI phone line was dirty?

Shelly's e-mail was open on the computer desktop, so Eve checked it but found she had no new mail.

"Guess we'll have to ask Anne after her nap," she said. "She might have a forwarding address or something. Want me to wake her up?"

"Not yet."

They finished with Perez by proposing a follow-up after Shelly reached 'whoever it was' at 12:02 p.m.

"We'd better have Bartow sweep these phones again too," Grant said. "Why would the man call Brownsville?"

Becoming more excited by the speed of the chase, Grant focused his thoughts. If he was on the right track, he knew the clues would find him.

*Suppose this person is Bret,* he thought. *Then he must want to give us some information. What does he have? Does he know about Lane, or could he have been an accomplice to the disappearance?*

Eve and Grant reviewed the "Bret" message on the wall of facts. How did Bret know the FBI was involved? How much contact did he have with Lane after the "Bret" e-mail? Maybe he knew where Lane was. Maybe Bret was Lane. Rob said he had a laptop with a modem.

The hotel service waiter arrived with a pot of coffee just about the time Eve was thinking about a cup. She decided it must have been a positive brainwave that had brought the fresh cup in the door at the perfect time. Mojo. Eve offered a cup to Grant and poured hers. Being in the same room with him was starting to feel normal. She decided to try the brainwave thing on him and get another dinner.

As the conversation reached a stall, Eve became impatient. She picked up the phone and dialed Big Houston to get the log information from Darrell McCullock.

The answer was yes, he had it, but he was waiting on the details for some of the log registration data that was missing. There were some alterations to an entry in 1971. The name was clearly Lawrence Collier, but the agency-department classification had been redacted with a black marker. Yet another entry, in 1978, showed the name Deborah Bearing-Haas; her department classification also was redacted.

Eve made notes and asked McCullock some questions pertaining to FBI file sequence numbers and who the file librarian had been on those dates. Unfortunately, both charge librarians were now retired, but McCullock would get their phone numbers to see whether either person had recollection of any unusual events occurring in 1971 or '78. Although he didn't hold much hope for those leads, he did initiate search strings on Lawrence Collier and Deborah Bearing-Haas.

After Eve ended the call, she was sure it had been an inside job. The files were accessible to properly documented representatives from other agencies, but no one could alter the logs—except perhaps someone on staff at the FBI, and it had to be someone high enough in the organization not to gather attention from the librarian. This wasn't a normal occurrence, and someone was accountable.

This was definitely a job for Internal Affairs, and Eve needed to issue a report immediately to flag the breach of security. Even though the breach had occurred years ago, someone hadn't followed the rules. Of course, she thought, it was amusing that the first person she should notify was sitting at the table next to her, as she thought about having dinner at a romantic outpost on the Rio Grande and "lookin' for a lost shaker of salt."

Eve relayed the news about the impropriety within the Bureau and explained the redaction of the agency name and the staff levels of two file users. This complicated things for Grant, because he had hoped to find out which agency had screwed with the file. However, Eve and Grant both concluded that if they could retrieve the missing information from the Kansas City office, it would lead them in the direction of the responsible party.

Even so, discovery would only be half the job, because there was still the cover-up, and finding out who had crossed that line would be in Eve's court. Tampering with those documents, and the file, was a felony. It might not be 'walking the plank' bad, but it was definitely 'hard time' bad.

Grant decided to check with Houston as well, in hopes that he and Eve could get their normal duties handled before Shelly returned for the chat session. It seemed awkward, Grant thought. Shelly's computer contact in the case was important, but currently she knew nothing about it.

Grant punched the Houston number on the phone. "When Shelly gets on the chat screen, I'll bet we cut to the chase," he told Eve.

Of course, there were the unspoken words. The contact with Bret had added a new sense of urgency to the timeline. If this was a cover-up of biological warfare, then lives were about to become cheap.

After a repeated study of the wall of facts, Grant made mental summaries as he sorted through his notes and waited for Houston. As it turned out, Georgia didn't have any more info from David Lasorta, but she did have the transit plan for the wounded in Vietnam. In the Quang Tri area, the first stop would have been the 636 MASH unit or the Third Medical Battalion Hospital at Quang Tri, then offshore to the Navy hospital ship *Repose*. For those requiring recovery time, it was either Guam or Manila, and for those headed home, the destination was Pearl Harbor. After this, they could have gone anywhere stateside.

Tracking back this far, in order to find any information, would be a fine madness, particularly if someone on the inside didn't want the information to get to the outside. Someone, knowing what others didn't know, could have used the twenty-five years to make sure the records ceased to exist. An example was the FBI's own file, and now, each new fact the FBI uncovered seemed more significant.

*Of course,* Grant thought, *if we're talking about germ warfare, "deep cover" would be no great surprise. In fact, it would be essential.*

At this point it would be a good idea to talk to Lane's physician and review his medical records, so Grant asked Georgia to call and get an appointment for later in the day and to let him know.

In the ensuing silence, Grant thought about calling and waking Agent Shelly to see exactly what, and how long, she needed to prepare for the chat session. He questioned Eve, but she didn't think Shelly had gotten nearly enough sleep and voted for giving her a few more minutes until after eleven thirty.

By this time, Grant wondered how to approach Eve about joining him for lunch, but those Evec eyes saw right through him, and she spoke first. "After this chat thing is over, maybe you'll join me for lunch, my treat."

Grant smiled and wondered if Eve had planted a bug in his mind; it seemed she knew everything he was thinking. "FBI's buying," he said. "I was getting ready to ask you the same thing."

Eve intentionally responded like a schoolgirl. "I know who's paying, but I asked you first." She gazed at him with her penetrating eyes. "I was hoping to help you look for that new recipe."

Their compatibility scored another point, but before they could continue the thread, the ringing of the phone suspended the conversation.

Rob had returned to HiLite, and Grant updated him on the upcoming chat session. Rob told them he would use a packet sniffer to locate the packet direction coming into the chat room and to see if he could locate the address of the sender. He tried to explain how he could position himself to get between the location and the sender, and backtrack the packet route. He told Grant to go ahead and wake Shelly, because computer people didn't need much sleep. Besides, she'd want to know where her information was taking them and how fast it was moving.

Eve called Shelly's room while Grant concluded his conversation with Rob.

Everything was going smoothly; Shelly was on the way down, and it was almost eleven thirty anyway. Thirty-two minutes—the countdown was on for a new set of clues that could prove pivotal in the investigation.

*Be there, Bret. Come in*, Grant thought.

It had to be Bret, and it was time to find out what he knew. Grant was pondering the value of interrogation techniques on a computer in real-time. Could you really believe what you saw or read without a face-to-face? He was forced to admit that what you see may not be what you get. The answers may lie in what Bret didn't say.

* * *

When Agent Shelly comfortably occupied her chair at Little Houston, they discussed the phone conversation with Brownsville.

After hearing of her contact, Shelly wrote her own sticky note, which read, "COMMAND CENTRAL." She placed it over her computer as she awaited the modem tone for confirmation that she was logged on to the Internet.

Youth had its way of either imitating, or maintaining, normalcy. Shelly looked extremely rested, refreshed, and excited. Eve complimented her appearance and wondered what brand of makeup she used, or if she had washed her face with Coca-Cola. Shelly was amused by the comment and countered that her appearance was due to a combination of very little sleep and a lot of cold water.

By Grant's estimation, the next thirty minutes was at least two hours long. He finally got up and walked down the hall with the knowledge that the pot wouldn't boil while he was watching it. His feelings of uneasiness generated from the knowledge that this was the first live, direct contact with a 'player' since the Monday morning meeting with Jackson. Then he remembered that he had vowed to slow down and relax.

It was refreshing to walk out and see the fountain, the palms, the lush undergrowth, and birds sipping from the water in the concrete birdbath. McAllen was at approximately the same latitude as Miami Beach, and although the temperature was in the seventies, it seemed warmer. He thought about how cold it had been in Houston a few mornings before—and in his life a few mornings before.

As he studied the amenities, his mind recaptured visions of Eve. He sensed a commonality in the way they approached the pace of the day. As his knowledge of her grew, he saw a deep and extreme pattern in her actions.

*What propels her life with such a passion?* He wondered. *Carried a step further, is this what she was talking about when I mentioned love?*

He thought about it for a moment.

*Passion...is it a quest? Is it something you have or a way you are? Is it a noun or an adjective? And if you have it, do you have it naturally, or is it something you choose, something you can even acquire? People like Eve experience life at a different level.*

Grant realized that because of her he was chasing a very special feeling. Two mourning doves flew away from the concrete birdbath, and Grant's dialogue with himself was suspended, but it was a good conversation.

* * *

Upon his return to the office, Grant joined Eve and Shelly in their talk about the chat room. In preparation, Shelly had located and book-marked the chat room so she could find it quickly. She also familiarized herself with the site and talked with Rob about the packet sniffer. She was acquainted with the technique and expected they would be able to get a trace.

As the clock approached high noon, the atmosphere at Little Houston became tense.

Shelly's fingers tapped the keyboard, then she smiled. "Some people spend far too many hours in chat rooms. Anybody read those stories? No one's in here right now. Think I'll just sit here for a minute and see how this is supposed to start. Does anyone's watch show Greenwich Mean Time?"

As they waited, Grant and Eve positioned themselves to see the screen. Then it happened.

On the screen appeared, "Ashell?"

Shelly quickly replied, "Here. Who r u?"

"Go to 205.51.417.99. U only have 5 sec to save."

Shelly quickly typed in the address and went to the new location. It was another chat room.

She sat there and until the next message appeared, "Location far nw laos, pilot who flew drop reassigned, next day I recovered 6, 4 damaged, 3 required isolation."

Shelly saved the note, and just as suddenly, it disappeared.

She typed, "R we safe here?"

"Nowhere."

That answer disappeared too.

"What was Lane trying to find out?"

"Wolf?" came the reply.

"Yes."

"Go to 206.10.401.221."

Shelly realized he was moving around rapidly with the expectation that the conversation was being monitored. She recognized the address as the previous location and complied.

A new message appeared. "Wolf forgot, wondering if he killed anyone. Scorpion said no. Saved them, blew it up, got contaminated."

"Where is Wolf?"

"Hiding."

The screen went blank again, and Shelly said, "I forgot to save that. Someone had better take notes."

Eve told her she had been keeping notes, so not to worry.

Grant suggested, "See if you can get anything more about the mission."

Shelly typed, "Who is Scorpion?"

"Mission cleanup."

"Where is he now?"

"Won't say."

"I need to find Wolf."

"Good luck."

"No, I need your help."

The screen was emptied again, and Shelly waited. "Damn it, Bret, come back!" she said.

"Tomorrow."

The message immediately was erased. The room and the keyboard were silent.

"Bret?" She typed.

Nothing happened. She returned to the other address and reentered her question, but it sat there alone, white on a black screen.

She commented, "Around the world with someone you don't know, in two minutes."

"I'll bet he's going to check with Lane," Grant said, "and find out if it's all right to tell us where he is." He hesitated with a bit of disappointment, and when no one commented, he continued, "We've learned a lot. I mean, what were they doing with biological weapons in northwest Laos in the first place? This is getting worse. It's no wonder they want to keep this thing quiet…and Lane must have screwed it up for them. Four damaged…isolation. It sounds like we have to find Scorpion some way or another."

Eve pointed to one of the sticky notes on the wall. "Well, Bret was the pilot. He said, 'I recovered six.' 'B-ret'—Blue Retriever. Starfinder was reassigned to who knows where, and here's something more for tomorrow…who's King Arthur?"

The phone rang, and Grant picked it up.

"Hey, Rob, what did you get?"

"I identified the location for one of them and got a trace started on the other."

"What do you mean, 'the other'?"

"There was the one guy on chat and another monitoring the whole thing."

"Are you kidding me?"

"No, someone was monitoring the conversation between Agent Shelly and the first guy. I couldn't watch. What'd they say?"

Grant recapped the chat conversation while Rob listened.

Rob replied, "I had Joe Guerra, our systems guy, check the route. The address of the guy doing the eavesdropping is in a series of class-three licenses controlled by—are you ready for this, Grant?—the UN."

"United Nations?"

"One and only…"

"Conveniently in bed with 'our military' and the CIA? This isn't right. Something is off with this. What's going on?"

This was becoming far too complicated. Grant needed to give some thought to the data and where it was leading before he could divine the strategy. He told Rob to keep tracing the route and to see if he could get the address for Bret. They agreed to meet at three o'clock at Little Houston, which would give Grant and Eve time to line up additional assistance from Big Houston.

They had spent a little more than two days on the case, but it felt like a week. The UN was some way connected to biological weapons tests in Laos. There is a *Fire in the Sky*!

"Anne, I need you to design a sting to catch those people who are trailing Bret and watching your conversations. They may be UN, but they're tied to US intelligence, and most likely they're the ones who tracked and hacked Lane. Maybe you can figure out something by posting to the newsgroup. Anyway, see if you can come up with a plan—and let me know it—before three."

"Sure." Anne Shelly was confident, and it was apparent she enjoyed her work. "That sweet roll's not going to hold me for very long, so would you guys pick me up a greasy hamburger and some fries, if you're going out?"

Grant smiled at Shelly and spoke to Eve. "OK, 'Wednesday,' I guess we can go find a quick lunch. The Houston crew won't be back for an hour."

"Wednesday?" Shelly said. "What's that about?"

Eve responded, "That's a whole conversation…I'll tell you later. You have my cell phone number if anything more comes through."

They left Shelly with her assignment and went out to get some lunch. Eve reminded Grant it was her treat, but he corrected her again.

As they departed, Grant looked back at the wall. Shelly was putting up more Post-it notes, increasing the facts in the quest for understanding the disappearance of B.W. Lane.

# CHAPTER TEN

Lunch didn't carry the romantic overtones of dinner the night before, but Grant didn't expect he and Eve would connect at the same level every minute they spent together. Thinking about the speed of the chase and the value of time, he tried to untangle the short answers delivered by Bret's chat session. They were very short answers, but it was a thirty-year-old question. Fortunately, he had found a partner to share his time with as he sorted through the complexities of the case.

Eve and Grant went trolling for seafood and found Joe's Crab Shack, "an embarrassment to any neighborhood," or so stated the marquee. They were acquainted with Joe's, as the chain was also located in Houston.

In the silence after they ordered, Eve became serious for a moment and asked Grant, "If you had to explain it all right now, what would you say is going on with this?"

Grant hunted through the maze and down the halls of his mind. "I wish you hadn't asked me that right now, because I feel like an idiot. By this time on a case, I generally have an idea of what's going on, but this is different. It's possible that I don't want to admit some things to myself. When we discovered the UN is involved in some way, the scenario went beyond my worst expectations. We have a lot of leads, but they're all cold. All the clues are gone, covered up... It all happened so long ago."

"Well, it may have been yesterday's problem, but a part of it is still happening now. Lane's gone. Where do we go from here? Grant, I know you're thinking something."

"I'm thinking the timing is getting critical. I think those people were infecting *somebody* with *something*."

"If Lane didn't remember anything, maybe that's why they left him alone."

"No. It doesn't make sense that they didn't take him out." Grant continued as if he were making an outline of the day's activities. "We need to get to Lane's doctor and see his medical records, and I wish Kansas City would get back to us about the microfiche. We also need to see how your man Darrell's doing with turning up the heat in his hunt for Jackson. If we put enough pressure on the CIA, we'll force them to make a move. I want to know if David Lasorta found out anything about those two, Collier and Bearing-Haas, who had Lane's file. Then we have to find Scorpion, whoever he is."

"If Bret talked to him, then he must still be in the mix…somewhere."

"Without Bret's help, we'll play hell finding him." Grant paused as he gazed into Eve's eyes. "We need to task a group to research chemical or biological weapons used in Southeast Asia. Bet we get a lot of help with that one. Want to watch Washington run for cover?" Thoughtfully, he continued, "Here's another big question. Why is the UN involved?"

After listening to Grant's review, Eve responded, "I'm not liking what our military is involved in."

"Eve, it may not be the military. Besides, you've always known there's more out there than what we know."

She looked distantly to the side, then back at Grant. "We don't know what's going on, and we're on the inside. It probably shouldn't freak me out, but I was never this close to it." She reached across the table and touched Grant's hand. "Do you think Lane's all right?"

"I didn't think so Monday because I knew the CIA wanted him, and they have a heavy network that's notorious for getting what it wants… no rules. I wouldn't be surprised if they put a contract out on him, but I think he's shrewd. He lost them, and right now he could be anywhere. The big thing is that he apparently hasn't broken silence. No one knows where to look. I also think Blue Retriever knows more, but he's not talking. He knows he's being watched."

As the discussion progressed to the next series of moves, and what they needed to do upon their return to Little Houston, Eve seemed a little more relaxed. "Can I change the subject?" she asked.

"Sure, go ahead."

"I like being on this case with you. It's like... Oh, well, just... I'm glad I've had a chance to get to know you better."

Grant smiled at the possibility. "Don't stop now. I'm planning on your having a lot of chances." He gave her his Magnum wink, and she smiled back with those Evee eyes. Going with the mood, he continued, "I marked some good parts of the screenplay to show you—about a walk on the beach and... By the way, how do you like riding merry-go-rounds?"

"I love them, and I love the beach. No shoes or... Well, never mind."

"No shoes or what?"

"No shoes or inhibitions."

As she smiled, Grant wondered if this was an addition to their other conversation when she didn't want "to go there." He returned her smile and sought retreat—sometimes the finer part of valor.

He thought about his past relationships, how they seemed to end, and though he was enjoying her companionship, somewhere within himself he felt fear. It was probably from taking down his wall, giving Eve the bricks, opening up, and both hoping and fearing he could give her more... or maybe it was the music. ABBA was singing "The Winner Takes It All."

Lunch progressed as a combination of business and a little flirting on the side. E. Justine Wednesday was almost her schoolgirl self, but she could turn it on and off, if the conversation merited the change. It was interesting. She felt confident enough in all the complicated parts of herself to be comfortable sharing from each of them.

Suddenly, without changing his mood and manner, Grant smiled but became serious with his voice at the same time. He looked at Eve and instructed, "Keep smiling, and act like we're having a romantic conversation."

"Well, to a degree—"

"Don't look right now, but two guys just walked in. I saw them yesterday at the hotel registration desk, and I think I saw them tailing me this morning when I went to meet Rob for breakfast. They may be the guys we're after."

"What are you going to do?"

"Just smile at me and think about how we can find out who they work for."

Eve smiled and reached for Grant's hand. "OK. Remember, I have my phone."

"Why don't you go to the ladies' room and call Bartow? Tell him… Let's see… Tell him we're going to lead these guys to the Holiday Inn, down the street, the Holidome. We'll make them think you and I are going to meet someone. Yeah, we've contacted somebody for a meeting. They'll believe that. Tell him to get one of his agents over to the Holiday Inn's check-in desk and act like a manager or something, and when… Let's see… After we come in and ask a few questions, they'll be following us to try and find out where we're going and why. Tell Bartow to make them show badges and credentials, something to tell us who they are. We'll leave the desk people a note telling them what to say."

"What makes you think they'll want to follow us so closely?"

"If they had anything going right now, they wouldn't be tailing us at all. They'd be going after Lane. One thing's for sure. They don't have him yet. The best we can do for now is let them know we're on Lane's trail. They'll stay with us, and it'll be like a tied game."

"And we have the ball."

"Exactly."

This suited Eve, because now she'd actually be doing field-agent work, and she could do it with the best investigator in the program. It was time to turn up the heat.

Since she and Grant already ordered their food, Eve slid out of the booth and walked to the ladies' room. Grant looked at his watch, hoping to get the spies thinking about the time, like he was planning to be at an appointment.

He pondered a Plan B in case the fish didn't bite. The best he could come up with was letting them have some type of information that would lead them back to Rob. Knowing the intelligence hook-up, Rob could get something out of them this time, without their knowledge of course. Grant knew if he approached them directly, nothing would happen— just like nothing was happening with Jackson.

When Eve returned and sat down, she smiled pleasantly and started the conversation as Grant looked at his watch again to solidify the effect.

"Bartow said he'll have someone over there in about twenty minutes, and I told him that should be fine, because we haven't been served yet. He said there's no problem. He's acquainted with the management at the Holiday Inn, and they'll work with him. How'd I do?"

Grant couldn't lose the opportunity to respond. "I hope we plan to stay on the same team. We need to call Shelly and tell her to cover for us if we're late for the meeting."

Eve replied that she already called Shelly and told her about the plan. She and Grant would try to return before Rob came at three—and, yes, they would bring her a greasy burger.

Lunch concluded, and it was now the hour of the chase. This time the fox was leading the hounds instead of running from them.

The two left casually so as not to alert the targets regarding the setup. As they walked to the exit, Grant glanced at the table and saw one of the men hail the server for the check.

Continuing out the door at a slow pace, and on to the car, they were soon driving out of the parking lot with the two men not far behind. Grant took his time pulling out of the parking lot to make sure the men didn't lose the tail. It was only about five or six blocks to the Holiday Inn, which Grant had passed on the drive to the restaurant.

While he was driving, he asked Eve to write two notes for the desk clerk. The first one read, "Is one of you Mr. Lane?" The second read, "Mr. Lane, please meet us by the pool."

The two found a parking space near the entrance and entered the lobby. As they approached the desk, Grant recognized an agent from the McAllen Bureau. He couldn't remember her name, but it didn't matter. He introduced Eve and himself and spoke to the clerk in charge of the desk while the agent listened.

"One or two guys will follow us in here in a minute. Just ask this question," he handed them the note asking if either one was Lane. "They'll say no and probably ask you something else…something official-sounding. Just make them show identification and look closely at their credentials. We need to know what agency they're with. Be very cooperative and show them this note. Tell them someone left this for Lane."

He handed them the second note about waiting by the pool.

"After they're gone, call us at the Casa de Palmas, and let us know what you found out. We're going to go out the other door and lose them."

Grant and Eve walked through the lobby to the dome section and doubled back through the restaurant, where they could view the lobby without being noticed.

After a few minutes, the two men entered the hotel from a side door. As they walked across the lobby, Grant and Eve went through the outside entrance to the restaurant, got into the car, and left for Little Houston. The trap was laid.

As they drove back to the hotel, the conversation continued about Shelly and what she might be doing about chasing the UN eavesdroppers.

* * *

It was a little after two-thirty when Eve and Grant walked into Little Houston with the greasy burger and fries for the Coke-a-holic. Eve updated Shelly about the trap that was in place at the Holiday Inn and asked about the plans to catch whoever had been monitoring her conversation with Bret.

Shelly explained, in some detail, about creating two different presences on the Internet. This way she could talk to herself and keep both identities a secret. If she left a clue trail, it would lead the eavesdropper to a different location. At the same time, she could contact Bret. In this way, the two of them would have a more secure conversation, and she might get more information about Lane and Scorpion.

It sounded reasonable to Grant, so he sat down to call Houston. It took about fifteen minutes to get through his housekeeping Q-and-A regarding the regional office. Although he knew it was important, Grant was more interested in getting the information collected and disseminated to the correct parties. This way it would be temporarily off his plate, and he could get on with talking to David Lasorta.

While he handled the Houston business, Eve did likewise with Internal Affairs. She found out the Kansas City records had been merged with others over the past decade and transferred to the FBI's Western Regional Computer Support Center in Pocatello, Idaho. They had received and processed her request and retrieved the Lane files for the period between 1965 and 1970. They were making copies and faxing the results to Houston; she should have the information within the next hour or so.

Eve's conversation with Darrell McCullock revealed that Agent Jackson couldn't be traced through any normal channels. McCullock managed to locate and talk to an acquaintance of Jackson who lived in the same apartment complex. The neighbor said Jackson was from Atlanta and had lived in the apartment for about a month or so. He added that Jackson was very much a loner, but he didn't offer any other information about him.

McCullock had also contacted the CIA. He told them that he was with FBI Internal Affairs, and further, that there was a problem with some information that was missing from Benjamin Lane's FBI file. He asked the CIA to research their files for the names Lawrence Collier and Deborah Bearing-Haas. He also told them that the FBI was continuing to investigate Lane's disappearance and didn't expect any interference. McCullock was sharp. It sounded like he was shaking the trees—and building a pretty good fire.

After her conversation with McCullock was completed, Eve focused her attention on Grant, who'd phoned Lasorta.

"Lawrence Collier, who referenced the file in the period between nineteen sixty-eight and seventy-one, was an employee of the Department of Defense," Lasorta told Grant. "He was transferred to other government posts during the seventies and early eighties, including assistant to the Deputy Secretary of Defense, who oversaw Military and Tactical Intelligence."

"Sounds like we're getting close."

"Yes, but this one leads nowhere. He retired in nineteen eighty-seven and died of a heart attack in eighty-eight. That's called a dead end."

Grant laughed. "Cute, Lasorta. Cute."

He wrote "DOD," and added the word "DECEASED" on a sticky note and handed it to Eve, then pointed to the facts wall and mouthed the word "Collier." Eve posted the note and continued to listen.

"The word is still out on Bearing-Haas. She was an FBI special agent who moved to the Houston office in nineteen seventy-two, was promoted to SAC of the DC Intelligence Unit in seventy-six, and then

Deputy Assistant Director in seventy-eight. It's not evident when the file was tampered with, but it could easily have been during this period."

"Anything else?"

"Maybe. Something happened during the Carter administration in the late seventies, and she transferred out of the FBI to a post with the World Health Organization."

"Well, get that! There's a tie to the UN!"

"Grant, it was a political appointment, and finding out what happened after this is going to take some doing. I've located her, and she's still active with WHO in some consulting capacity, but no one wanted to give me any specifics. They say you have to talk to her. Nobody over there knows anything. I mean, they won't say jack."

Grant was thinking, *I hope we own somebody over there.*

Lasorta excused himself for a moment then returned. "Delaney's man McCullock buzzed up. He just received the information from Pocatello, so we can compare their file with ours and see what's missing. I'll call you back in five or ten minutes."

Grant stalled him. "Also, get me a rundown on that blood sample from M.D. Anderson. There's something funny about that too."

With a promise to return quickly, Lasorta ended the call. Grant told Eve and a curious Anne Shelly about the status of Bearing-Haas—formerly FBI, currently with the World Health Organization, and no one was talking. This might be the information they needed to start squeezing until someone yelled.

Although the day wasn't over, Grant complimented his associates on their excellent performance. Two days of the Wolf were behind them. "FBI" and "WHO" became Post-it notes and joined the others on the wall—facts regarding the disappearance of B.W. Lane.

# CHAPTER ELEVEN

The atmosphere in Little Houston was decidedly intensifying. Waiting—they were waiting for Lasorta and McCullock, waiting for Bartow's agent to call from the Holiday Inn, waiting for Rob to show up for the three-o'clock meeting, waiting until tomorrow...when Shelly could again touch the keyboard and get to Bret, the Blue Retriever.

Grant stared at the notes on the wall, sorted his thoughts, and knew they were finally shining a light into the tunnel of the mystery. Eve answered the phone and, after a brief conversation, broke the silence.

"We have an appointment with Blanca at Dr. Sanchez's office between four and four-thirty. She called Veronica Lane and received permission to show us Lane's medical records. Anything else you need me to do?"

Grant looked at his watch; it was almost three. The ringing phone signaled the arrival of more information, and this time Grant answered it. He was silent for a moment.

"National Security Agency. Anything else? By authority of the DCI... OK. That's it. I'll call you later tonight or in the morning, and we'll sort this out. We'll probably leave for Houston tomorrow." He paused and listened. "OK, and we appreciate your work on this. Tell your agents 'Good job.'"

Replacing the phone, Grant said to Shelly and Eve, "Well, the gang's all here. Those guys tailing us are NSA. The CIA director sent them."

Grant thought for a moment about the history of the intelligence community. He used to spend time in the library studying law enforcement and was somewhat of an expert in the field. He also welcomed the opportunity to share his knowledge.

The facts were becoming more complex. Grant went on to explain to Shelly, who wasn't aware of the complexities of the intelligence network and the so-called "community," that the National Security Act of 1947 had created the Intelligence Community—known as the IC—to control and coordinate national security. The IC, Grant pointed out, wasn't properly named. It was bankrupt of reason, honor, and intelligence as far as he was concerned, but it still received billions of dollars in government funding. At any rate, it was organized to aid the president and other decision-makers in staying abreast of information to assist in the formulation of domestic and foreign policy.

In 1952, President Truman established the National Security Agency as a separately organized agency within the Department of Defense, the DOD. While not a military organization, the NSA was one of several agencies within the Intelligence Community administered by the Department of Defense and was therefore related to Defense Intelligence, DIA, which coordinated intelligence within the armed services. This was also the area where most covert actions originated. The worst, in Grant's opinion, was DSD, the Defense Security Division. They had plenty of money, but no one could find the boss.

The CIA was independent in foreign intelligence and counterintelligence, and they were OK at what they did—as long as it was all they did. The FBI was responsible for counterintelligence within the United States, maintaining basic domestic safety and dealing with federal crimes. Shelly needed to know this information because it was a complex web and the clues were tied neatly together with intelligence and the military.

Some questions remained. Why northwest Laos? What was the payload on the missile, who was in charge, and what happened on the mission? Furthermore, what happened to B. W. Lane?

Shelly was glad to have the historical heads-up, and Eve enjoyed watching Grant give a lecture that, to her, resembled a performance. She noticed how Special Agent Shelly was glued to 'Professor' Harris's narrative and questioned her own continuing education.

As Eve smiled to herself, Grant interrupted her thoughts. "What are you smiling about, Special Agent Delaney?"

"Nothing much. I was just thinking about something…uh…"

"Can we go there yet?"

Eve was thinking of a response when the door opened and Rob sauntered in. Grant looked at his watch. Rob was ten minutes late, but computer people were never very concerned about time. Since his information traveled at a speed of nearly 1.5 million bytes per second, Rob didn't seem concerned about minor details -- like minutes.

"So these are Special Agents Anne Shelly and Evangeline Delaney? Closing in on the trail of the men in shades and trench coats."

They stood and shook hands then completed a formal round of introductions. Shelly offered Rob a Coke, but he opted for coffee. They replenished their drinks and, without much formality or preparation, began the recap of events.

Rob watched the wall as Grant analyzed the notes and bits of paper containing the clues that had been ascertained throughout the day. The only item of which Rob was unaware, regarded the information uncovered a few minutes earlier in the 'Great Lunch Caper' which had revealed the identity of the NSA agents. It was three o'clock plus twenty minutes, now two days and seven hours into the case.

Rob was silent until Grant finished his summary, then he repeated, "So everyone is tied together with the IC and the director of the CIA. You won't be surprised to know that the UN class-threes—the licenses we discussed earlier for those Internet addresses—were not the UN after all. They're in the UN block but have a sub-assignment to your friend over there." He pointed to the note indicating "WHO."

"The World Health Organization?"

"Right on, Grant. We have the Internet address. It means we can e-mail them directly or dump anonymous notes in their mailbox. We can make them think we've decided to chase them for a while. What do you think, Shelly?"

It was evident to Grant, and probably Eve and Shelly, that Rob was trying to impress his new, young acquaintance, but the idea had a nice sound to it. After all, Grant was trying to figure out how to smoke them out, and this was probably what Lane had in mind all along. It was the reason for his disappearance—to complete the sting.

Shelly took the bait and sparred with Rob. "I set up two different aliases with my laptop and Lane's computer. One shows a university computer through On Ramp with a Dallas hub, and the other is a single user with Inet in Houston." She continued as if she were a TV announcer. "The locations are real. Only the names have been changed to catch the hackers."

"Sounds like a plan," Rob said. "What are you going to tell them?"

Grant spoke up. "Tell them we have the information regarding Diamondstrike and give them some of it. Make them nervous. Turn up the heat. Then we'll give them another place and time to get back to us…like Bret did earlier."

The cat was out of the bag, and everyone seemed to be talking at once. They divided in two groups, Rob and Shelly were talking about how to keep the trail covered electronically, as Eve and Grant were discussing how to properly bait the communication without tipping their hand. The end result of the next fifteen minutes' work was that the computer geeks were ready to get underway, and Grant had written an e-mail to send to WHO.

Anne Shelly typed the message as the group looked on.

*Re: Population Control, NW Laos, 1969. Please be advised that Diamondstrike and your chemical/biological involvement were discovered and will be made public after the investigation is complete. Notify King Arthur.*

Shelly signed it, "Spoiler."

Rob stopped her before she sent it.

"Hold it. Let me go over to HiLite and follow the traffic in and out of the site and see what I can find out from the activity level after they receive the e-mail. Wait about fifteen minutes, say about four o'clock or so, and then call me. I'll be on by then."

Shelly agreed, and Rob left in a hurry.

The phone rang, and Eve answered. It was Darrell McCullock; he was with Lasorta.

As they all listened attentively to the speakerphone, they heard the information that was now in the re-created FBI file but wasn't in the current Lane file.

"Here's what I have, Agent Delaney. The missing details include the complete investigation for top-security clearance, and all the security info checks out, but this medical thing is complicated. There are lots of records. I mean, a big stack of them. I've never seen this type of information in a file. I think a doctor will have to interpret the results. There are lots of blood profiles and test results. I have no knowledge of this stuff, but there are some points of interest in some of the memos here with the documents and samples…comments regarding things like deoxythymidine, one of the DNA building blocks."

Eve stopped him. "You can skip over that. I don't understand it either."

"But some of this sounds important," McCullock said. "The research comments state that 'In human white blood cells, certain proteins can stimulate or inhibit the creation of the cells themselves. Fewer white cells mean less resistance to disease—immune system dysfunction.' " McCullock hesitated. "Why would they have been studying Lane for that?"

Eve nodded a confirmation and responded. "He was evidently contaminated with something, and that's what we need to find out."

McCullock went on to say that an important routing was found in the notes. Lasorta discovered that the copies of the test results, in the late sixties and early seventies, had been forwarded to the Naval Medical Center in Bethesda, Maryland.

There was a handwritten note on top of one of the file summaries that wasn't very clear. It appeared to say, 'Galileo's Wine' and had a circle around it. Other than a winery in Napa Valley, an extended file search hadn't located any other reference to the name or anything similar.

Grant recalled his earlier conversation with Veronica Lane. "Lane's wife said he never got sick. Lasorta, did you find out any more about that blood, those five pints at Anderson?"

"Yes. It's low in the cell count. Hemoglobin or whatever."

"If that's true, the person who used it should have been sick a lot, right? Am I understanding this right?"

"Sounds logical to me."

"Do me a favor and send a fax to our medical department in Houston. Send the information and see if this makes any sense to them. Ask them what it means if a guy has a very low white-cell count but is never sick. Let me know what they come up with."

As the conversation ended, the Houston team agreed to track the Bethesda lead and to be available for another conference call around five o'clock.

*It's the last lap*, Grant thought. He gazed at the wall of facts then realized he was being watched. Turning, he discovered Eve studying him as intently as he had been studying the wall. He smiled, and her penetrating eyes smiled in response.

As Shelly intently pecked the keyboard, Grant invited Eve to take a walk down the hall, and they excused themselves for a minute. The 'Super Hacker of Casa de Palmas' smiled and readied the e-mail for its trip to WHO.

In the remote silence of the hallway, Grant slipped his hand around Eve's. "Evangeline Justine Wednesday, this has been quite a day."

They headed outside. He had located a secluded area earlier in the day where the view was quiet, peaceful, and romantic.

Eve knew the answer, but she asked the question anyway. "Is this starting to get complicated?"

"The case…or us?"

"Both."

"The case…less, I think, but my feelings for you are getting more… Not really complicated… Let's say 'stronger.' I don't know if that means 'complicated' or not."

They stopped at the isolated romantic location where he saw the doves earlier, and he gently touched her shoulder as she turned toward him. He was speechless as he looked at the beautiful fountain in the background and then into those gorgeous eyes.

Not knowing whether to be serious, Grant recited as if he were reading from a dime novel. "Evangeline Wednesday, framed in the beauty of a perfect setting, fell into his arms and surrendered to his passion!"

Eve tried to maintain a straight face, but as a light snicker and smile overcame her, they hugged and laughed. She looked into his eyes, and he into hers, until they found themselves more serious, and they both knew. 'Complicated' was all right.

It was acceptable to be close, and in the moment, Grant didn't feel threatened. Nothing could have kept them from this chance meeting. It was a fine destiny for two people who hadn't known each other well to touch each other so completely.

As Eve's smile slowly dissolved into a serene gaze, Grant was paralyzed by her beauty. He stood motionless. She moved her hand deliberately up and around his neck, then he pulled her mouth slowly to his. The world stopped as she relaxed in his embrace.

In a kiss that lasted perhaps twenty seconds, she felt the serenity some people never feel in a lifetime. As for Grant, his re-entry into a world that held reason and purpose felt electrifying.

After slowly easing away from Eve, he felt a surge within himself, and he looked longingly into her eyes. He leaned toward her once more and touched her lips again, this time with a stronger passion. He tasted her lips and allowed himself to feel her body press firmly against his. As his arms encircled her, the encounter ignited a feeling that had been absent from both their lives; the inflamed embrace continued until Grant heard someone coming through the mezzanine door.

Although they parted for the moment, he continued to hold her hands.

Eve had never felt such complete affection and admitted her feeling. "Don't let this end."

Again, Grant embraced his new love. "It'll take both of us."

After a time they returned to reality, and Eve interrupted the silence. "Do you think…?"

"No, I never think."

"Don't we have some work to do?"

"I thought you said you didn't want this to end."

"You know what I mean."

She laughed and hugged him once more before they started back to Little Houston.

When they walked in, Shelly was popping the top off a Coke can and watching the computer screen. She had sent the message but hadn't received a response. Rob, however, had called and was checking on activity from the site after the e-mail was received. He agreed to get back to Shelly in a few minutes.

Grant decided he should wait at Little Houston while Eve handled the doctor's visit without him. This way, if she was detained, he could still get the five-o'clock conference going with Houston and be available to sort out the information on WHO.

Eve, still confident and aggressive, knew she could manage the assignment. Having received the directions to the doctor's office, she took Grant's keys and departed to complete the medical side of the investigation.

This was a good time to get away for a break, to sort out the complexities of her thoughts. Eve needed time to think—about her career, the change in her path, her life in general…and Grant in particular. Two days ago, she was thinking, they were just coworkers in an office in downtown Houston. They might have been friends, but only from a distance. Now she felt drawn to him with a magnetism that left a void with his absence, and she wanted him.

Eve remembered a few months before, at the office party, when she had tried to get close but could not. She relived the thoughts of today's embrace, and she wanted more. Even so, she had a chaperone in her mind that interrupted her pleasant thoughts and told her not to move too quickly.

*Don't come on too fast*, she thought.

OK, the actions were on hold, but the feelings weren't.

* * *

After escorting Eve to the car, Grant returned to the office. He watched Shelly peck on the keyboard and then combed the facts wall for some thread that might have escaped his attention.

As the minutes crept toward five o'clock, he telephoned David Lasorta. Something was up; he could tell by the tone of Lasorta's voice.

"Meyers is here with me. He's got some good news and some not-so-good news."

Grant knew that Ruben Meyers, the AO, or administrative officer, wouldn't be needed on this case unless something big was happening.

"Seems the boss has a heart problem or something," Lasorta said, "and he's taking his retirement early, namely today. They say he'll be all right, but you're the new SAC for Houston."

This was it—the promotion Grant knew was his, just a year earlier than he'd expected.

Lasorta continued, "Here, I think your AO wants to talk to you. I'll get back to you in a minute."

Meyers took the phone, exchanged greetings, and dropped the bomb. "The director called from Washington and asked you to get off the Lane case and back to Houston double time."

"Doesn't he know the CIA got us on this in the first place? Remember, they asked for our help finding this guy. We're talking kidnapping here!"

Meyers responded firmly. "Evidently not, Grant, or it doesn't matter…because that's not what's coming down. He didn't give you any options."

Grant had to stop for a minute to catch his thoughts and his breath. A promotion, and then an immediate command to separate himself from the case. His first instinct was to simply disagree, but he knew he couldn't.

He immediately reorganized his thoughts to defuse the situation as quickly as possible and confine the communication to as few people as were now involved. *Keep this quiet for a while*, he thought. One thing he knew for sure—he wasn't getting off this case until he had the answers to his questions.

"OK, Meyers. I'll start closing this down today and get back to Houston tomorrow. Keep this on the short list until I get there. Did the director have anything else to say?"

"No, he just said to call him if you need clarification. He's sending a news release and some internal paperwork announcing your appointment. We should have it in the morning. He wants you in Washington in the next week or so for a formal ceremony and a photo session. 'Big Time in the Beltway.' Good luck…Boss."

Grant Harris was the newly appointed Special Agent in Charge, Houston Region, probably one of the youngest SACs in the business. Either the search for Jackson, the leaning on the NSA, or the e-mail must have punched the right button at the CIA, or somewhere higher up, because Grant was sure his promotion was a setup to get him off the case. It had to be from a superior source, or this would never happen.

It was an ideal circumstance. He was going to get the promotion anyway, but why now? In some way it seemed a hollow victory if leaving Lane in harm's way was the payoff. But the game wasn't over yet.

Eve could be obtaining some of the missing components, and there still was the possibility of solving the case today. If not, at least he had bought tomorrow…and one more conversation with the Blue Retriever.

Meyers signed off and left Lasorta to talk privately with Grant, who was questioning which particular issue authored the early retirement of his boss, Will Masters.

Lasorta explained that something must have happened because Will Masters had called in from his holiday to check on the Lane case.

"Grant, this is complicated. Masters called me this morning and said that he told the DCI that he didn't have any information and that you were handling it. Then he asked me for details and I told him how far we were. When the boss apprised them of the situation, the DCI told him the NSA didn't want any help. Also, they said that Jackson should not have contacted you and that they had it under control. Will must have drawn his own conclusions and refused take you off the case until he had a briefing from you."

Grant was adapting his assumptions as Lasorta continued, "They probably didn't like the answer, and my guess is Will was too stubborn to give in. That means you're too close! They want you back in Houston now—'now' as in 'yesterday.' And this is how they're going to do it."

"So they blamed it on Jackson, and then he disappeared? I wouldn't want to be in his shoes—they might be made out of concrete. Maybe he's the stick in this thing…or maybe he was just exposing it. Do you know where this is going?"

"Yes," Lasorta said. "I'm sure getting a clear picture now. Cover and hide. What are you going to do?"

"I told Meyers to tell them I'd close up shop and be back in Houston tomorrow. That answer should defuse both sides and give us a couple of hours to catch our breath. We've got to find Lane quick, before they do, and before they can get me out of the picture."

As the two sorted through the confusion of the last move, the second phone rang, and Agent Shelly answered. It was Eve.

Shelly interrupted Grant's conversation and said it was important, so he excused himself and, it appeared, took the position of dispatcher, with a phone in each hand.

Eve's information wasn't good. Blanca, at Sanchez's office, couldn't locate Lane's medical file. Upon further questioning, Eve discovered the office had been broken into two days before, on the preceding Monday, and a small amount of drugs had been taken. The office staff hadn't noticed anything else missing or violated and had assumed the heist was strictly drug-related.

Even without the file, however, the staff was able to confirm that Lane's annual blood samples, perhaps as many as three, had been sent to a medical research hospital. They supplied a copy of the address and an air bill for one of the shipments.

Under direct questioning, no one at the office said they could confirm that Lane was aware of the samples' disposition. They assumed he knew, since it had been occurring for a while.

The only other information came from Deanna, the nurse who had drawn the samples. She offered that they always sent three hundred cc's, which was considered a large sample, but Lane never complained.

Grant continued to hold both phones and talked back to Lasorta. "I'll get back to you, Dave. Eve says Lane's medical records are missing. If we don't do something soon, it's going to be hard to prove this guy ever existed. Oh, also, stay on that Jackson thing, too."

As he returned one phone to its cradle, he spoke to Eve. He asked her to return quickly, since they had a confusing array of information to consider and time appeared to be running out. Grant hesitated in saying anything about his promotion, thinking it would be better if he told her in person.

Shelly followed up on the air bill by typing in "fedex.com," the domain for Federal Express, and entering the number that Eve dictated.

Rob eventually called and passed along the word that there was significant activity from the WHO server after the e-mail was received. Although he didn't trace all the sites, he did establish that most of the movement was in the .gov realm—NSA and others—which meant the majority of the Internet traffic was going out of WHO, as a notice to other government agencies.

This came as no surprise, since less than an hour later the message had come down to Grant about stopping his work on this case and blurring the focus. Government cover-up? A vast government conspiracy could never happen—not with this subject and not on this scale. Or could it?

Within a few minutes, Eve returned. She had a copy of the air bill, and Shelly had determined it was received by R. Cockrell, Institute for Disease Control Research in Arlington, Virginia. The address placed the Institute off US Highway 66, inside the Loop.

Shelly was doing her best to locate some information on the institute but wasn't having much luck with the Internet. Grant decided it was probably a front for some other affiliation of WHO. He decided against contacting the Washington Bureau for fear of letting anyone know he was still following leads.

He asked Shelly to try to contact Bret again through the chat or news sources and to tell him the importance of contacting Lane or Scorpion immediately.

After Eve completed her business with Shelly, Grant invited her to take a walk so he could tell her privately about the news he'd received while she was tracking the medical leads.

The two walked down to the verandah lounge that overlooked the pool and fountain. Grant found a private corner, and he and Eve sat on the love seat.

When the waitress came by, he ordered two glasses of Chardonnay. The wine sounded inviting to Eve; it had been quite a long day—long in terms of the intricate weaving of her emotions and even longer in regard to the disturbing facts that appeared along the path to locating Benjamin Lane.

# CHAPTER TWELVE

Although Grant had awaited this achievement for years, in fact his entire career, it didn't seem like the right time to celebrate the new appointment. It was almost a backhanded promotion, and advancing in this manner took the polish off, even though he deserved it.

Then, there were his thoughts of the SACs he'd known in the past, how principled and honest they were, how "above reproach." In a matter of a minute or two, he felt guilty, wondering whether he was doing the right thing, accepting the promotion under these circumstances.

These thoughts continued to disturb him throughout his conversation with Eve.

Eve was elated, even after Grant explained, in detail, the state of affairs regarding his returning to Houston and leaving the NSA to their devices. The only bright spot was amnesty until the following day.

Since he hadn't told Meyers what time they would be returning to Houston, he felt the group could use most of the day without arousing suspicion; it would buy them a little more time. Grant knew he had to gather enough data to continue on to Washington and meet with the director. If he didn't stay after it right now, this case would never be solved. It was already obscured, and getting more so.

Grant secretly hoped to stay for the weekend and take Eve to South Padre Island to enjoy some sun and sand, to do as Lane's character had done in the screenplay—ride a merry-go-round and take a romantic walk on the beach.

Maybe he'd find the opportunity to fall in love. Who knows?

Still, he was too shy to tell Eve the plan.

The wine came, and the waitress set the tray on the table in front of them.

"Congratulations!" Eve exclaimed. She held up her glass, and they toasted the promotion. Then she made a rapid return to seriousness. It was evident she was struggling with a comment. "Grant, what are you going to do? I mean, about the director? You can't disregard his order."

He was very confident in his response. "We took an oath to uphold the laws of the United States against all terrorists from outside or inside. Eve, if these people are doing what we think they're doing, it's criminal at every level. I'm going to hold on to our oath while we get the rest of the answers. If any of our agencies have been compromised, we have an obligation to get the facts. Do you agree?"

Eve cautiously approved the thought. "I like your idea about going to Washington and explaining the actual situation. Lane might be an embarrassment to the NSA by exposing US involvement in this dark business, but it doesn't mean the NSA gets to kill him. It's evident that they let a guy slip through their net, one with a conscience, and now someone on the inside has got to stand up with him. It sure looks like the guy needs some backup."

She thought for a moment. "I love it. We've got to help…regardless of what happens. *'Out of this rabble, come men who will defy kings.'*"

"What's that?"

"It's what some British soldier said after the colonists beat the British at Yorktown. It's about defiance—like there's a limit to what you can make me do. It reminds me of this situation." She looked at Grant seriously. "Like staying on the edge."

Grant's expression changed with the conviction that was crystallizing in his mind. "We don't have much choice. I—or should I say 'we'— will have to make a major break on this thing before tomorrow's over. Then I can go to Washington."

He hesitated, wondering whether he should share all his suppositions with Eve in the moment. He decided it was OK, even though he was afraid to get ahead of himself and possibly be wrong with his conclusions.

"Here's what I think," he said. "See if you agree and don't think I'm a conspiracy freak, Eve, I'm not; but this whole affair was evidently started by the military. I think they wanted the virus to use as a weapon, but someone found out and co-opted it for a different reason and ended up trying to manipulate the world's population. How sick is that?"

Eve dropped her head but didn't respond, so Grant continued. "They needed Lane, because no one knew how to load the triggering mechanism on the Diamondhead missile. When they wanted to fire it on civilians, he told 'em to shove it, dumped the warhead into a tree or something, and ended up contaminating himself and some of the others. It didn't kill him, so evidently he either had or developed the antibodies to fight the effects of whatever it was, and they're using his blood. That's the only reason they didn't take him out. They were using his blood for research or something."

"That sounds right on to me," Eve responded then asked, "Do you think Lane's OK?"

"I hope he's doing better than Jackson. It looks like his own guys might have already taken him out. Lasorta thinks they're mad at Jackson for bringing us into the picture. Nobody can find him, and no one's talking. I can't believe he'd make a move like that, contacting us, without someone else directing it. Those guys don't think for themselves. There's something real strange about that."

"Well, he's CIA, and they're NSA. This may be what confused the situation. Remember, back in your office Jackson told us to get back in touch if we needed more information. He didn't sound like he was planning on going anywhere."

Grant continued her thought. "Good point. Maybe the CIA is in the dark on this too."

"But what about Lane?" Eve asked.

"About Lane…" Grant smiled as he pondered the question in silence. "If I were hiding," he said, "and I had Lane's background and training, I'd be in the woods somewhere, but he's probably in Mexico, or in a cheap hotel down the street, watching us and waiting for something to happen."

Having completed their discussion of the revelations of this extraordinary Wednesday afternoon, they prepared to return to Shelly and Little Houston, for what was hastily becoming the final search for the truth.

Eve and Grant agreed on one thing—a positive outcome wouldn't be possible if they compromised or surrendered. Neither could, and neither would.

As they headed toward the conference room, Grant touched Eve's hand then grasped it more tightly. "In Lane's movie there's a part that says, 'You don't lose if you never quit.' I don't think he's going to quit, and I'm not ready to give it up either."

Eve said, "I'm with you…as far as it goes."

Upon return to the mini-office, they found the atmosphere with Shelly approximately as they had left it. She was intent at the keyboard with one or the other of her aliases, and she was evidently getting somewhere.

She stopped for a moment. "There you are, Grant. Here's the reply to your WHO message."

Grant and Eve joined her at the screen. The message was a reply to their population control and Diamondhead email, over two hours prior. It read simply, "'Do not make your findings public until you have all the information. Who are you?' "

It was unsigned except for the Internet address.

Grant responded, "OK, let's think this through before we respond. I'll call Lasorta and see if they had any luck with anything else."

As Grant dialed Houston, Eve watched him. She reviewed all the notes on the facts wall and began to appreciate the pace of the last twenty-four hours. She realized the questions were getting more challenging.

How many things could be understood from one short note? Was the WHO response the final word? It did sound as though they were giving up the chase. But it could be a baited response to find out who was getting close. "All the information"? That could be a long list and take forever to complete. Since their suppositions weren't definitive in any way, they still had many angles to consider. They needed to know, with some certainty, whether it was WHO acting alone or whether other parties were in collusion and, if so, how many.

Despite all the areas of speculation, Lasorta agreed that the WHO response was very encouraging. It sounded more like a plea than anything else—a request to confirm the information, with a focus on the accuracy.

Different ideas emerged until the case started to make a directional sense, and all directions pointed to a whistleblower, someone on the inside wanting to get the information outside. They all agreed with this position. There was a big hole in the dike, and it was impossible to keep the dam from breaking.

But what was the importance of who was asking? It didn't really matter who was stopping the parade.

After a prolonged discussion, it appeared the biggest dilemma the FBI faced was that it was bluffing. Although they were conveying their lead in the chase, they didn't have all the information…and where the hell was Jackson?

Shelly made her prediction. The FBI had uncovered its own Deep Throat, an insider to fill in the blanks. The question, "Who are you?" was simply to clarify who would be making the information public. Obviously, there were illegalities involved, and the insider probably wanted immunity from prosecution in exchange for more information. This was certainly something to consider.

All of them, including Lasorta, exchanged ideas for a few minutes, but the deliberations came up short of a verdict. Lasorta excused himself and told Grant to call him at home if anything urgent emerged. It was after six thirty, and he was sure his wife would be expecting him soon.

However, no one was going home in Little Houston's war room. In fact, it appeared things were speeding up instead of slowing down.

Eve suggested using another alias and not revealing their identity to the mole…not yet. They should use something associated with Lane and see if more information could be resurrected before they turned up the heat.

Whether it was a good idea, or because it was Eve who had made the proposal, Grant thought it had merit. At least their entire hand wouldn't be exposed for a while longer.

"OK, Anne. Let's ask them this. 'What information do you have? Will you phone or chat?' That should give us a chance to find out how cooperative they want to be, but we won't tell them who we are. E-mail it to them, and see what happens."

"I'll bet they're sitting on top of that mailbox," Eve supposed.

Shelly changed the configuration and put in another phony alias then sent the e-mail through the anonymous Oklahoma ISP. "Now it's your turn," she muttered to the computer screen, then switched over to Lane's computer.

After pointing the browser address to Bret's chat room and posting as "Ashell," she sat back and sipped from a newly opened frosty Coke. Relaxing for a moment, she looked through distant eyes toward the facts wall. Then she took another sip and looked longingly at the Coke can.

The sight was pictorial. Grant commented that she would make a good advertisement for the product.

Eve kidded her about joining the Pepsi generation, but her comment received a look of disgust from Shelly.

The e-mail program announced an incoming message, and they all read the screen.

"Not NW Laos. Look further. Who are you?"

Grant told Shelly to respond through the same "Spoiler" alias she already had used. "Just ask. 'Much further? FBI.' "

Shelly complied. There was a significant pause as the next message came through. Grant supposed the party was having second thoughts.

Then came the response. "Not much. More later."

Grant wanted more now, but he decided not to push it. He summarized his thoughts with the others. "Next message—we'll tell them we have Bearing-Haas in a felony and see if we get more cooperation."

Agreeing to stall the response for a few minutes, they sat and stared at one another. No one really had a feeling for how long "later" was.

Grant thought out loud and said to his young associate, "Not much further… Can we find a map of Southeast Asia and look at northwest Laos?

"Yes," Shelly responded.

At the same time, Eve said, "China."

Grant grimaced. "That was what I was thinking, but I was hoping I was wrong."

He thought about the ramifications of US involvement in covert activities in Communist China at the time of the Tet Offensive. It was a possibility, of course, since the Chinese communists supplied most of the weaponry to the North Vietnamese army. Yet somehow this didn't make any sense in a reasonable thought process. Attacking a civilian area, remote in relation to the front—there was no military advantage to that move. Even so, he was forced to remember that this was somebody's covert op.

*Could it be?* He wondered. *Maybe…if you're talking about population control. Maybe China would be a good place to start it, and a war might be a good time to provide the cover.*

Eve considered the information. Because she understood and believed the evidence, her thoughts became painful. To chemically or biologically affect an innocent population was a step too far; it was a reflection of man's inhumanity toward man, power versus innocent targets for political gain. *What are they telling us?* She thought? *That we're saving the planet?*

Who would conceive of such an endeavor? Grant reasoned this was *not* a renegade unit; it was a strategically planned initiative. And he wouldn't believe it was *our* country, and he didn't believe it was *our* military. Further, he hadn't seen anything that made him think Lane would have agreed to such a mission.

Trying to establish an answer for who was coordinating this destructive scheme, Grant searched the facts wall intently, then backtracked slowly into a dark corner of his calculating mind.

Bearing-Haas was involved, but was she the pawn or the king? Was she the informant or was it someone else at WHO? If there was a scale, who was more guilty, the one who pulled the trigger or the one who gave the order?

*Maybe there should be another category of guilt,* Grant thought, *one for those people who knew what was happening but didn't try to stop it.*

Grant didn't like the questions he was asking himself, or the answers he was thinking, so he stopped short of further judgment with the knowledge that he didn't have all the facts.

His expression grew stern, and he asked Eve, "Can we take a short walk? I had an epiphany."

Eve, becoming accustomed to Grant's desire to be alone with her, accepted the invitation. They walked to the mezzanine again, the one that overlooked the pool. No one else was around, and in the seclusion, Grant gazed distantly through the window. Her stare joined his in the distance as she calmly awaited his next comment.

She knew his thoughts had been running at a hundred and five—five past critical—all day, and she wanted desperately to help him, to offer a release, or to aid in organizing the complexities and finding a conclusion. She wondered how the two of them would communicate on a normal day, in a normal relationship, outside of a critical situation.

Grant broke the silence. "Eve, this dog won't hunt. I've got to go to Washington tomorrow. We know who the enemy is, and they're chasing Lane like he's the enemy. We know enough about this. Everybody does. So we know this whole thing is *not* going away."

Her hand rested on the railing as if asking for assurance, and he placed his hand on hers. "If we don't expose this now, we'll lose the chance. The confirmation is there, and it's too big. But the evidence is disappearing as fast as we find it. I don't think we can wait until we have all the answers. It goes too far up."

Grant continued to explain. Trying to untie the uncooperative details in one day wasn't realistic, and trying to work around the director would prove to be a flawed move in an already difficult game.

Eve agreed that a proper presentation to the number-one man in the FBI should allow him to continue the investigation. At worst, if Grant was forced to discontinue the pursuit, he might have an idea where the command had been made—in other words, how far up. Then he could act on whatever information he had at the time and stay committed all the way.

When they returned to Little Houston, nothing had transpired as far as the returned e-mail was concerned. Rob, however, had called and said he had located Bret on a computer link at Audie L. Murphy Veterans Hospital in San Antonio. The Alamo City was about 250 miles due north of McAllen.

Shelly said she questioned Rob about how he had located Bret, but he said, "Don't ask!"

It probably didn't matter. Rob Garza had been known to hack into places where no one was supposed to be, and he hadn't given Shelly root access, which was a mark against him. Either he didn't trust her, or he had an agenda of his own.

Grant asked Shelly if she knew who Audie Murphy was, and she said she knew he was a famous film actor in the fifties. Grant told her that he also was the most highly decorated veteran of World War II. With the revelation, Shelly was somewhat stunned by her lack of knowledge. Why hadn't she known this piece of trivia? Sometimes the system that educates youth omits some very important facts.

After a couple of minutes of silent deliberation, Eve offered an idea. "If you're going to Washington tomorrow, Grant, I think I'll go to San Antonio and see if I can get some personal cooperation from the Blue Retriever. If he knows for sure that we're real people and that we're on Lane's side, maybe he'll be more helpful with the information we need. It could be that Lane's there anyway."

Grant didn't respond immediately. He didn't like the idea of Eve going on a dangerous mission without him, but he did see the logic in trying to make the contact. They discussed the fact that the FBI had other field agents to do this kind of work, but Eve wasn't buying into this excuse.

"I know you're in charge, Grant, and I'll do what you say, but don't you think we should keep this in as small a sphere as possible? The fewer people who know about it, the better."

Eve was right, and Grant knew it. The problem, which he wouldn't admit to himself, was that he didn't want to be away from her right now. He thought about how silly his feeling was. After all, since he was going to Washington, he couldn't go to San Antonio himself; but he did have another sentiment at stake. He was concerned for Eve's safety, so he told her.

Shelly, the 'Mad Hacker of the Mexican Border,' interjected, "I'll go to San Antonio with you, Eve. There's nothing I can do here that I can't do on my cellular modem, and I'm not going back to Dallas until this is resolved. Right?"

Grant knew he would have to make the final decision, but the situation was like a runaway train on a private railroad. He smiled, thinking about how badly outnumbered he was; there were two of them.

Still, they were all in this together, jointly entangled in the same web of intrigue, a web that continued to unveil concealed facts about the disappearance of B.W. Lane.

# CHAPTER THIRTEEN

Over the next hour, there was little to no increase in the intensity of the chase. Shelly returned to her room for a break, leaving Eve and Grant with an opportunity to discuss their private thoughts. The time flew from seven to eight p.m. while they waited for WHO to answer the email, and the silence was making both of them a little uneasy.

Grant asked, "When we get back to Houston, would you say yes to spending some time with me?"

Eve took her time then toyed with him in response. "Doing what in particular?"

Grant recalled her previous remarks regarding romanticism. "Oh, go to the park, walk and talk, wait for a rainstorm…do like Lane's song and 'paint mountains where there aren't any.'"

Although they were seated at the table in cumbersome office chairs, Eve moved closer to Grant, carefully placed her fingers to silence his lips, and quietly answered, "And surrender to your passion."

Again, Grant was immediately overcome by another type of awareness, an understanding of what two people could share in the midst of extreme situations. What was it—some distorted definition of peace?

His awareness was drawn into those splendid eyes, the ones that could make him relinquish inhibition. As if mesmerized, he leaned forward and touched her lips with his. This time the kiss seemed destined for tomorrow. As a trivia link crossed his mind, he remembered a line from the movie *The Princess Bride*, something about one of the greatest kisses of all time. He was certain this kiss would make the top ten.

Finally, Grant forced his heart beyond his fear. Her presence consumed him. She relaxed in his embrace as his arms awkwardly encircled her. He almost fell out of his chair, but Eve held on to him and helped him regain his balance.

They laughed, and she hugged him.

"I keep wondering how life is going to be for us. When something happens naturally, and before we even get started, we have to say good-bye," Eve concluded.

Her comment made Grant become more serious. "Don't say good-bye, there's no such thing as a *good bye*."

He held her sensitively, gently played with her hair, and pushed her bangs aside, which allowed him to kiss her on the forehead. Then he returned to her eyes and her lips. Grant didn't want the moment to get away, but he began to worry about it, about saying goodbye.

Falling for Eve might make life harder. When a relationship starts, it makes a path that will continue—that is, until it reaches an end. Lane's song said, "The days and the seasons and the years they go by…like a two-minute ending on a ten-second song."

*Will it be over too soon?* Grant wondered.

He started to second-guess his ability to make this a permanent arrangement. The last thing he wanted was a long ending on short song.

*Can I admit I'm afraid?* He thought.

He looked into Eve's eyes and prepared to say something.

"You were going to say something?" she asked.

"I guess, but I didn't like the question, so never mind."

"What?"

"I don't know…"

"Well, when will you know?" Eve wouldn't let him get past the automatic response and stayed after him, "Better than that, say 'I know but I won't tell…' "

"You won't let me get away with anything, will you?"

"No. I don't think you want to. I think you want this. I think you want *us*."

Grant finally answered her question, "I was wondering how long *we* are going to last."

"What brought that on?" Eve sat back, looking a little stunned. "Where's this coming from? 'The cake out in the rain' thing?"

Grant was silent, and Eve continued to quiz him. "Are you confusing me with the girl from 'MacArthur Park'?"

He didn't respond.

"Tell me about it."

Grant stalled a minute then realized she was going to make him respond.

"I told you, in college she went out with a guy I didn't like."

"So what happened?"

"I went to her place, pulled out a record album, played 'Softly Now I Leave You,' and I did. I walked out of her life."

"So twenty years later you bring it up with me? What's it got to do with me?"

Grant returned his eyes to her inquisitive gaze and, after a moment, admitted, "Guess I'm going back there…and I realized that's probably when I started building my wall."

"Grant, I hear you. I understand. You're taking it down. You're being honest. I want you to be. Just remember you can't hang on to what happened years ago and use it to keep your distance from me, or anyone else for that matter."

"You know that's not what I want.

Eve lessened the intensity of the moment. "Then don't make it end before it starts."

Grant was silent.

Eve smiled sheepishly. "You're not going to come into my room and pick out a song, play it for me, and walk out of my life, are you?"

"No." He hesitated as he thought about her words. "I'm just not used to being this open. I never have been before."

"I know. You're a big, strong, he-man FBI agent, and nothing makes you show emotion, right?"

"Can't be weak…"

"I've got news for you. Emotion is not a weakness."

Grant squeezed her hand. "You're reading me like a book."

She smiled with those dazzling eyes. "Good read."

He kissed her gently. "Don't you have any fears?"

She relaxed and moved close to him. "Not like yours. If I'm ever hurt again, I'll just live with it. But I'm not going to live in fear of it…

and if I were you, I'd give fear up. The carnival's not over. We're not Pierrot and Columbine."

Grant surrendered what was left of his hesitation. He was being held prisoner in the moment and decided he liked it.

"Who were they?" he asked. "You almost told me that time at the party."

"They were characters in a French mime play. Columbine loved flowers. Pierrot fell in love with her and sold his shirt to get money to buy her a flower. She loved the flower, but Harlequin, the rich kid, saw how much she liked the flower and gave her a lot of them, so she went with him."

Eve paused as Grant listened, and she continued.

"So Pierrot traded his flower for a rope and hanged himself." She hesitated knowingly, looked directly into Grant's eyes, and cautiously continued, "Columbine found out and died of a broken heart."

"I don't like the ending."

Eve continued. "She was reincarnated as a flower."

"I still don't like the ending."

"Neither do I, but it doesn't have to be us." She smiled, "Like I said, the carnival's not over. In fact, it's not even going good yet."

Grant relaxed as Eve held his face in her hands. She looked at him attentively. "Just walk with me, Grant. Hold my hand. We'll dance like no one's watching and love like it's never going to hurt."

As Grant hugged her again, the sound of someone coming in the room disrupted their momentary paradise. Although they unlocked from their embrace, they didn't try to separate themselves, either quickly or distantly, and the situation relaxed. It was Shelly returning from a break.

Agent Shelly, though somewhat interested, wasn't inquisitive about the relationship between her FBI associates. She didn't give much attention to anything except the computer—or computers, as was currently the case.

She stopped in the door and asked if she was interrupting anything but was told to come on in.

Grant responded humorously, telling her Eve was in the process of writing him up for allowing Internal Affairs and Investigative Services to start doing fieldwork. The response, of course, regarded their decision to travel to the San Antonio VA the following morning.

After Shelly entered and sat down, Grant suggested they reconnect with WHO, whether the organization was ready or not. The message took the shape of the one previously suggested, explaining the obvious involvement of Bearing-Haas in a felony crime. This was all it said.

Grant picked up the phone and called Lasorta at his home. He wanted him to have all the information about the plans for tomorrow.

Lasorta was a twenty-four-year veteran of the FBI and, as evidenced by his productivity over the preceding twenty-four hours, he was as capable as anyone in the unit. He knew his job, spent a lot of time taking in the strategies of police work, and like his longtime friend Grant, could find substance where others found obscurity. He had an unusual talent for knowing where to look for information others might have overlooked. Many times he helped Grant develop leads in cases that were completely stalemated. He was also the kind of person who a guy like Grant needed, someone to brainstorm with, as well as a trusted friend.

Lasorta agreed that the inclusion of the chief in Washington was the right stroke for the hour, especially since this case would create considerable questions and hostility from somewhere higher up in the Washington power train.

The question was whether Grant could convince his boss that the FBI shouldn't cover up the covert intelligence activity. As an FBI Agent and an SAC, Grant couldn't stomach the idea of the intelligence community being a hammer and the FBI being the nail. As he concluded earlier, if he was called off the case, at least he would know from which height the decisions were being directed.

After he hung up the phone, Grant returned to thoughts of Lane—where he was, what he was doing, and what he must be thinking or planning.

*Does he know the FBI is closing in?* He wondered. *Will he know we've uncovered this much information from two days in McAllen?*

The lack of an immediate response from WHO, or specifically Bearing-Haas, gave Grant time to think about the evening and dream silently of another quiet dinner alone with Evee J. Wednesday.

He wanted to continue the conversation about his "bricks" and also determine which Eve she'd be tomorrow, before they were separated for a time.

The two decided to break for dinner, which was fine with the Super Hacker of Little Houston, who by this time was hitting chat rooms and following her own trail with the packet sniffer located on the other computer. Grant and Eve promised to gather some kind of junk food on their return. Grant told Shelly he wasn't very worried about her condition, since the room-service people had delivered a fresh snack cart and replenished her Coke supply.

* * *

Neither agent spoke much at first. It probably had to do with the depth of their earlier discussion, which hadn't had time to settle. Besides, how could they maintain the level of emotions from the mezzanine rendezvous and the subsequent conversation? They needed to establish another pace for their relationship, a pace that would allow them to manage their emotions in the unchained drama that was rapidly unfolding before them.

Grant couldn't believe he had been so truthful about his feelings, but he knew Eve was good with it. He reminded himself of her earlier comment, "Dance like no one's watching, and love like it's never going to hurt." He had committed it to memory. The fact that she wanted to know him intimately was the special connection.

The Italian restaurant they chose was as romantic as the name, Iannelli's. It was on the beaten path, and Grant had passed it several times on his travels around McAllen. He had started to mention the restaurant the night before, when he and Eve were returning to the hotel from the evening on B. W. Lane's ground. When they passed it, however, he remembered the saying about "Coming back someday and taking a particle of the night's silence…and the day's honesty."

Remembering that the remark had openly intensified the emotional exchanges with Eve, he didn't regret the restaurant oversight. However, he was glad the opportunity was returning. It is as if some moves weren't meant to be natural, and this one was.

As they walked into the restaurant, the sounds of Pavarotti played delicately in the background, and they chatted with the maître d', who held the last name of Iannelli. Grant mentioned being from Houston and that the restaurant had been recommended by Veronica Lane.

They were directed to a table on the mezzanine, which the maître d' said Lane favored. It overlooked a lower seating area, as well as a balcony above an even lower downstairs area with a large mural painted on the wall. It showed an ocean-side Mediterranean village in the distance, and the atmosphere of the restaurant was remarkable.

The mood light and candles, like stars of the night, seemed to attend to Eve and Grant as they continued to captivate each other. They discussed their lives and loves, families, his children, and her ability to accept them should their relationship become committed. They agreed that living in the present was better than the past, and Eve established her belief that every day was its own. She loved children and supposed Grant's kids would probably have more trouble accepting her than she would them.

Grant was glad to have discussed this concern at the beginning of their relationship, because he wanted their lives to become entwined. The longer he was with Eve, the more of her he wanted.

After dinner was finished, and when the conversation conferred a break, he asked what name Evee J. would be using the following day. She didn't know which one for sure, but she thought it would be either E. Jay or Justine Thursday.

Later, he asked which name would be the best for a field agent in the San Antonio investigation.

She smiled secretively. "I'll think about it and let you know. No big deal anyway."

He held out for an answer, but it wasn't coming from her lips, at least not this evening.

Grant teased her inquisitively, "Eve, you can tell me anything. I've been telling you everything."

"Yes, Grant. I know. Believe me. We're going fast, and I need to hold on to a few thoughts while I get my feet a little closer to the ground. After all, I've only known you for two days."

"Longer than that." Grant smiled as he looked at her hand then reached for it. He knew she was right to not give all of herself to him under the circumstances. Their emotions had reached the boiling point. He also knew something was there, something worth waiting for. He was confident the relationship could stand the stress of the events and situation, so he sat silently and prayed the name she wouldn't disclose was Evangeline Harris Thursday, or E. Justine Friday Harris, or E.J. Christmas Harris, or any one of them on all the other days.

The night succeeded in joining the two searching souls on the Mexican border. The fire had gone from the sky, only to rekindle itself in the lives of those who had so closely lived the day. Each sought relevance in reaching out for someone they did not know…and found passion and inspiration in the quest. Connecting to each other, they found feelings of love. For Grant it was the start of a new recipe; for Eve, it was a start at being truly loved.

* * *

In the car, as they returned to the hotel, silence owned the conversation. Both were afraid to speak for fear of interrupting the intimate vibrations.

As Eve tenderly squeezed Grant's hand, she broke the silence. "I guess I'll probably be back in Houston by Friday."

Grant knew this was a question as to when he might be back. Although he didn't know how long this business would take, he knew it would be determined by the amount of support he could get from the director. If any clues drove them toward Washington political schemes, all bets were off.

He responded, "I'll take the jet so I can try to get back tomorrow night."

They both knew this would be next to impossible, but Eve realized he was as eager to return to her arms as she was to his.

As if they were given a reprieve from a clumsy discussion, Shelly called Eve and announced she had received the anticipated response from WHO. Grant was right. It was Bearing-Haas.

The response, as Shelly read it, was, "Get Lane to safety. It's critical. I have the proof and the details. We'll meet in your office in Washington tomorrow at noon. B-H."

Eve relayed the information to Grant as he drove the car into the hotel parking lot.

He smiled and excitedly slapped his hand against the steering wheel. "Perfect."

Then he stopped for an instant re-think. *Not so fast.* "What? As far as Bearing-Haas is concerned, this sounds easy." He spoke aloud as he wondered what was behind Bearing-Haas's response. Mumbling under his breath but loud enough for Eve to hear, he said, "How does she think we can get him to safety by noon tomorrow? She thinks we have him? We don't even know where he is."

"She didn't say get him back by noon tomorrow. That's just the schedule for her to meet with you...and it still means we have some time."

"Well, it's evident for now that they don't have him. That's a point for the home team."

They went into Little Houston, and Shelly seemed very intent at the computer. "Nothing has really happened until just now when I called you, and now there's all kinds of activity."

"Activity? Like what?" Grant asked.

"I've been all over the place—all over the Internet—and I found out I'm getting a tail out of HiLite. Someone, Rob or somebody over there, is tracking everywhere I go."

"What do you mean? Say it in English."

"Well, when I go to a site, I watch what's happening at HiLite," she explained, motioning to the other computer, which registered an address from the traced route. "It's like a reverse look-up. And it's always the same static IP. It's in the HiLite class-threes."

Although Grant didn't understand the specifics, he did understand that someone from HiLite was monitoring Shelly's Internet activity. He said he would handle the situation with Rob then suggested his two associates prepare for their early-morning departure to San Antonio. Since it was late, they needed to get some sleep. It was a little after eleven p.m., and the next day would hold a busy schedule and a long car ride.

What Grant didn't say was that he wanted to talk to Rob in private.

He proposed, "I'll have a snack down here at six thirty. If you leave at seven, you should be in San Antonio by noon. It seems like there's a fix on high noon. Lord, I feel like Gary Cooper."

Shelly packed up her laptop computer and excused herself to her room. Eve stayed for a moment with Grant.

"What does this mean with Rob?" she asked.

Grant was slow to respond. "He knows more than he's saying, but I thought something like that."

Eve smiled and gave him a brief but very sexy kiss. "So did I. Guess you're a good teacher. What are you going to do about it?"

"I need to find out his secret and why he's keeping it. I know he's honest, but he knows Lane, and he's trying to serve too many masters. I think he's covering for Lane, probably has been all along. He may know where the guy is. That's why he didn't let Anne have the root access. If there were other contacts, she could have traced where they were coming from. Hell, Lane may be back at home."

Probing, Eve continued, "You don't really think so, do you?"

"No. It would be too dangerous...and he knows it."

Eve kissed him again, very lightly, and said goodnight. He held her hand and stopped her from leaving, then forcefully drew her back into his arms.

"Don't kiss me like we're married," he said. "Kiss me like we're lovers."

She did, the second time, like they were lovers. Her eyes reached for his like a bridge built on a beacon of light.

Sighs became gasps, they embraced, and Grant began to feel an uncontrollable urge, one that Eve felt as well. As he held her body close to his, he thought about what she had come to mean to him in such a short period. She had detected his wall and helped him remove some bricks and get past his fear of the outcome. As he felt her body mold into his, he wished that his shirt was off and that her blouse was off as well.

Through the intensity of his embrace, Eve also realized the heat of their passion. The feeling was right, but the timing wasn't. Although it was what she wanted, she hesitated at the thought of being too bold.

*Am I coming on too strong?* She worried. *Will Grant think I'm easy?* She gently pulled away. "Guess I should see you in the morning."

Although neither wanted the instant to pass, they knew it was destined.

In the stillness of Eve's departure, Grant sat down at the table in Little Houston. He thought about all the activity that had taken place in this room over the last thirty hours.

His thoughts became fixed on Eve. *Though the carnival is over, I will love you till I die.* He hoped that didn't happen anytime soon.

While appreciating the silence, he reviewed the facts that dominated the wall and made notes in his mind. All the pieces were lining up in some order, even if he didn't yet understand the ultimate arrangement. Although he didn't have a summation of the answers, he knew the players. He also knew intuitively he could find the remaining answers if he could buy the time.

Grant called FBI travel dispatch and arranged for the plane to be in McAllen for a seven thirty a.m. departure to Washington. He might be late by a kiss, but he needed to make sure his associates were on their assigned mission before he was airborne on his. Thanks to the magic of modern electronic communications, Shelly could be on her computer and Eve on her cellular phone, and he could be in touch with both of them while flying on the *Dixie Express,* the name David Lasorta had given the FBI plane.

Grant called Bartow for a final briefing and to request that he return Lane's computer and screenplay to Lane's wife. He would tell Mrs. Lane that the group had departed to various locations while continuing the search and promise to give her updates on a daily basis.

Grant picked up the phone for the most important call. He dialed the number for HiLite and received a recording. Since he didn't have Rob's home number and couldn't get it until the following morning, he decided to leave a message.

"Rob, you sorry, no-good son of a…intelligence agent… What the hell are you doing chasing my computer guru around? I've been leveling with you, but you're not leveling with me. Why do you want to know what I'm after? You know the answers. He's your boss and I know you're hiding something. You know more than you're telling me. I just hope I don't get any further into this and find out you have any misplaced loyalties. I'm on Lane's side, in case you haven't figured it out! Or are you riding shotgun for the DSD?

"You be where I can talk to you sometime early tomorrow, or I'm going to be mad, and you know what it's like when I get mad. You're going to talk to Bret, and then you're going to tell me who Scorpion is, and then I'm going to want to know where Lane is. Don't think about it, Rob. Just do it! Tomorrow…early!"

He paused momentarily, wondering if there was anything else. Then he closed the one-sided conversation very calmly. "I need your help in a hurry. I'll call you."

Grant looked at the phone and placed it back in the cradle. "Well, there went my New Year's resolution." Honestly, he was a little surprised he'd made it this long.

Did he do it right, or would Rob be chased away with his vigilance?

Tomorrow would be one of the most eventful days of Grant's life, or at least in his new career as Houston's youngest Special Agent in Charge. Not feeling very new, young, or special, he gathered up his papers and prepared to go to his room.

It could have been a better ending to an eventful day. A lot had happened on all fronts of this complex case. The team had found many answers that, in turn, created even more questions. He spent the day with E. Justine Wednesday, and it was a gorgeous day with a *Fire in the Sky*. He received his promotion, but more important, it was the day he decided to stay on the edge and not be intimidated by those who had caused the disappearance of B.W. Lane.

# CHAPTER FOURTEEN

The night did not favor sound sleeping, but Grant accrued a few hours between light dreams of the upcoming San Antonio trip and his Washington venture.

As his brain sorted information through the apparitions of slumber, he felt he had won the battle... uneasily, however. He awoke with a light sweat and a realization that he remained surrounded by a phantom enemy that prevented him from enjoying the victory.

*How could I win but feel like I lost?* He asked himself. *Is it a victory or rather a defeat disguised as a victory?*

He shuddered. It was uncomfortable, even if it was only a dream.

Although the night resisted as long as it could, the morning eventually rescued him from the failed sleep. Maybe he could take a catnap on the plane. He took a shower, shaved, and went down to what was quickly disappearing as Little Houston.

It was a little after six twenty, and all was quiet. The day was about to begin. It was Thursday, the fourth day for Grant and his team, but the sixth day for Benjamin Wells Lane. By high noon, he would be meeting with the director in Washington, and Bearing-Haas would be there as well. Eve and Shelly would be confronting Bret, if they could find him, and Rob may have supplied Lane's location, if all went according to plan.

After Grant ordered coffee and a Coke from room service, he peeled the sticky notes off the wall. As he finished packing his briefcase, Eve and Shelly arrived. Eve looked her ravishing, professional self, while Shelly was dressed casually in a pair of tight jeans and cowboy boots. Eve remarked comically that they should be able to meet with anyone, king or commoner. In either contingency, one of them would be properly attired.

Shelly didn't bring her travel bag and, after noticing Eve was carrying hers, retreated to the room. In the brief moment, Eve Thursday and Grant Magnum kissed their farewell until whenever.

Although they shared an optimism for the day's plan, something was missing in the confidence. As Eve explained, she had a revelation during the night that was similar to the one Grant felt: a dream that echoed, "There is no winner here."

In the seriousness of the morning shadows, Grant held her closely as he tried to put his mind at ease. He and Eve had both been loved before but never with the same intensity which they felt now. The two locked in an embrace, feeling like inexperienced lovers not knowing how to express themselves, but they were destined to try.

With a tight-lipped smile, Eve said, "I wish tomorrow would be today."

Then Shelly returned, and they went to the car.

Grant could only say, "Eve, don't take any chances. Be careful."

Eve responded with her eyes while her lips mouthed silently, "And you."

In a moment Eve and Shelly were disappearing from Grant's sight and heading toward US Highway 281, which would take them to San Antonio and the Blue Retriever. Although the latter wasn't for certain, it had to be. For Benjamin Lane's sake, it had to be.

* * *

Eve was a confident driver and took pride in not having had any accidents. In fact, she hadn't received a traffic ticket since she was eighteen years old. As the senior party of the twosome settled in at the wheel, the rookie began to set up her cellular modem and configure it for the trip.

After Shelly completed the connection, she logged on to the Internet and kicked into cyberspace with a trip to Bret's favorite chat room. She commented to Eve, "I don't know how long we'll be out of tower range, but it shouldn't be more than a half-hour at a time."

She typed, "Bret, wake up, expect me at noon, in person," but she didn't say where they would be…and she didn't sign it.

Even while "Ashell" was remaining anonymous, Bret would know who she was. Anonymity was preferable, however, because she didn't know whether she was being watched or by whom. She questioned herself about becoming overly paranoid but didn't want to take any chances, especially considering Grant's lesson on the intelligence community.

* * *

Meanwhile, slightly closer to the border, Grant was riding in the Casa de Palmas courtesy van to McCreery Aviation, the fixed-based operator, FBO, for private air traffic at McAllen Miller International Field. As they drove across Wichita Street toward the building, Grant saw a black-and-silver Learjet on the taxiway beyond. It wasn't the Gulfstream he'd expected to see, but what the heck? It was a late call, and there's was no telling what the plane pool looked like at midnight.

He exited the van, tipped the driver, and carried his bag and briefcase toward the plane. Two pilots met him near the steps, and since they were not Grant's normal crew, they introduced themselves. The younger of the two, the copilot, carried Grant's bag to the cargo hold at the rear of the plane. Grant boarded and sat in the right-side, face-forward position in a large overstuffed leather seat.

It was a luxury jet—smaller and perhaps a bit nicer than the plane he was accustomed to, but he thought, *what the heck?* He was now the SAC. Maybe he rated an upgrade. In questioning he thought, *I still like the Grumman.*

The pilot already had gone to the cockpit. The copilot closed the cabin door and asked Grant if he needed anything before takeoff. When Grant declined, he went into the forward cabin and closed the curtain behind him.

Grant looked around the plane and spotted some magazines as well as a phone in the mahogany console near his right hand—a first-class addition to any plane.

He thought, *who do I need to call?* It was almost seven thirty. He decided to call Lasorta, who was always in the office early. He could check on the progress of the research on biological warfare and see whether there were any other updates.

Lasorta answered on his direct line with a degree of urgency. "Yeah, Grant. Where are you?"

"On the plane, waiting for clearance to taxi."

"Grant, don't act like anything is up, but get off that plane!" Lasorta said frantically. "I couldn't get a hold of you. Our plane was held up because of some radar glitch. It may have been sabotage. It's running twenty minutes late."

Grant's heart rate doubled. He looked toward the forward cabin. Through the slit between the door panel and the curtain, he saw the pilots were busy setting the VOR for instrument flight rules and talking to the tower. Since the curtain door was almost closed, he knew he wasn't being watched.

Lasorta exclaimed, "Come on, Grant. Get the hell out of there. That's a *no-name* plane!"

"Oh, man!" Grant mumbled to himself as he placed the phone softly in its console and, using his left foot, shoved his briefcase toward the door.

He didn't have access to his weapon, which, at the moment, resided in his travel bag in the cargo bay.

*Damn it! Why didn't I carry it?*

He removed his seatbelt then inched toward the door as he kept an eye on the cockpit curtain. He listened to the pilots chatter with the tower. Just as the pilot revved the turbines for taxi, Grant frantically turned the door handle, pushed down the stairs, and vaulted to the runway.

He stumbled slightly but managed not to fall as he ran quickly toward the FBO offices. He heard the turbines slow down as he ran the seventy or so yards, but he didn't wait or look back.

Suddenly he heard the unexpected—a zing, followed immediately by the report of the pistol that intended to shorten the life of the newest SAC in the FBI.

*Not in the cards today, you son of a bitch!* He thought.

He dodged sideways in a sprint. He was almost there. As he heard the third shot fly past, he dove behind a planter box in front of the office door. He saw people scurrying around inside but motioned for them to stay back.

As he completed his escape, he heard the turbines wind up again. Looking between the plants, he saw the door lift up and the plane begin its takeoff roll.

Grant stood up and ran inside the building where the staff was calling the tower to report the emergency. The FBO manager stayed connected while waiting for a trace on the plane's route.

The Learjet never stopped. It continued down taxiway CC next to Runway 18 and didn't slow down. No one who witnessed the sight could believe it. Planes don't take off on taxiways, yet this one wound down the open taxiway, nosed up at a forty-degree angle, and took off like a missile, heading south. By Grant's calculation it was in Mexico within twenty seconds.

*Close call,* he thought.

Amid the noise and confusion, he managed to get a hold of the McAllen FBI office to request Bartow's immediate follow-up, only to find out he was at the Casa de Palmas reclaiming Mrs. Lane's items which were being attended by hotel security.

Grant remained on the line, and while he was holding, the aviation clerk received a call on another line. It was Bartow. He had an urgent message for Grant. The FBI plane was delayed. Also, when retrieving the computer, he had located a bug. A small microphone transmitter had been planted on the room-service delivery cart which had been in the room the previous day.

So that's it! The enemy had overheard all the conversations of the previous evening.

In the midst of his many uneasy thoughts, Grant decided rather quickly to make some drastic changes in his communication options. This was the nineties, and 'urgent' was taking on a new meaning. He needed more up-to-date equipment—an alphanumeric pager was no longer the latest device. He needed a cell phone like Eve's.

Grant had flatly refused to carry one, because he thought they were too big and cumbersome. His original thinking was that everyone knew where he was and how to reach him, and he didn't like interruptions. Now he could see the importance; what worked yesterday wasn't any good for today, and it almost cost him everything.

As Grant sat down to gather his nerves, he noticed the ripped knees on his suit pants. No matter. Clothes were unimportant. What was critical was that the rules had changed. Violence had been introduced. Secretly, Grant had hoped that deadly force could be avoided, but he was forced to admit his miscalculation.

*Wishful thinking,* he thought. *It's Murphy's Law, "If something can go wrong, it will."*

Grant's travel bag and his .38 were on a one-way trip to an unknown destination, most likely foreign, and he was going to Washington, DC, with torn pants.

He thought about his private, personal conversations regarding death. Quickly however, he reminded himself of his mission. He would continue doing what he had to do and leave the analysis for another time. Continue…until it was done.

Bartow was on his way to the airport, Officer Rice was coming from the McAllen PD, and SAC Harris was listening to his Grumman landing in the distance. Gathering his thoughts and putting his mind back in gear, he tried to reconnect with the conversations of the previous evening.

What exact information did the intelligence community learn after planting the bug?

Suddenly he recalled, and began to fear, his dreams of the early morning. Last night they had discussed Eve and Shelly going to San Antonio, as well as the time. He had called for the plane. Grant knew they had heard that schedule, and he had laid out everything for Rob.

*Damn! I laid it all out for Rob!*

In doing so, Grant had compromised everyone: Bret, Rob, Scorpion, and Lane—if Rob knew where he was.

*What am I, a rookie?* He asked himself. *Why didn't I just run an ad in the damn newspaper?*

Grant was overcome by a terrible feeling for his associates, who were now en route to danger. Bartow arrived within ten minutes, and Grant briefed him before his departure to Washington. He left instructions for Bartow to keep in touch with Detective Rice about the safety of Mrs. Lane and the children. They were already investigating the plane's call sign but held little hope it would have a legitimate registration.

Grant knew the pilots on the second plane, but Bartow insisted on checking their credentials anyway. Then Grant boarded the Grumman and prepared to take off again, this time on an FBI plane. He should have trusted his instincts about the first one, but questioning the pilots would have got him shot. The crooks would have thrown him on board, and left the same way they did.

*Can't second-guess everything*, he thought. He decided to be creative. *What can I do to change the things I screwed up?* Unkind thoughts jumbled in his brain as he owned his own set of facts. It was his job to stay ahead of the game, and he had let his team fall behind.

Grant picked up the plane phone and called Eve's cellular number. He knew he could contact her. She always kept the phone on "roam."

The response was, "Sorry. All circuits are temporarily busy. Please try your call again later."

Grant put down the phone and tried again, only to receive the same response.

*Oh no,* he thought. *They've taken out the tower.*

He got out his address book and called Bartow, then Hector Perez, but received the same responses.

Grant began to panic. He was shut off from both Eve and Shelly. They were in danger and unaware of it.

In addition, someone had tried to kill him. This vicious attempt elevated the case to a level totally out of control. When someone attempts the assassination of an SAC to keep a secret, it's an unqualified state of panic and there are no rules for this game.

Grant was aware of this new fact, but his team wasn't. He wondered whether Eve and Shelly had their firearms with them. They weren't field agents, so they weren't expected to carry weapons all the time. Of course, they weren't supposed to be in the field in any regard.

The security of the team was unraveling at each level, and Grant felt helpless. He was out of touch—airborne—two hours and forty minutes from the Beltway at just short of the speed of sound.

He went to the cabin and asked the pilot, Jerry Longren, about their flight plan. They were filed for landing at Fairfax Municipal, south of Dulles, and closer to the Beltway. Grant advised them of his suspicions about the dangers that could lie ahead at some point. He told Longren to prepare for anything and to be ready to wing a change in plans if circumstances dictated. Longren, a former Navy pilot, read into the situation instinctively and knew to let Grant know if anything unusual occurred during the flight.

Grant returned to his seat and called Lasorta.

"What the hell happened?" Lasorta asked.

"Guess I was touched by an angel. I don't know why I called you when I did, but it was perfect. I beat the shakedown by about fifteen seconds."

All was silent on both ends. Grant finally owned the tragedy that had been so, so close. "That's as close as I've ever been," he said.

Lasorta remained silent. He knew what Grant was talking about.

Grant took a deep breath and sighed. "Thanks for being at work early."

Both felt the emotion of twenty thousand feet vertical distance and three hundred miles, but they understood the meaning of friendship.

Grant regained his control of the situation. "Now I really need your help. They tried to kill me, so we understand how serious this is. I think Delaney and Shelly are probably in trouble. I can't reach anyone in this lata's cellular network. I think the bastards must have taken out the tower, or they're jamming it somehow."

The two discussed all the relevant information they had lost to the enemy. They also considered their options and covered a lot in a couple of minutes, but before anything could be decided, Lasorta wanted to complete a quick sweep of all phone lines the FBI would be using for the day.

In the same conversation, Grant authorized code clearance for the third and fourth floors in Houston. No one would be allowed on those floors except those with FBI security clearance. If they had to do battle with the whole damned intelligence community, they'd make sure everyone played by the rules.

The new SAC also asked Lasorta to check out Rob Garza's file and see what he was doing in sixty-eight. Finally, he left Lasorta with a serious message. "Do something to help Delaney and Shelly. I don't know what. Highway Patrol, roadblock, get them an escort…but do something. And keep it quiet…no APB."

Actually, Lasorta knew this was a given.

As the conversation concluded, Grant thought about Rob. When he called HiLite, the phone connected but Rob wasn't there. However, Grant was able to obtain his home number from one of the employees.

"Be at home, you son of a bitch. I need you now."

He dialed the number, and Rob sleepily answered.

"Wake up fast, Rob. This is all going to be over by noon, and you're a party to this bull—"

"What's happening?"

"It hit the fan. That's what! To start with, I got on a plane where the pilots had another idea about where I ought to be going. They shot at me with real damned bullets! And now they've jammed or wiped out cellular communications for the whole Rio Grande damned Valley! I can't get hold of Delaney, and I think they're after her and Shelly. Now wake your ass up!"

"OK, OK. Just a minute."

"Come on, Rob. Start telling me what you know. I don't give a hoot when you knew it, but I need to get in touch with Bret and tell him it's a setup. We're leading the enemy right to his door! I also have to reach Shelly by modem and let her know they're probably being followed. What do I do?"

Starting to wake up, Rob responded, "Meet me at HiLite in twenty minutes."

"I can't. I'm almost over Houston at thirty-one thousand feet."

"OK. Be difficult," he responded facetiously. "Don't get out. I'll take care of it." Rob was thinking, *it must be a jammer because he's talking to me.*

Grant was astonished. "Rob, you and Lane set the whole damn thing up, and now it's collapsing on my head!"

"Hey, Grant! Cool it! I told Lane yours was the best head. As for Shelly and Delaney, they're good, and if you're good, and I'm good, it'll all turn out the way it's supposed to, so *you* pull it together."

If Grant Harris ever had a weakness, it was thinking he had all the answers all the time, not just part of them but all of them. At that point, he was pleased to admit he didn't have them all. He needed to relax, lie back for a minute, and regroup. He had lost his cool and broken his New Year's resolution…again.

Rob was right. Eve and Shelly and Rob and Lasorta and the rest of those he could trust—they were the best, and they were all with him. He could count on that.

It wasn't much consolation, though. Grant didn't like the fact that he was headed for Washington and leaving everyone else in jeopardy.

He started to second-guess whether his romantic relationship with Eve had caused him to lose focus, but he acknowledged it hadn't. The relationship only gave his life more meaning. A new urgency, however, was appearing, which was to make sure his people, and the others concerned, were safe. Then he could re-concentrate on the final facts about Lane.

# CHAPTER FIFTEEN

As Grant reviewed the specifics from the skies over eastern Louisiana, Rob had reached Shelly in the chat room. She confirmed that her cell phone wasn't working and supposed there was a problem with the bands or a limitation in the bandwidth, because the modem did connect. And yes, they were being followed.

A dark sedan appeared to have been with them since they had passed through Edinburg, a little north of McAllen. It was probably the same intelligence team that had followed Grant and Eve the day before. The sedan hadn't tried to overtake them. It only trailed from a distance, but Shelly said they didn't plan to stop. They should reach San Antonio by eleven or a little later and would go immediately to the VA hospital.

Although Shelly had a city map and a general idea of the veteran's hospital location, Rob e-mailed the directions for the fastest route. They'd take the Interstate 410 West Loop to the Babcock exit, turn left for three lights and then right. They should see it from there. He told Shelly to stay off chat, because Bret knew she was coming. Since the traitors knew the FBI's objective, he was prepared and would be in Ward B, on the second floor in the recreation lounge area.

Shelly read the information to Eve as they continued their drive between George West and Three Rivers. "You need to carry your weapons from now on," Rob told her in the note. "After what happened to Grant, you may need them."

As Shelly read this part aloud, Eve glanced over quickly and lost her concentration. The car swerved, but Eve quickly recovered and then looked back.

She was frantic. "What happened to Grant?"

"He didn't say anything else. I'll e-mail him back and see if he'll answer."

This was all Eve needed to hear. She took a few deep breaths as she tried to reestablish control of the car.

*What happened?* She wondered.

Tears filled her eyes, and she held her lips tightly as she began to feel a hollow place somewhere within her. For a moment she felt overcome and out of control.

*Was it the alarming dream I described to Grant in the early morning? The dream that confirmed we were together but somehow remained separated by an unknown force and so far apart?*

She composed herself with a convincing assurance that Grant must be all right or Rob would have said more.

Anne Shelly was young but also bright and insightful. She recognized the pain her associate felt.

"Are you OK, Eve?"

"I think so. It just caught me off guard. I wasn't ready to hear that Grant was in trouble."

"Want to talk about it?"

"Not yet."

After a minute or so of silence, Eve asked Shelly, "Are you good with your weapon?"

Trying to add some humor, Shelly replied, "Which weapon? I've got an arsenal."

Eve smiled. "The one you use on bad guys."

The answer Shelly gave wasn't exactly definitive. "My mind is my best weapon." She hesitated for a beat and then realized she was skating around a proper answer to a serious question. She continued, "Not as good as I am with a computer, but I'm OK, I guess. I was the best woman in my class and third best overall." After another short silence, she added, "I don't know how I feel about shooting people, but I can, if they're shooting at me or somebody else. What about you, Eve? Could you kill somebody?"

"Yes. Right now I could."

Eve periodically checked the rearview mirror to see whether she could still spot the dark-colored sedan that stayed a quarter-mile or so behind them. It was there.

The car was silent except for the purring of the engine and the sound of the radials singing a drone-like song to the roadway.

Eve decided to keep the conversation going. "I don't like violence, but I have to admit, after I saw the movie *A Time to Kill*, that I guess there are times when it takes violence to stop violence." She paused momentarily. "If something happened to Grant, I'd be able to kill somebody."

Shelly wasn't surprised by Eve's remark and agreed. She stopped typing on her laptop and placed it beside her next to the console. She'd have to wait to connect with the next tower.

"How long have you known Agent Harris?" she asked.

Eve knew Shelly had noticed her attentions, which admittedly, had been focused on Grant.

"I've been in Houston for six years," she replied, "and I've known him for that long, but more or less from a distance. Until recently we only had minor contact, not a whole lot and not daily, since I'm in operations and he's in the field and senior management. I was single, and he was married."

She felt comfortable and continued.

"Grant was divorced about eight or nine months ago, but I wasn't the reason. If you want to know if I'm interested..." Eve glanced at Shelly. "...I am. I've always respected him as a gentleman and an agent, and he's always been a special person. I've wanted to know him better."

"Do you love him?"

"I think so. Yes, in a way. It's early on, but I know I'm going to love him more and more. We just need more time. We haven't ridden a merry-go-round or walked on the beach... you know what I mean?"

Shelly smiled, "I think I got it. 'Together' is an important word."

"Yes. It's important to me—and to him. We both know that it takes two, but he keeps remembering that 'love' and 'pain' are both four-letter words. So we have to let go of the past."

With this, Eve changed the subject. "How about you? Is there someone important in your life?"

Agent Shelly smiled. "Lots of them would like to be, but I haven't found anyone worth being with all the time, at least not yet."

They pursued a discussion of relationships and became more relaxed. Although the two had spent a significant amount of time together in two days, it didn't exactly constitute quality time. Things seemed to be different now. They were in the same boat, so to speak, with someone in pursuit, and heading into dangerous waters.

As they continued to approach San Antonio, Shelly's e-mail program sounded Rob's response. It described the circumstances surrounding Grant's short-lived kidnapping. The e-mail detailed his escape from the pilot impersonators at the airport and said that Grant had jumped out of the plane as it began to taxi. They shot at him and missed. Currently, he was headed for Washington on the real FBI jet.

Eve breathed a long sigh, more relaxed knowing Grant was all right, at least for the moment.

Rob relayed more information, which included Lasorta's notification of security at the VA. He advised the hospital that someone was tailing their agents.

Special Agent Shelly reached to the rear seat and unzipped the side pouch of her briefcase. She retrieved an M1191A1; it was a .45 caliber semiautomatic. She held it in her hand, looked at it, laid it down, and retrieved a box of shells; then placed one full clip to the side and loaded seven shells in each of three remaining clips. With confident authority she picked up the weapon and slid one clip into it. She didn't cock it, but it was easily ready if needed.

She put the other three clips in the cup holder on the console and calmly placed the pistol in the door pocket.

As Eve watched in her peripheral vision, Shelly said, "Just in case those bastards decide to get any closer."

Eve answered, "I haven't heard you use such, uh…descriptive language before."

"It needed saying. I don't like the fact that they were shooting at Grant either."

Eve looked over toward Shelly and then at the .45. It wasn't the normal-issue Smith & Wesson she had chosen. Shelly explained that it was the same weapon used as a military issue for the US Marine Corps. It had a higher muzzle velocity of 253 meters per second and a higher maximum effective range of twenty-five meters, or a little more than eighty feet. Although it was heavier, she felt more comfortable using it to shoot a target a little farther away.

Eve was impressed. "You don't come across as a major warrior. Now I find out you're G.I. Jane."

"You may not believe it," she joked, "but I'm actually Xena the Warrior Princess in disguise."

"Well, tell me more. What did you do in high school?"

"I went to Coronado High in Lubbock. Uh…I like to ride horses."

"You're a cowgirl?" Eve added facetiously. "It's hard to tell from your clothes."

"No, I really wasn't too much of a 'kicker.' I was a cheerleader."

Eve laughed and scolded her. "Anne Shelly, you don't know me well enough to lie to me."

Shelly smiled. "I'm serious. I really was."

"How did a cowgirl cheerleader end up as a computer whiz kid with the FBI?" Shelly stalled with the answer, but Eve continued to hunt for the answer. "Well?"

"I made pretty good grades."

"How good is pretty good?"

"I was valedictorian."

Eve looked at her young associate and smiled. "OK, OK, enough," she told Shelly. "Stop talking. You're starting to intimidate me."

Recognizing the upcoming exit for I-410 West, they headed right, then up and left over a triple-deck overpass.

Eve watched as the dark sedan made the same maneuver.

"Still there," she said. "What was the name of the exit?"

"Babcock, but it's probably another fifteen miles or so."

As they passed a billboard for the Sea World exit, Eve picked up her cell phone and this time reached a tone.

"Well, I guess they haven't taken out San Antonio." She handed the phone to Shelly. "Try Houston."

After Shelly dialed the number, the phone offered a funny tone but didn't connect. *I'll bet they're jamming the frequency*, she thought.

Eve studied the reflection in the rearview mirror and saw the sedan following menacingly in its trailing orbit.

Shelly asked, "What are we going to do when we get there?"

"We'll go in quickly. I think I'll leave you at the front to guard the car and see if they're going to follow us in. If they both do, you come up to the second floor. Ward B lounge, right?"

Shelly responded affirmatively.

"If one of them hangs around our car, you need to hide and watch."

"But you won't know if I'm coming or not. You'll be alone."

"Not totally. I'll have Bret."

"You hope. We're still not sure about that."

\* \* \*

As they neared their destination, someone else was deep in thought about what was going on in San Antonio.

Grant Harris was over the border between Virginia and northwest North Carolina, about thirty-five minutes from Washington. He had been in contact with Lasorta and learned the security at the VA had been alerted. Lasorta had given Rob the information to relay to Shelly. As far as everyone knew, security verified it could take care of anyone pursuing Eve and Shelly, at least temporarily.

Grant felt a little more relieved about their safety.

After a follow-up conversation with Rob, Lasorta confirmed Shelly's receipt of the earlier communication; everything was OK. She and Eve were prepared and had their weapons.

When the update was completed, Lasorta dropped the first of his series of bombshells on Grant's Washington parade.

"Rob Garza was in Vietnam in sixty-eight and part of sixty-nine. He was listed as a gunnery sergeant with an armored unit stationed at… guess where?"

"Quang Tri."

"Right. Also, he was referenced as a field specialist with a classified specialty and top-secret clearance. Want his code name?"

Grant answered this before Lasorta could. "Scorpion."

"Bingo!"

Grant was quiet as he tried to plug the information into his already overcrowded brain.

"I knew there was something about this that didn't ring true. Son of a bitch, Rob. You took me out on that one." *I knew you must have been in on this from the start, now I know for sure,* Grant thought.

"Grant, I told Rob I was going to call you with this information. He said it didn't matter and that nothing changes. Eve still needs to talk to Bret to find out what he knows about Lane's location, because Rob doesn't know where he is. Lane posted a page that his son Wade found, telling everyone he was all right. Rob said he traced it to a Houston source.

"Rob also said he didn't know much more about the mission than you did. He was just there on the recovery. Three of the six people were injured. Lane was one of them. They were battered by small pellet-type wounds in numerous places on their bodies. Two people, other than Lane, were very sick, but Lane wasn't. As Rob recalled, Lane had other injuries: a cut on his left leg, a dislocated shoulder, broken ribs, and a head wound. He and the Retriever delivered them to a secure non-military position outside the Quang Tri base. This was the extent of what Rob knew."

Grant assessed the information as Lasorta continued the briefing.

"When Rob met Lane years later, they never discussed it. He didn't think Lane remembered him or anything, until recently, like the letter said. When Lane's e-mail got hacked, he told Rob about it. Rob decided to help him, since he knew more about the mission than Lane remembered. He told Lane he'd get you in to solve the mystery. Then Lane received the message in which Bret told him to hide. That's all."

"Nothing else?"

"Rob said he was sorry for keeping you in the dark, but he needed your help to find out who was after Lane. He decided the chain must have gone way up, like *ionosphere high up*, but he didn't think you'd believe him until you confirmed it for yourself."

Lasorta knew Grant was putting it together in his mind and continued, "The conspiracy-theory people will have a field day with this."

"Yeah, it almost sounds too crazy to be true," Grant murmured. Then he thought, *the press will make sure this never sees the light of day.*

Lasorta added, "It does sound super crazy." When Grant didn't respond, he continued, "Rob also said to tell you he doesn't know anything about the WHO involvement, or where the mission originated. He just knew about Defense Security, no more."

After a brief silence, Lasorta continued, "Grant, we now know *who*, and I also think we know *why*. I found something else. Listen to this."

He prepared to start his dissertation, but Grant interrupted.

"Are we sure no one's bugging your line?"

"It's OK." Lasorta said. The FBI's Internal Security team had swept and certified the third and fourth floors as being clear of electronic surveillance equipment or bugs.

"Sorry I interrupted, go ahead."

"OK, this is it. I found a book titled *Emerging Viruses* by Dr. Leonard G. Horowitz, and although I haven't had time to read it all, I did read a review by JoAnn Hartmangruber.

"Here are some quotes from the review, 'Different stories have been told as to how Acquired Immune Deficiency Syndrome (AIDS) got its start. Most people...' So on and so forth... 'Dr. Leonard Horowitz researched and investigated the origins of the AIDS, Marburg, and Ebola viruses...' et cetera, et cetera. Oh, here. Listen to this.

"Dr. Horowitz claims that 'after the original research, in nineteen sixty-nine...' Got the date, Grant? '...the Department of Defense requested and received from Congress ten million dollars to contract for the development of immune-system destroying agents for germ warfare'... and so on.

"There's more. 'Thus, beginning in the latter part of the nineteen sixties,' says Horowitz, 'scientists in government laboratories worked on developing immunosuppressant or AIDS-like viruses, cancer viruses, and vaccines. Some of the work was also contracted out to private firms.'

"Here it is. Get this name. 'Dr. Robert Gallo.' Ring a bell? Galileo's wine. 'Gallo was one of the chief scientists working in these areas,' says Horowitz. 'Although he was credited for having discovered the virus that causes AIDS, published materials reveal a different fact. Dr. Gallo actually discovered how to manufacture AIDS-like viruses in the seventies. He did not openly admit to this.'

"It goes on to say, 'Dr. Gallo was ashamed to admit he had created the AIDS-like virus years earlier in the sixties. This may be why he tried to block its discovery, as he was afraid it would be traced back to his research in biological warfare.'

"One more item here. 'It's no secret that the World Health Organization, governments, including the United States in conjunction with the UN, and certain non-government organizations, including environmentalists, have been looking into the control and reduction of the world's population,' and there's the *why*. Does that get you to China?"

Grant was silent before he replied, "Lasorta, you've outdone yourself this time. The director has to give us an extension on this now. It can't look like anything but some type of conspiracy and cover-up, regardless of how you dress it."

Lasorta said, "I followed up, and I have one more for you. What I just read about Defense getting the ten million in sixty-nine. Get this. 'Dr. D.M. McArtor, then Deputy Director of Research and Technology for the Department of Defense, appeared before the House Subcommittee on Appropriations to request funding for a project to produce a synthetic biological agent for which humans have not yet acquired a natural immunity.

" 'Dr. McArtor asked for the funds to produce this agent over the next five to ten years. The Congressional record reveals that according to the plan for the development of this germ agent, the most important characteristic of the new disease would be that it might be refractory'—meaning, 'resistant—to the immunological and therapeutic processes upon which we depend to maintain our relative freedom from infectious disease.' "

Grant concluded, "So Congress gave them the money to develop AIDS—and this 'McArtor' has got to be 'King Arthur.' Is that your take?"

Lasorta agreed. "We have a winner!"

"You think they were using Lane for research?"

Lasorta answered, "I asked the doctor at Anderson the question about low white-cell counts for a person who was never sick. He said the person must have had a perfect immune system, so he didn't need them. How about a vaccine?"

"So that's why they left him alone. A vaccine...so he was just a blood bank...they couldn't kill him." Grant projected, "So they just *made him* forget everything."

"I gave the doctors the rest of the info out of Lane's file, and they said the blood in those samples is consistent with some of these conclusions, but it'll take a while to complete an analysis. I suggested that they stay on top of it, just in case something in there holds the cure for AIDS or Ebola."

After Lasorta was off the line, Grant gazed through the window and scanned the tops of the noon winter clouds which carpeted the sky floor below the plane. As they started to descend, he saw the pictures come into focus in his mind.

Lane had a natural or developed immunity to the original strains of one of those manmade diseases. That's why they needed him, to supply the blood…but the people at WHO didn't want the world to know they started it, and they couldn't afford to have Lane out there talking about it.

Eve and Shelly were moving in on the VA, toward Bret and Lane, and Grant was closing in on Bearing-Haas.

*High noon!*

Grant knew WHO couldn't hide from the information the FBI had in its possession. Soon everyone would be able to see through the shadows and hopefully to the location of B.W. Lane.

# CHAPTER SIXTEEN

After the exit onto Babcock, the hospital was easy to locate. The intelligence tail, in the dark sedan, pursued as expected. "Thursday, High Noon"—it seemed a good name for the showdown.

Eve thought about the previous Monday, the commute into downtown Houston, meeting with Grant and Agent Jackson, the beginning of the chase—not *Three Days of the Condor*, as Grant related it to Georgia, but *Four Days of the Wolf*.

Then came the unexpected—allowing herself to fall in love with one of her friends and having the love returned, and from a guy who agreed, like she did, that a woman should be named Dulcinea. If he would only continue to take down those bricks…

She considered her attachment to Grant, the way he talked and shared himself with her, held her, and the gentle way he touched her. She could talk about anything, and he would be interested. She could be her loving, silly self, and he didn't care. He supported her in every way she needed, *almost*, but the desire was there, and she could manage the intensification when the time was right.

The number of puzzle pieces in her life had increased. Eve considered her work, this case, and the serious parts of her life. All were important, but it was also essential that she recognize and allow her emotions to thrive. Not all things can be the same degree of serious.

\* \* \*

The reality of the situation was reborn in the flash of the sign that read, AUDIE L. MURPHY MEMORIAL VA HOSPITAL. Eve steered into the parking area to a reserved space in front of the main entrance.

"Ready?" she asked Shelly, the 'Cowgirl Rose of San Antone.'

As they exited the vehicle, a security guard came toward the car. "May I help you?"

His tone was both kind and professional.

Eve told him they were FBI agents, offered their credentials, and said they were expected by someone in Ward B named Bret. The guard was very obliging and told them Bret had been notified. Lasorta had made arrangements with the hospital in advance.

Shelly surveyed the distance and saw the sedan as it circled slowly in the entrance boulevard.

"They must be calling for instructions," she told Shelly. "They're not coming in."

The guard introduced himself as Harry Lumperman. "Ladies, the security of Audie VA is at your disposal. We'll watch your vehicle and those guys. Don't worry. We won't let them interfere with your investigation."

Eve felt somewhat uneasy about the comfort level with which Officer Lumperman tried to put them at ease. She wasn't relieved. He was only a security guard.

Lumperman realized her hesitation. "Sorry. I don't mean to be forward."

He confidently pulled open his jacket and revealed his brass, a Navy SEALS emblem and a Navy Cross.

This time he spoke with a definite air of assurance. "We would love to get a piece of those guys, ma'am, if they get in your way."

Eve smiled and relaxed, realizing they had a real escort, someone who could win a contest with any opponent. SEALS were born and bred for war, and this one probably hadn't seen any action in twenty years.

Eve replied, "Thank you, sir."

Lumperman smiled. "Bret's one of us. He works Ward B, and he's waiting for you."

So the Blue Retriever, a former military helicopter pilot, was also with security at the hospital. He likely had his own brass of some kind. Eve recalled the legends about the vets who returned from Vietnam, how many of them couldn't make it outside, in a world where anti-war protests had brought them humiliation. They were heroes, reviled without reason instead of being appreciated for loyalty.

Of course, no one came back from Southeast Asia and felt good about the experience, because war is war. But in the case of the US press corps, it became a *political war,* and the battles were actually fought at Berkeley and the 'peace' tables of Paris, over bottles of wine or brandy. The real problem was that sixty thousand American boys didn't come home, and a twenty-year-old named B.W. Lane grew older with recurring nightmares of his own involvement. That was a fact.

The reality returned. As Eve and Shelly continued into the main entrance, Lumperman fed them information. He sounded like a mission commander giving the last-minute drill to his unit before a raid—very low-key and factual, with no emotion.

"You'll enter through the main entry and then make a left down a hall," Lumperman told the agents. "At the end of the hall, you'll turn right and proceed to a group of elevators about halfway down the hall. You'll enter the elevators, and a man in a wheelchair will meet you on the second floor. He'll take you to Bret. I'll remain here to guard the rear and protect your vehicle. If you need anything else…"

This guy was on top of the situation.

He handed Eve a radio. "You're set on frequency, and I think you'll have more help than you'll need."

Eve was preparing to thank Lumperman for his help and support, when youth intervened its inevitable quest for a perfect way to communicate. Although Lumperman was certainly old enough to be her father and maybe because of the fact, Anne Shelly felt compelled to kiss him on the cheek.

This attention was very well received, and as Lumperman blushed, Agent Shelly boldly stated, "Thanks. I know everything will be OK."

*It feels good to know you have backup,* Eve thought. She knew if Robin Hood, the Lone Ranger, or Superman were around today, they would have been disguised as Special Forces: Rangers, SEALS, Green Berets, Delta. Certainly the FBI had whatever it needed to wage a war with the Intelligence Community or their henchmen right there in San Antonio, or anywhere else.

Anne and Eve walked into the elevator and punched the button for the second floor. When they arrived and the door exposed the unknown territory, there sat a middle-aged black man in a wheelchair.

"Agents Shelly and Delaney?" They responded, and he turned his wheelchair around. "Please follow me."

They went down the hall, left, then right again, over the main hall they had traveled below. As they entered a lounge, they saw a group of eight or nine patients and a couple of nurses. They didn't take the time to size up the gathering. All eyes were on them as they entered the room, and all were hushed.

There was a silence, as if the patients were inmates waiting for someone to give a command or speak. Eve did. Honest and direct was the only way.

"Where's Bret?" she said, to no one in particular. During a moment with no response, she thought about Bret's circumstances. Since she didn't have knowledge of Rob's e-mail introduction or Lasorta's phone contact, she determined Bret must be "checking her out." She added, "I'm very sorry to intrude, but we have a problem, and we need your help. You communicated with Ashell." She motioned to indicate her companion as the room watched.

"This is Anne Shelly."

The room remained silent.

"You want me to keep going? Do I need to say more? About thirty years ago, a man named Lane went to Vietnam as an operative on a classified mission. We know he's being hunted. That's why we're here."

She continued in a more stern tone, "We need your help now, Bret. Get with the program."

After a momentary silence, a voice projected from behind a partition wall. "How do we know you'll help him, not just set him up?"

Remaining composed, Eve responded almost apologetically, "I guess you don't have any guarantees." She spoke more boldly. "But I spent an evening with Lane's wife and kids, and they want him back." She hesitated in the hush. "We all have to believe in one side or the other." She paused again, then added, "Believe in something, Bret. Lane's time's running out."

A figure walked out from behind the curtain wall. He wasn't a large man, but he was very powerful and rugged looking, like one might picture a common-man-turned-hero, as all soldiers are. He walked across the room to where the women stood.

In a low voice, he responded, "OK, you're in. Lane is at the Alabama-Coushatta Indian Reservation in East Texas. To find him, ask for Three Owls, and tell him, 'Endeavor to persevere.' It's the password to talk to Wolf. It's what the white man told the American Indians every time they broke a treaty…more or less what they tell veterans now."

Eve held back her emotion. Then she looked at Shelly and recognized the shared feeling.

Eve dropped her head slightly and responded, "We'll bring him in, I promise. Is there anything else?"

The Blue Retriever shook his head. Then he changed his mind and added, "When you talk to Wolf, tell him nobody ever found J.J."

"Who's J.J.?" Eve asked.

"Jimmy Jackson. Another one of the guys."

"What information did you have on him?"

"He never came back from Nam. That's all we know."

"Who's 'we'?" In the obvious silence, Eve realized she was continuing past Bret's comfort zone and with that, the conversation was over. Only slightly convincingly, she continued, "We'll tell him."

As they turned to leave, the very intuitive Anne Shelly rejoined the conversation and spoke in the direction of the patients. "We will too… endeavor to persevere."

One of the patients started to clap his hands. It was like a slow, soft chant, very deliberate and on a mark. A couple of others joined him in the mystic rhythmic sound, and it echoed like harmony in a mute choir as the two retreated toward the elevator.

Eve keyed the microphone on the radio. "Lumperman, come in."

"You got me, Delaney."

"We're heading back to the elevator."

Lumperman interrupted and told them to slow down. One of the sentries had seen another suspicious vehicle enter the grounds from the north entrance and turn toward the rear of the hospital where the emergency entrance was located. This change in events needed a monitor. It was strange that the men parked on the street in front hadn't followed the agents inside. The spooks were evidently content to wait and pick up the chase when the women departed the premises.

Eve knew they needed a plan in order to lose the tail. Changing their destination to East Texas would be easy enough, but the concern was in not leading the IC to the target. At this point, she was unsure whether to run or to make a stand…and then run.

Lumperman came back on the radio.

"Leyman," he said to their escort in the wheelchair, "get the Retriever and take the agents to the cafeteria fire-escape door. I'll slow these guys down, the ones out front, and direct them away from Delaney's car."

Leyman wheeled down the hall and returned just as rapidly with Bret wheeling him. He motioned to the agents to follow, and they continued down the hall past the elevators, toward the other end of the building.

"Is your car parked in front?" he asked.

Eve told him the location as they continued.

With the intent of alleviating the pressure, Bret remarked, "Ashell, when this is over, I want you for a pen pal. You stay in touch."

Shelly smiled nervously. "OK with me," she agreed as they scurried down the hall.

\* \* \*

At the front entrance, Lumperman walked toward the dark sedan that was parked on the roadway just beyond the front entrance. As he approached the vehicle, he instinctively unbuckled the strap on his .45 semiautomatic, which was similar to Shelly's.

The players in the automobile decided to temporarily take themselves out of the game. Spotting the guard approaching them, they made a quick U-turn and sped back toward Babcock. Lumperman watched for a second, confirmed the retreat, and radioed the information to Bret.

"Let's get them to the car now, and then we'll sidetrack the guys coming through the emergency exit."

Bret agreed and added, "Those guys who got down the road are probably in touch with these guys. We need a diversion."

Although Eve and Shelly were unaware of the details of the previous communications with Scorpion, they began to realize that Bret was as committed to the success of this mission as they were.

In accordance, Bret also knew they needed to get to East Texas in a hurry. Still talking in the radio, he continued, "I think I'll let the ladies take my Jeep. They won't be followed if they leave through the north entry in a different vehicle."

It was a good plan, except for how and when they would exchange cars. But first things first... Getting out of there without being tailed would be primary. Then they could regroup with a plan.

Bret summarized, "I know we're all on the same team, so you get out of here and then we'll talk. Just go."

Shelly stopped for a moment. "I need my laptop and our stuff from the other car. Can we...?"

"If we hurry, you can get your things before those other guys can come in through the back."

As they went out the cafeteria exit door, Bret said, "Leyman, we're gonna leave you here. Don't let anyone follow us." He confirmed with Eve, "Is that a rental car?"

She responded, "Alamo," and Bret gave her his Jeep keys.

"Are the papers in it?"

As they continued hastily toward the car, Eve responded, "Visor" and handed him the keys.

"I'll turn it in for you later, after I make sure those guys watch it for a while."

The agents retrieved their bags and the laptop and proceeded a short distance across the parking lot to Bret's Jeep.

Eve asked, "What are you going to do after we leave?"

"Just take the Jeep and do what you need to do," Bret said. "I'll be backing you up."

"I don't understand."

"Don't worry about it. I'll be there. Look for me tomorrow in the Big Thicket. I'll find you."

With quick thanks to the heroes of Audie Murphy, the departing FBI agents fixed their focus on the east side of Texas, and Bret quickly reentered the building.

As they departed in the Jeep, Eve shook her head. *Grant's not going to believe we stole Bret's Jeep*, she thought. *Well, it's not really theft, but it certainly can be classified as an unusual occurrence, but this whole case is about unusual occurrences, isn't it?*

Eve knew the general direction toward the 'piney woods' of East Texas, the location of the Alabama-Coushatta reservation. The reservation, only an hour or two north of Houston, had been given to the Indians by Sam Houston when he was president of Texas. This ultimately would make sense to Grant, because the Alabama were relatives of the Cherokee, the tribe to which Lane claimed heritage.

This would be a five-to-six hour drive, and Eve thought about locating a map after they made sure they weren't being followed.

* * *

When they turned onto the freeway, Shelly called the Houston office for an update session; both ends of the equation needed one. This time, her wireless phone made its connection. She asked for Lasorta and reached him. He relayed his conversation with Grant, adding they had some new facts that revealed the identity of King Arthur, and most likely, Galileo's wine.

Eve voiced, and Shelly relayed that they were going to the reservation where Lane was hiding. The desired conclusion would be for Grant to connect with them at that location, if he could get back to Texas after his meeting in DC. She said they had changed vehicles, but Shelley didn't give the details, as the story was too long for this call. Lasorta said he would pass the info along and get back to them as soon as he knew anything. Grant was still using the company plane, the *Dixie Express,* but hadn't scheduled a return. Lasorta agreed to have Grant call her, since her cell phone was now functioning.

Shelly logged on to the Internet with her laptop and found a Texas map. The reservation, east of Livingston, was about halfway to Woodville on 190, in an area known to Texans as the 'piney woods' or, in a larger sense, the Big Thicket. The best route was to take Interstate 10 to Houston and then travel north on US 59 to Livingston, then drive east about fourteen miles out in the woods.

This route, through Houston, would allow Eve to stop at her apartment and replenish her wardrobe with something more casual for the reservation trip. Since it was the middle of winter, it would be dark by six, but with any luck, they would be back on the road quickly. Since there was an airport in Livingston, they discussed advising Grant that they could meet the plane whenever he returned.

In a moment of silence, while Shelly typed on the laptop, Eve took the opportunity to reflect on her special three days with Grant. Although they had been separated for only about five or six hours, the distance had grown to over fifteen hundred miles and a thousand dangers. She owned a new feeling. She wasn't afraid for herself, but she was becoming afraid for him.

The phone interrupted her thoughts, and Lasorta relayed some up-to-the-minute issues that were still being dealt with at the VA. The SEAL security team had subverted the IC in its pursuit by completing some unauthorized maintenance on their vehicle. They took the chance, while the second group had entered through the emergency entrance, to covertly disassemble enough of the vehicle to prevent its rejoining the chase.

During the undertaking, however, they noticed an unusual piece of equipment in the auto. It resembled a small reception disk, like those used in cable TV, with some other electronic equipment attached. It was likely a signal-interceptor radio for the capture of cellular, microwave communication. The IC was either bugging the airwaves or jamming them.

Since the fellows in the dark sedan had disappeared again, Eve and Anne were warned to watch out for the tail. Beyond this, they needed to be wary of communicating anything important on their cell phones.

Then it was time for Eve to feel like a rookie. She reminded Lasorta of their previous calls regarding the possible location of "you know who" and "we said where" and the timetable as well. So how about some more spilled milk? They signed off. It was time to stay alert.

Shelly asked, "If we're stopping in Houston, can we have your office get some special equipment for us? There might be a few items I could use to help us catch these guys."

"Sure, go ahead and email David Lasorta. He can get anything you need." Under her breath, she added, "Except Lane."

As the Jeep and its passengers continued eastbound toward their destination, Big Houston, conversation slowed. The telephone poles and fence posts counted the miles and the time.

Shelly had been on the computer for a while when suddenly she broke the silence. "What? I can't believe this! What…?"

Eve glanced over at her. "What is it, Shell?"

"Just a minute. Let me read a little more." An uncomfortable silence continued until Shelly explained. "You're not going to believe this. Remember Bret said something about Jimmy Jackson? J.J.? He was with Lane on the mission. Well…I've been playing with some differ-ent search-engine inquiries, and I got a million hits on James Jackson. There were too many, so I narrowed the search through Quang Tri and Vietnam, and you're not…" She dramatically emphasized, "You're not *even* going to believe this."

She began to read. " 'September twenty-first will mark the twenty-fifth anniversary of the day Marine Lance Corporal James W. Jackson, Jr., of Atlanta walked into a Navy Hospital in Vietnam and vanished into thin air. Since that day in nineteen sixty-nine there has been absolutely no trace of Jackson nor any indication how or why he was swallowed up the moment he stepped through the doors of the Third Medical Battalion Hospital in Quang Tri for treatment of minor shrapnel wounds.' Eve, can you believe this?"

"Minor shrapnel wounds? No, I can't."

" 'Of the more than twenty-two hundred cases of men who were prisoners, missing or unaccounted for, in Southeast Asia, Jackson's may be the most bizarre. Jackson's disappearance is like the war itself, a rid-dle without an answer, a mystery without a solution, an unsatisfactory and frustrating end to youth and innocence.' What do you think, Eve?"

Eve stared down the road, almost as if she were in a trance. She asked Shelly to continue.

Shelly read silently for a moment, as if editing parts of the manu-script.

"He was just a nineteen-year-old kid from Atlanta." She started to read again. " 'It is an indictment of a system that failed Jackson and his family in nineteen sixty-nine and continues to fail other missing men and their families. Jackson's case is unique, because he was not lost in the jungle while on patrol. He was not in a helicopter or an airplane that crashed or was shot down. He did not wander off into the seamier sections of Saigon or Da Nang. He simply walked into a hospital in the middle of the busy Quang Tri Combat Base and vanished from the face of the Earth.' "

"Where is that coming from?" Eve asked.

"The article is titled, 'The Strange Disappearance of Lance Corporal James W. Jackson, Jr.,' written in 1994 by Ron Martz, Special Liaison to the *US Veteran Dispatch*."

"Wow, Shell, this is huge! See if there's anything else…any clues."

Shelly scanned the article for other details. "The military said it was a real embarrassment to them. I'll bet it was!" She continued, " 'For Jackson's mother, the answer was simple. "The Marine Corps lost my son," she said. "I had prepared myself for the possibility that my son might die in Vietnam," she added. "I was ready for him to be wounded or captured or any of the things you expect in war, because I was the mother of a Marine, but I wasn't ready for him to be lost without any explanation and that's just what happened." The last time he was seen alive was when two corpsmen took him into the triage unit in the hospital, and it was six weeks before it was discovered that he was missing.' Can you believe this? Grant said intelligence guys don't play by the rules."

Eve looked over at Shelly as she saved the information to the hard disk. "Sounds like Diamondstrike claimed at least one victim…a long time ago."

Eve's gaze returned to the road as she thought about her SAC, or VSAC, Very Special Agent in Charge, and wondered if he needed this upsetting information now or later. She decided it could wait until they spoke again. There was certainly nothing they could do for Jackson.

"James W. Jackson," Eve repeated.

Suddenly a thought jumped into her mind. *Jackson. That's the same name as the agent who started all this.*

Eve began to wonder.

*What if James Jackson was related to Jackson, the CIA puppet in Houston? No, that would be too much of a coincidence.*

Still, she thought about it until she reached the 651-mile marker, and then she changed her mind.

Maybe none of this was a coincidence at all.

Eve asked Shelly to use the modem to send Darrell McCullock an e-mail. "Tell him the info you have on Jackson's family in Atlanta, and see if we can find out if he had any relatives named Eldridge Jackson… and tell him to stay after this. It may have something to do with the fact that we can't find Agent Jackson of the CIA."

The women continued to add miles as they added thoughts, but they were unable to draw a conclusion.

Interstate 10 welcomed the souped-up Jeep as it accelerated down the highway in the early afternoon of the sunny winter day. The trees had lost their leaves, the grasses their color, and it appeared, humanity its direction.

Eve was reminded of an old saying that her father had repeated as she grew up, "All it takes for evil to triumph is for good men to do nothing."

She thought the saying was a fair summation for their current position as well as a byline to the *High Noon* day. Corruption appeared to be winning in the bureaucratic scheme of things, as it wrestled the world for control and power. While everyone slept, its companion, Evil, designed the death of the innocents.

*High Noon* was happening every day, and it was time for a showdown on this particular day. Someone had to answer for the disappearances of James W. Jackson, Eldridge Jackson, and B.W. Lane.

# CHAPTER SEVENTEEN

The *Dixie Express* touched down without event at Fairfax Airport, outside the Beltway in Arlington, Virginia.

After some minor surveillance of the grounds, checking for opponents with illegitimate orders, Grant chose a caution tactic and took a taxi to the capitol in lieu of a vehicle from the government interagency motor pool. He hadn't totally recovered from being the target of bad guys carrying government credentials, and he felt an anonymous cab ride would offer more safety.

He also had designs on taking a quick detour to buy some new pants before his meeting. In addition, there was the continuing problem of a wardrobe, however minimal, to help him get through the day, until he could get back to Houston. Since his current state of disrepair, and the loss of his bag, had been a result of the attempted kidnapping, he questioned whether the purchase of new clothes was a legitimate business expense.

He'd probably get audited by his own IRS. Another day at the office. It was like Eve had said before, "I love a nine-to-five."

Grant admitted his life was becoming complicated because of Evee J. Thursday. He was needing to think "serious," yet he found himself trying to think "calm." It had only been half a day, and he was already missing Eve's companionship, her smile, her touch. After his last update from Lasorta, he knew his final destination for the evening would be someplace other than Houston. He hoped to find her there.

The Grumman completed its taxi to the tarmac, and Grant instructed the pilots to keep a close surveillance on the plane and be prepared to leave for Houston, or wherever, on short notice. Grant calculated the fastest he could get to the FBI building was about forty-five minutes, so he would try to return by three thirty or four. He would let them know by phone so they could file the flight plan and be ready for an immediate departure when he returned. It seemed like a tough schedule, but sometimes schedules had to be.

Although it had been an impossible day up to this point, he still thought of recapturing Eve's affection by night…whatever the location. His new relationship, or friendship, or whatever it was, occupied more and more of his thoughts as he walked toward the airport building. It was an interesting focus, but he was getting used to it—two mindsets within the same time frame.

As he waited in the FBO office for the cab, he picked up the courtesy phone, dialed in his credit card and a number, and reached Eve on her cell phone. She was so glad to hear his voice and know he was safe.

Immediately, Eve warned him not to say anything that could be used by the enemy, because of the surveillance equipment located in the IC vehicle at Audie Murphy. Grant understood.

He expressed his concern for their safety and told Eve, "I'll see you tonight," before he cleared the connection.

For Eve, the comment meant one thing. Grant had been in contact with David Lasorta and knew where she would be and when. It was the answer she wanted.

Great! He was already making plans to re-traverse the country to find a place in her arms before the day was over. She wanted to experience him again, in another beautiful but unfamiliar location, to find herself in a perfect setting with a good cold-night companion, to fall into his arms and surrender to his passion, to be his "new recipe."

She smiled. Shelly looked at her and smiled too, as if she were doing some mind-reading.

"What are you smiling about?" Shelly asked.

"I was just thinking about Grant and a 'cake out in the rain.' "

"What's that about?"

"I'll tell you later, if it turns out to be true."

Eve kept smiling as they passed the 703-mile marker.

Some people don't know how far it is across Texas. Those mile markers started in El Paso.

\* \* \*

SAC Harris had more work to do before he could find time to give Eve the attention he desired. The objective for the day was to obtain support from the FBI director so he could continue his investigative quest. He had contacted the office and was cleared for an appointment immediately upon his arrival. Houston had notified the Washington office about the attempted kidnapping incident earlier in the day.

It was unusual to have the director of the FBI so available, but this was bordering on a very silent national emergency. The urgencies from his previous day's communication, together with the attempt on his life, warranted the hastily planned visit.

Unfortunately, Grant couldn't continue directly to the meeting without his necessary stop. The cab dropped him at Foley's department store on the inbound path of US Highway 66. He completed the hasty shopping trip in which he picked up three changes of clothes. First was a sports coat and slacks replacement, not at all formal, but he didn't have time for a suit alteration. His other purchases included casual clothes— denim jeans and a heavy hunting-style jacket for the colder night and the day tomorrow. He added a pair of all-purpose boots, some gloves, and a duffel bag, then changed into the new apparel.

He hurriedly visited the drugstore on the way out and bought a toothbrush and shaving supplies. As usual, his typical shopping trip was twenty-five minutes and he was out the door.

Grant pushed open the heavy mall doors and surveyed the parking lot and the cab for signs of anything unusual; then cleared himself for the ride downtown. In thirty minutes he would be in the middle of DC, and in an hour he hoped to be returning. Of course, in the interim he needed to obtain the director's approval to continue the case.

Good plan.

As he returned to the cab, Grant made mental notes regarding the facts of the disappearance and in what order he would present them. His presentation would be like a summation to the jury, and Bearing-Haas would be his corroborating witness.

Director Spires would give him the approval. Then he could bring Lane in, uncover and arrest the covert operators, and force the controlling powers to release the information they had on AIDS and the other viruses—along with the cures.

While questioning how many more diseases were hiding in the Defense vaults, he thought about a headline, "FBI Uncovers Covert World Health Organization Activities." A Headline like this would never see a newspaper; he knew that.

As the cab arrived at the Federal Building, across the street from Justice and down the street from the Capitol, Grant began to have second thoughts; he started to become nervous.

*This is a huge scheme. What if the government part of the conspiracy goes beyond the IC?* He thought. *What if it encompasses Justice and, in fact, includes the FBI?* It was frightening to admit the government was getting so expansive; it was uncontrollable within the purview of its own responsibility. *The government was simply too big.*

Some instinct, however, told him it couldn't be this bad yet. Further, he wouldn't have time to sort out contingencies regarding this idea before his meeting. That would be over the top, so Grant assured himself that it couldn't happen.

If this scenario was true, and the FBI was somehow involved, he had lost. He asked the cab driver to wait for him then entered the FBI building.

Although Grant had been at headquarters a few times, this trip was different. No socializing or hobnobbing today. Whether it was his new title or the urgent case he was pursuing, there was an entirely different feel for his purpose. Most of the time, he completed his job from a desk—from a distance, in isolation, usually only involving a few people. This case, however, involved many people, and he would have to hold the system accountable, but first he had to prove it.

As was usual in the building, he had to clear security. If he had his firearm, he would have checked it, but unfortunately his weapon had taken a side trip earlier in the day. After heading through the passageway, he moved through the outer offices and into the protected lobby.

Grant was greeted by all those who saw him and introduced to some staff he hadn't met before. Then he was escorted into the office of the Director of the FBI.

They shook hands and after the salutations, Director Spires asked the others to leave so he and Grant could have some privacy. All of

Grant's presentation planning went out the window, and the director gave him the briefing.

"Grant, the DCI called me yesterday…"

Grant remembered telling Shelly about the Director of Central Intelligence and the web of secrecy that emanated from the agency.

"…and told me we were interfering with one of their investigations," Director Spires continued. "I figured he was leading me on, so I talked to Meyers. He said you were on to something, but he wasn't sure what. Then we had the interruption… By the way, I hope his heart problem isn't very serious." Realizing Grant was unaware, he added, "The last report we got a few minutes ago said he was doing better but they were going to keep him for observation."

So it was his health, Grant thought. This was major news he wished he'd known earlier. At least Will Masters' situation was not linked to the case.

Although his thoughts were interrupted, he recovered his attention as the director continued.

"Anyway, I put out the message to hold everything until I talked to you, and this morning, things started happening. First, I heard about your episode in Texas, and right after that, the CIA director called me again. This time he requested our assistance. He did a one-eighty on us, Grant. Seemed he didn't have his information straight."

Grant listened. He knew this meant the CIA director didn't have a clue as to what his own people were doing.

Spires mentioned, as an aside, "I don't believe him on that. He said they lost an 'item,' and I think it's the same item you've been chasing since Monday. In any case, they do want our assistance in bringing him in, or so they said. I don't believe that either, and besides, it's way out of their jurisdiction…as if it matters."

Grant responded, "Sir, did they say why they wanted him?"

"He stole something years back. It had something to do with some unusual blood, biological research. Don't ask me why somebody would want it, much less why it would be important enough to kill you to get it."

Grant sorted the information in his mind as the director continued "Evidently it's a very hush-hush, top-secret matter. What I really think,

Grant, is that they have a covert operation running away from them, and they called 'no joy' and are bringing it in and you caught them where they weren't supposed to be."

Grant responded, "Did the CIA director say anything about Deborah Bearing-Haas with the World Health Organization?"

"Yes, he mentioned the name and asked whether we made contact with her. He said to let him know where she is as well."

"Has she made any contact with us, sir?"

"Not that I'm aware of..." Spires hesitated. "...I don't believe we have..."

"She was supposed to meet me here around noon."

"Well, then, come to think of it, maybe we have. There was something going on this morning in the Washington..." The chief interrupted himself, "We have our guys working on something that we received in the mail. We got a tape."

As Spires moved back toward his desk, Grant asked, "Did the CIA director say anything specific about our investigation?"

They seated themselves, and Spires responded, "Yes, they were working closely with you, and they had three teams available to 'assist' you. I hope it wasn't the bunch at the airport."

Grant responded, "Well, I think it was. I know for sure the NSA is involved, so it had to be the IC, or their hired help, who tried to kidnap me. They don't want to work with us. They want to keep us from finding the truth. This thing is very dirty. I think they're following us just because they know we can find their man and they haven't been able to."

Spires was naturally curious about the details and the way the IC was handling it. It had to be a covert operation, probably a renegade NSA unit that was now off the grid.

Grant related more of the details regarding the airport incident and the entire investigation, this being the third complete day. He stated, "Here are some facts we've uncovered. The 'item' is a guy named Benjamin Lane, who was somehow involved in a covert mission involving germ warfare. Evidently he has immunity to one of the viruses they made...most likely to kill a bunch of people in the third world. It may be the original strain of HIV or Ebola and we do know it's important enough to cover up."

With Spire's silence, he continued. "The virus was developed in the 1960s by a doctor named Gallo who worked for Defense. The military developed it as a weapon, and it should have stopped there. But World Health co-opted it for its own motives, and they want Lane back because they've used his blood for developing vaccines. At least that's what we believe, because it would have been easier to eliminate him."

The director listened attentively. "Keep going."

Grant continued. "We know the Department of Defense was involved, but how deep we don't know. Other than World Health and the NSA, we don't know which other rogue operations are in on it. In short, sir, we don't know who they are, or how far it goes."

Grant looked at his watch. It was twelve forty-five, but he was still on Central Standard, so Bearing-Haas was at least an hour-and-a-half late, Eastern Time. Again he mentioned Bearing-Haas and her desire to meet them to provide critical details regarding the scheme.

Spires interrupted. "I told you someone sent us something. Stop here, and listen to this." He pulled out his desk drawer. "We received this in the interoffice mail this morning, unmarked. I didn't know what to do with it. It may not tell us who we're chasing, but see if this fits with your scenario."

He pushed the button on a tape recorder. It was a woman's somewhat nervous voice with a message, which seemingly had been made in haste. However, the tone was very deliberate and controlled. She said, "If I don't get there, call my office and ask for Elizabeth. Somebody's after me... Strike Two went to Africa... World Health is the disease, and Lane's the cure."

"That's her, sir. That has to be Bearing-Haas. She's telling us the other strike group went to Africa."

"What does it mean?"

"Lane, the guy we're after... The covert mission went across the southern border of China. It was code-named Diamondstrike One. We think it was intended to contaminate people and start the virus, but Lane refused to fire the missile into a civilian village; he destroyed the weapon. He and a couple of others in the group were contaminated, but the virus didn't kill him. Originally we thought WHO was using his blood for research or maybe for more weapons, but now we think they were using him to create the vaccine."

"A vaccine for AIDS? Why didn't they get him and hold him?"

"No reason. He didn't know anything about it. He was injured, and while he was recuperating, they deprogrammed him with drugs and shock treatments. He thought it was amnesia, but he hasn't known anything about this since sixty-nine, or at least not until a couple of weeks ago. As soon as he had an idea of what was happening, he skipped."

"So who's Bearing-Haas?"

"She was an FBI assistant in Houston in the early seventies, here in DC after that, and then transferred to World Health. We found her while we were examining the logs on Lane's file. Her name was there, and information had been taken out of the file and the logs altered."

"So you think she's in our camp now?"

Grant responded affirmatively.

"Can Intelligence get to his family?" The director asked. "Could this end up in a hostage situation?"

The answer would depend on how far this spread and how fast, but Grant knew the FBI was in a position to move quickly.

He responded. "Sir, I'll make sure the family's safe, and I think I can get Lane in safely as well. My people have located him in East Texas."

"What do you need?"

"Sir, all I need is your go-ahead…and a call to the CIA director to tell him we will cooperate fully. If you agree to help them, maybe it'll keep the heat off me for twenty-four hours. I think that'll be enough time."

"Anything else?"

"Yes. I need to find out about Bearing-Haas. If she's with us, she may be in danger. Also, she's the one person we'll need on our side to explain this mess once we get the pieces together. Can you give me some backup with the DC office while I try to find her?"

"Anything you need, Grant."

"Also, what she said about Diamondstrike Two made reference to Africa. Can we get research to find out how many cases of AIDS and Ebola they've had in Africa and compare it to the number of cases in China? Those might be interesting statistics."

"What do you think it'll show?"

"That the disease could have spread twice as fast."

"You've got it," Spires said, and then he became more personal. "I know you've been a bright star in this organization since you became an agent, Grant. I trust you'll do what's right to uphold the image and reputation of the Bureau." He paused in closing. "I'll tell Frederick…"

Grant knew he was talking about Keith Frederick, his assistant.

"…to give your people help, research, or whatever you need. I'll bring Van Camp on board to help you with whatever you need here in Washington. I'll give her a quick heads-up…and, Grant, keep me in the mix."

"You've got it, sir."

They exchanged farewells, and Grant went to the outer office to meet with Keith Frederick.

Grant requested a stop at the FBI armory to pick up some equipment. First he needed a handgun and some ammunition. If they were going to do battle with the IC in Washington now, and in the piney woods later, he needed some weapons. Frederick requisitioned some basic items: radios, vests, a riot gun, a 39mm sniper rifle, and a small quantity of tear gas. When they were delivered, the items were placed in a black weapons case.

Grant found his personal taxi, which had been waiting in an emergency-waiting zone. As he paid the taxi and let him leave, he thought about his feelings from an hour earlier. Although no one else knew it, the cab was his primary escape vehicle to Texas if something had gone awry at his meeting with Spires. Thankfully, the winds today were blowing in a favorable direction.

SAC Lois Van Camp was an acquaintance of Grant's, even though they had never worked together on any cases. She was in her late fifties and as spry and active as anyone in the Washington Bureau. She was also three times as sharp as almost everybody else. Grant thought Washington, DC, was probably the toughest of all places to be, and Van Camp had the added pressure of having to deal with politicians.

While in the reception area waiting for Van Camp, Grant called long-distance information and obtained the number for the World

Health Organization in New York. After reaching the main switchboard, he asked to speak to Deborah Bearing-Haas.

A secretary or receptionist answered, "Ms. Bearing-Haas's office."

"This is Grant Harris, Ms. Bearing-Haas requested I ask for Elizabeth."

"One moment, please."

As Grant waited for the other party, he thought about the dangers that lay ahead. WHO was extorting assistance from the IC because of the Defense connection, and together they were in pursuit, attempting to prevent any further damage from the leak about the deadly game. *Imagine*, Grant thought, *attempting to selectively control the world's population.*

Whose choice was it to decide how many lives they would take and which ones?

Finally a voice responded, "This is Elizabeth. May I help you?"

"Grant Harris, FBI."

"Mr. Harris, Ms. Bearing-Haas left a message for you." Her message was a website, and she spelled it out, "www.who.sw/ds1/loc.shtml." "I hope that will mean something to you. She left in a big hurry yesterday evening, and we haven't heard from her today."

"Give me her cellular number, home number and address, and license plate numbers—anything I can use to trace her."

To obtain the information, Elizabeth excused herself temporarily.

As Grant continued to hold, he asked Lois Van Camp's executive assistant, Vicki, to look up the Internet address he had written down.

"Mr. Harris, I found it."

"Print me a hard copy, will you?"

Vicki hit the print key, and Grant watched as the Hewlett Packard LaserJet discharged two pages into the tray. She handed them to Grant, and he glanced quickly at both pages. The first sheet was a couple of paragraphs written in memorandum form, and the second was a crudely drawn map.

He began by reading the letter. "Mr. Harris..."

Grant hesitated. *How did she know my name? It hasn't been mentioned in any communications, and I haven't talked to anyone at World Health until now. Something's going on here*, he thought, and then returned to the letter.

*I don't know who started this program, but someone with the DSD found out there was a cure. They developed a hugely profitable black market for the sale of the HIV/AIDS antibodies from Lane. His DNA has the capability of re-creating the base components of nucleic acids that affect cell reproduction. It isn't important that you understand it, but it is important that he is located. We need him. It's time to stop this.*

Grant considered her summary. *They started a virus and spread it all over the world, and now they want to cure it. Brilliant. Selective harvesting...*

Grant had written on the subject for a college humanities class. How does a man justify premeditated murder as a worldview? What mindset is that? He couldn't allow himself to believe something like this actually could take place. Then again, there was Hitler.

But this was even more bizarre. What started out as a biological weapon had become a tool for reducing the world's population, which then morphed into an unrestrained opportunity for a bunch of government crooks to make a lot of money. Now it was a case of greed. But Grant had seen this before.

The Mena syndrome. Do something acceptable like smuggle weapons to freedom fighters, then do something unacceptable like fill up the plane with cocaine for the return flight. Government undercover operations always had more to do with business and dirty money than they ever did with politics.

He continued to read.

*The Global Programme on AIDS started in 1987 within WHO and was funded by the Rockefeller Foundation. This may be the entity that has sought to make antibodies available to certain people at very high prices while continuing to show progress in the hunt for the cure. Someone on the inside of the NSA, or higher up, found out about the black market scheme and contacted Lane.*

*I don't know who leaked it, but now they have to release the new therapies and take drastic measures to prevent a disclosure of the details.*

Knowing that desperation made for different decision-making processes and strange bedfellows, Grant wondered how to shorten his standard analytical process. Bearing-Haas sounded frantic. This thing was
going down quickly unless he could come up with a plan to stop it.

As Grant continued to hold, still waiting for Elizabeth, he studied
the hand-drawn map. It wasn't very professional looking, but some
details were there, including names and numbers.

Finally, Elizabeth returned with some—but not all—of the information he'd requested. She offered the address and telephone number of
Bearing-Haas, a phone number for her daughter in Philadelphia, and
a cellular telephone number. Her vehicle was an auto from the interagency motor pool, but Elizabeth was unable to determine the number,
style, or license number of the vehicle in use at present. She agreed to
pursue the description and follow up shortly.

Grant obtained Van Camp's cellular number from Vicki and relayed
it to Elizabeth so additional information could be forwarded.

* * *

It was approaching 1:10 Central Time and 2:10 Eastern when SAC
Van Camp returned to her office to meet Grant. After a quick update and
a look at the Internet clues, the two decided Bearing-Haas must have
traveled to the destination on the map—either that or there was something at the location she wanted them to find.

It appeared to be a remote point near a body of water called Mirror
Lake. The closest marked locations were labeled Browns Mill and a
road that turned off Highway 530. There were no compass markers, but
if the top of the map was north, the road was on the south side of the
lake. The problem was…where was Browns Mill?

Grant asked Vicki to recall the Internet site which Bearing-Haas had
provided, but the information had disappeared.

"Lois, it must have been one of those that's read once and it's gone."

"Yes, so no one else could read it. A self-monitoring program pulled it
after our hit. One of our undercover people told me it's how some foreign
agents communicate without using e-mail. Put up a webpage, and it disappears after the first hit. It's harder to track than e-mail."

Lois picked up the phone and called one of her agents. "Chris, there's a place called Browns Mill near Mirror Lake. I need to know where it is. Run a search on Virginia, Pennsylvania, New Jersey, Delaware, Maryland, and I guess New York, and get back to me as soon as you can."

Van Camp dialed another number. "Mary Anne, get me one of the Rangers ready to go with a full tank. Also, call Agents William Ranson and Carl Watts. See if they're available to join SAC Harris and me on a quick trip."

After she finished, Grant asked, "What do you think?"

"Hard to tell, Grant." She was thoughtful. "You know, I think I remember Bearing-Haas from the old days. She was some kind of a 'heavy' around here in Washington for a while, back when I was over in New York, but I do remember her name. Seem to recall she was from a rich family in the Ivy League somewhere. I remember her as one of those women who wanted to keep all her names out there, hyphens and so forth."

Within three or four minutes, the intercom announced Chris, who had more information.

"We have a Browns Mill in Virginia about eighteen miles west of DC. There's another one in Pennsylvania, about a hundred and fifty miles north of here, placing it about a hundred and twenty-five miles southwest of New York City. There's another one on the Jersey side, east of Philly about thirty miles."

Grant asked quickly, "Can you narrow the search to a Mirror Lake or a Highway 530? That's all we have."

"I'm running it now. I'll be right back."

The line went silent, and Grant smiled at Van Camp. "You have a pretty sharp group around here, don't you?"

"Damn right. Picked them and trained them myself. You must have a good group too. You started with nothing, and you've stirred up some pretty deep crap in three days."

Grant smiled. "I'm not sure we stirred it up, but we definitely got there in time to watch it hit the fan."

"In the briefing, Spires said they took a couple of shots at you this morning. You all right?"

"Yeah," Grant told her, "but I'd like to get a piece of those guys. Maybe we'll get the chance."

The intercom buzzed. It was Chris again.

"Got it. Browns Mill, New Jersey, on the west end of Mirror Lake. Take Highway 530 east out of Philly to Camden, then Mount Holly, then turn south at Browns Mill. Anything else?"

Van Camp responded, "Vicki will give you some information on Deborah Bearing-Haas and a relative. Check out the phone numbers, addresses, and maybe get the New York or Philadelphia offices to do a drive-by. Listen carefully and make sure everyone knows it. Although we want to find her very badly, we don't want an APB. We have to keep this tight, just with us, because the IC is more than likely after her as well. Get a ground force backup out of Philly ready to head over there if we need it. Thanks, Chris. Take care of it for me." She hesitated in thought for a moment. "That's all for now. If you need me, I'll be mobile."

The Washington SAC turned her attention to Grant. "Let's get some help and get over to Browns Mill for a quick look. You ready?"

Grant was ready, so Van Camp told her assistant to notify the pilots and agents to meet them at the heliport. It was time for a ride. They secured their weapons and Grant's bags from security as they headed to the heliport on the third-floor deck outside the main building.

Two Jet Ranger helicopters were on the deck, and one was being prepared for departure. Agents William Ranson and Carl Watts joined Grant and Van Camp at the heliport a few minutes later.

After Van Camp handed the pilots the map with the destination, she and Grant continued their conversation.

"Tell me more about what you have on these people so far," Van Camp said.

Grant explained, in some detail, about the Internet business Lane owned, the letter about his involvement with Defense in the sixties, and what had happened after he started to research the historical information regarding his "amnesia." He also discussed the contact with Bret, the tracing of the communications to the UN and WHO, and how Grant and his team had attempted to bluff Bearing-Haas into cooperating.

At this point, he had to admit his pursuit wasn't the main reason that Bearing-Haas was cooperating. Lane was the facilitator for someone else, someone on the inside who had exposed the origins and called attention to the game.

The pilot, Captain Lewis Toms, informed them they should arrive at Mirror Lake in less than thirty minutes, and after about half the time, he confirmed it. Grant brought Van Camp up to speed on the rest of the investigation, including the trek of Agents Delaney and Shelly to Audie Murphy Veterans Hospital.

The primary missing ingredient, as far as Grant was concerned, was what had happened to CIA Agent Eldridge Jackson. He had given the initial information, offered additional support if required, and then vanished. And still unsolved in Grant's crowded mind was how Lane had developed an immunity to a virus that had taken so long to evolve.

Since they had a few minutes before their arrival at the lake, SAC Van Camp offered the helicopter's radiophone to Grant so he could contact Shelly and Eve. He could update them on Bearing-Haas and also see whether they had any more information.

The two comrades were still on the Jeep ride and expected to be in Houston sometime after five o'clock. Although they'd be driving in rush hour traffic, at least they'd be going the preferential direction—against the traffic instead of in it.

Eve was glad to hear Grant's voice again, but after realizing the urgent circumstances behind the call, she didn't let her emotions play into the conversation. It was a noisy call anyway.

After the brief hello, she said, "I'm going to give you to Shell for an update on Jackson. Hold on."

"Hi, Mr. Harris. This is Shelly. We've been doing some inquiries and discovered there was a young marine we think was on the same mission as Lane. His name was James W. Jackson. Lane knew him by his code name, J.J. He was from Atlanta. Jackson mysteriously disappeared from the hospital at Quang Tri in nineteen sixty-nine and hasn't been heard from since. We've checked out his family back in Atlanta and found he had a younger brother named Eldridge. Eldridge Jackson. What do you think?"

"Eldridge Jackson. The CIA."

"We think so, sir."

"I'll be damned."

"What do you want us to do?"

"When you get to Houston, fax all the information you have to SAC Van Camp's office in Washington," Grant told her. "I don't know what time we'll get back there, but leave a message with Lasorta as to your plans. I'll stay in touch with you through him. We have to find Deborah Bearing-Haas. She didn't show for the meeting. We think she's in trouble."

"The same kind of trouble as Lane and Jackson?"

"Probably. Thanks, Anne. Could you put Eve on the line?"

After Eve took the phone again, Grant assured her he would call again after they finished their trip to Browns Mill.

"Keep working on that 'recipe' for me," he said.

After signing off, Grant updated Van Camp on Jackson's history. This had to be more than a sheer coincidence. If Eldridge Jackson was indeed James Jackson's brother, then here was the clue that connected the CIA's current interest to Lane's past. He had to be the one who had followed this and then blown the whistle.

As Grant's thoughts continued to develop, he shared his suppositions with Van Camp. Eldridge Jackson may have been studying the case for years. With continuous research on his brother, he must have seen Lane's questions pop up on the Vietnam newsgroup. Then Bret answered with some information; Lane responded and that brought Scorpion in. Jackson ended up with remnants of the original unit. Then, some "big ears" were monitoring them. Jackson and Lane got too close, and like Lane's letter said, "They got really pissed." Lane got hacked and vanished and Jackson went to the FBI. This appeared to summarize the latest of the facts. The end result—both Lane and Jackson had disappeared.

About the same time as Grant finished his summary, Captain Toms showed his SACs the lake that stretched before them. Grant saw the town, Browns Mill, and the main highway. The area was heavily wooded, but they saw cabin tops intermittently nestled in the trees.

Captain Toms found what he believed to be the road on the map and followed it. Suddenly he pointed to a cabin roof near an open area. The clearing apparently had been built as a helicopter-landing pad. There was a peninsula just northeast of the "X" on the map, and it matched the same locale on the lake. This was the correct location.

At Van Camp's request, Captain Toms hovered while the four agents looked at the cabin and the surrounding area. There were no signs of a vehicle, but a small stream of smoke came from the cabin's chimney. They landed.

Agents Ranson and Watts disembarked, drew their weapons, and ran toward the cottage while Grant and Lois waited for them to complete an initial search. It was a precaution to make sure they weren't targets, setting themselves up in a DSD shooting gallery.

Perhaps the end result of the original search could have been anticipated…no one was home. It was too easy. After looking through the windows and completing a perusal of the grounds, they signaled "all clear" to the SACs and knocked on the cabin door.

There was no answer, so Watts shouted, "Federal agents. Anyone here?"

He tried the door, and it was unlocked. He opened it, stood at the doorway, and assessed the room's interior.

By this time, Van Camp and Harris had joined Watts and Ranson on the cabin porch.

Van Camp detailed her case. "We have an invitation to be here, so we don't need a warrant."

It was only a two-room dwelling, with a back bedroom and bath. The kitchen, living, and dining areas were all in the main room. Although it wasn't a large place, it was roomy enough for a comfortable couch, occasional chairs, and a dining table with four chairs. There was also a desk near a window that provided a beautiful view of the lake. On the desk was a computer on which a piece of yellow notepaper was taped.

Grant spotted the note, and handling it carefully by the edges, he un-taped it from the machine. "What do we have here?"

As he read the note silently, the others continued to look around the room. They moved cautiously without touching anything, for fear of disturbing potential clues or contaminating evidence.

"Bad news," Grant said.

He read out loud, " 'We have Bearing-Haas. Stop the investigation.' That's great. Well, at least we know they don't have Lane. So they think we're just going to drop the case?"

Van Camp thought about the proposition. "Idle threat. They know we're way past that point."

As an aside to Watts she said, "Carl, take a look around the outside. See if you find any other signs that they've been here...other than the fireplace there. Also, let's make a quick sweep for bugs, see if we're under any type of surveillance." She asked Grant, "Anything else in the note?"

"Nothing." Grant judiciously handed it to her and turned his attention to the computer. "Maybe there's something in this thing. Wish I had Anne Shelly here now."

"Grant, this may be a setup—trying to make us back off, just to buy time. Or maybe Bearing-Haas is in on the cover-up with them, and they just need time to skip..."

Grant responded, "We still can't figure out who *they* are. We're going to have to get some names. If we don't have Bearing-Haas, where are we going to get them?" He kept thinking out loud. "If we get Lane, it's over. We'll have proof of the original scheme. But what about the evidence...or lack of it? It's been a long time since sixty-nine, and Haas knows what's happened since then."

Van Camp added, "And who's involved."

After a brief pause, Grant said, "If they do have her, she's in deep doo-doo."

"She chose who she wanted to sleep with. I guess she'll have to pay the price."

In a matter of a few minutes, Watts returned from his browsing about the property. He had located an empty boathouse and found the fumed smell of a freshly started diesel engine. Nothing else appeared to be out of the ordinary.

"What do we know?" Grant said. "Let's say they knew Bearing-Haas was rolling over on them, and when she came here, they followed her and grabbed her. Something isn't right with that scenario. Why was she coming here? She was supposed to be in Washington at our meeting around noon. At least that's what she proposed yesterday."

Lois joined in. "Maybe she hasn't been here, and her note was a setup to lead us off the trail. They're buying time…to destroy evidence and find Lane—probably both."

Grant sat down in one of the dining chairs and offered one to Lois. She joined him. As the two brainstormed silently and then aloud, Grant suddenly stopped.

"There's more to it than this. Haas knew someone was after her, but she wanted us to find this place for a reason, whether or not she was here. This cabin has to be a front for something. I remember Watts showed me something when we were coming in. He made a passing remark about the size of the power lines that ran across the south part of the property, about a quarter-mile or so that way." He pointed south. "Watts said he wondered why the lines seemed to lead to nowhere. Let's get Watts and Ranson and go have a look around over that way."

"What are we going to look for?" Lois asked.

"Something in the woods. If there's nothing obvious, maybe it could be something underground."

"Sure you haven't been reading too many spy novels?"

Grant laughed. "No, just the news. Remember it was the CIA that started this, and it's their cousins that are shooting at us. They live in caves and holes in the ground."

The group started a trek in the general direction of the undergrowth. At the edge of the clearing they looked for a path through the trees but couldn't find one.

Ranson said, "Wish I had a machete." He looked through the trees and turned to Van Camp. "Lois, it's going to be rough getting through here. Why don't you and Mr. Harris wait here for us and give us a chance to get in there a little ways? We'll take a quick look."

"Works for me, Bill. Go ahead."

Watts and Ranson moved a few yards through an opening in the trees then disappeared into the overgrown forest. Suddenly Ranson tripped on something. Unfortunately, there was no time to react before a canister exploded with shrapnel, as smoke densely filled the air.

The percussion of the explosion blew back through the trees to the clearing; Grant grabbed Van Camp's arm, pulling her to the ground.

"Lois, you OK?"

"For now."

Very cautiously, Grant moved into the woods. While his eyes sought focus through the heavy haze, he gasped, "You OK, Watts? Ranson?"

There was silence.

Grant heard Watts as he coughed a response, "He's down. He's got blood on him. I don't think he's breathing. We've got to get him out of here."

Grant yelled to Lois, and she started back to the chopper.

As she hurriedly retreated from of the edge of the woods, Grant moved through the smoke and was able to locate Watts and Ranson. Watts, a former football player for Ohio State, was amply capable of handling Ranson's weight, so Grant bent branches and saplings as they half-pulled, half-carried Ranson. Finally, they could see through the trees to the clearing. As they reached the open area, they saw Van Camp at the helicopter, and Captain Toms had started the engine. The co-pilot, Al Bates, had unstrapped and was quickly coming to their aid carrying the copter's first-aid case.

At first Grant thought Ranson was dead, but he put his fingers on his neck and found a pulse.

Recalling his first-aid training, he quickly ripped open Ranson's shirt to find the source of the bleeding. Most of it was coming from a laceration on the lower-right side of his abdomen. Grant saw and removed a metal fragment from the gash. "Damn, this is bad." He made a quick assessment of the additional wounds on Ranson's legs, but determined he wasn't bleeding as liberally from them.

Watts applied pressure while Bates pulled gauze and bandages from the box. Then he dressed the wound while Grant started CPR. After about three inhalations, Ranson coughed and started to breathe on his own. Grant removed his coat and placed it over Ranson's battered body.

Watts quickly bound the leg wounds as best he could while Grant jogged back to Van Camp at the chopper. She was on the radiophone.

The pilot asked, "How's the agent?"

"Bad, but he's still alive. We have to get him to a hospital real quick. He's in shock and has three bad lacerations on his stomach and legs, as well as some burns. Watts is keeping pressure on the worst cut. How far are we from a hospital?"

"I can have you in Philadelphia in about fifteen minutes."

"Let's do it."

Van Camp was still talking on the phone, giving instructions to whomever; she nodded agreement as she quickly concluded the conversation. By that time, with assistance from Bates and adrenalin, Watts had carried his fallen comrade nearer to the helipad.

After the helicopter was airborne, the tail quickly pointed skyward and the blade plain tilted toward Philly. In chopper language, this configuration means a fast trip.

Ranson groaned painfully as Watts held on to him tightly. "We'll have you at the hospital in ten minutes, Bill. Hang in there."

He nodded and made a weak request. "Tell Sara I love her."

"No, Bill, damn it. Tell her yourself. Just hang on."

Van Camp told Grant that she had ordered the ground detail to cordon off the entire property as a crime scene. Local enforcement and the Philly team were on the way. What was hidden in those woods? Someone was harboring a big, dark secret... You don't protect 'nothing' with booby traps or landmines. All of this shouldn't have come as a huge surprise, and the SACs dealt with the private frustrations of being caught off-guard.

Van Camp also started an investigation of the property ownership. If whatever information they found was legitimate, the property would probably trace back to one of the friendly taxpayer-funded agencies, WHO, or maybe the Rockefeller Foundation.

Bates radioed the hospital and was told that trauma-center personnel would be waiting on the heliport when they arrived. It wasn't more than four or five minutes before Grant could see the metropolis of Philadelphia filling up the ground space below.

Van Camp asked Watts, "Do you think that was a landmine or what?"

"No, probably a grenade of some sort with a smoke bomb attached. If it had been a Claymore, it would have blown his legs off. This wasn't as powerful, mostly shrapnel, improvised...like guerrilla forces use."

When they landed, the trauma team took over. Having Ranson in the hands of doctors relieved the pressure temporarily, which offered Grant and Van Camp an opportunity to calculate the next move.

Van Camp wanted to return to the cabin quickly in order to supervise the investigation team upon their arrival. The other Jet Ranger from Washington was already en route. She requested another field backup and bomb squad from Philadelphia, and they were en route as well. Since Mirror Lake was only thirty miles from Philly, and a hundred and thirty or so air miles from DC, they were all planning to rendezvous there within the hour. Only about half that time remained.

Both SACs followed the medical team to the emergency room and waited for about fifteen minutes until they received their first report. The trauma surgeon felt that Ranson was strong and stable. His vital signs, though very weak, had stabilized. He was receiving a blood transfusion while they prepped him for surgery. The surgeon was most concerned about the extent of the internal injuries which were causing the bleeding. The leg wounds, though requiring attention, were more superficial. Although Ranson's injuries were extremely critical, the doctor assumed an air of optimism, though not overly so.

Knowing there was nothing more they could accomplish at the hospital, and with the knowledge Ranson was receiving proper care, Van Camp and Grant decided to rejoin to the investigation.

Before returning to the hospital helipad, Van Camp called her office and arranged to notify Ranson's family of his condition and provide for their transportation to Philadelphia. Then she and Grant departed.

The fast flight back to Mirror Lake was a somber one.

Grant told Lois the "X" on the map should have been a skull and crossbones. He assessed his appearance and hers and realized they were marked with Ranson's blood.

"Grant, do you think she knew? Bearing-Haas? Do you think she knew about the trap?"

"If the DSD is in on it, there's a chance she didn't. Since she was formerly with the FBI, she couldn't have liked the idea of dealing with them…and randomly killing people. This whole thing is sick."

Van Camp looked out the window then back at Grant. "We have to find whatever is out there in the woods. Do you think the trap was a warning?"

"I don't think so, they know we're coming," Grant told her. "It was probably an alarm to hold us up and notify 'em they had intruders."

Upon return to the scene, the cabin appeared to be transforming into an FBI ant farm. The local responders were joined by between twelve and fourteen agents who were attending to various parts of the small estate.

In a short time, the bomb squad had located seven more traps. The crude devices appeared to be centering around, and actually guarding, a concrete bunker buried within the overgrown forest. The team used sonar equipment to try to estimate the size of the structure, but the captain seemed to think it would be a couple of hours before they'd be ready to look for the entry. There was a continuing fear of more explosive activity in the ground-search area, and because of the dense undergrowth, they were proceeding very cautiously.

Meanwhile, the two SACs discussed Grant's need to return to Houston. If things were firing up this fast in the Washington sector, he was fearful for his team as they closed in on Lane's suspected location at the Alabama-Coushatta Reservation.

Van Camp agreed. She would continue with her end of the investigation, and both would stay in constant contact regarding any new information on Lane, Bearing-Haas, or Jackson.

"Grant, I lost a man in ninety-one." Van Camp was distant in her comment. "I want these guys, whoever they are. I'm going to stay on 'em hard."

Solemnly, Grant responded, "I'll get 'em in Texas."

"Where's your plane?"

"Fairfax."

"I'll have my helicopter take you back there. It'll save you some time and keep you out of downtown and the traffic. I'll stay with the investigation team here for a while longer and learn what we can about the bunker."

"The chief told me to keep him in the mix," Grant said. "Do you want to fill him in, or do you want me to?"

"I'll call him after you get out of here. He'll want to know more about the explosion and the details on Ranson."

After a brief farewell, Grant boarded the chopper and returned to the rear seat. He watched the activity through the window as Captain Toms busied himself with the flight instructions. The time allowed him some solitude to collect his thoughts and review the ugly reflections that had emanated from the Mirror incident.

The close call woke him up, the second time in one day. Grant thought about how many things he took for granted. He could have been the one who had tripped that wire. He said a prayer for Ranson then meditated on how much life had happened, had been experienced, since Monday morning. *It was becoming more evident that life's more than seconds ticking off a clock,* he thought.

Using the radiophone, he called his children in Houston. He hadn't talked to them since Tuesday. Jacob was home, but Laura was staying at a girlfriend's house. He told Jacob about his pursuing a case and that he would be back in Houston by Saturday. Thinking 'dad responsibility,' he suggested taking them to a movie, or something.

Although he didn't say it in the conversation, Grant wanted to introduce his children to Eve at the first available opportunity. The kids would like her, he was sure of it; everybody did.

The call was brief, but when Grant hung up, he felt better. At least he made the contact. So much had happened in a week, and as he looked at his bloodstained shirt, he recognized the week wasn't over.

He was relieved to have the unexpected victory with the cooperation of Director Spires and the FBI staff, but the confrontation at Mirror Lake had been more than unsettling. He was becoming very burdened by thoughts regarding the dangers that were unfolding as they closed in on the DSD.

*First in McAllen, then Washington*, he thought. *Where next? The piney woods?*

Grant decided to think more positively.

*Some things do work out right. Take Eve, for example. After all that happened today, he would still see her tonight.*

It was a little past six-thirty Eastern, five-thirty Central, and he had concluded this disastrous adventure with enough time allow for his return to Texas. The meeting produced the desired results and more. Some things were now certain, including the fact that he had received his promotion genuinely.

The worst occurrence of the day was Bill Ranson's injury, and of course, Grant held a continuing concern for Bearing-Haas. He admitted she was in harm's way, but no one had put her there. By her own choice, she had provided the testimony that would be the overwhelming clarification of the facts, particularly if the letter she posted on the Web could be confirmed. Even with Bearing-Haas's corroboration, Grant accepted that there was no hard evidence except Lane's blood.

Then he considered that no one had been killed in this scheme yet, except the innocents who were dying daily from the diseases paid for by US tax dollars…and maybe J.J. Jackson. Where was the media during all this?

* * *

As dusk moved in from behind him, the lights of DC appeared a little at a time in front of him. He considered the importance of this place and time.

He remembered *The Man of La Mancha*, Lane's favorite film, and the part where Alonzo Quijana, the aging Spanish gentleman, "lay down the melancholy burden of his sanity and considered how best to survive a world where evil breeds profit and virtue none at all."

Cervantes's novel, *Don Quixote*, on which the film was based, had been written more than three centuries before, halfway around the world. Nothing had changed. Good and evil remained at battle, and Grant was on the front line. This was what he'd wanted all his life, to be where the action was and to have a chance to make a difference.

As Eve said, he needed to "stay on the edge."

Knowing the amount of traffic in the airwaves of Washington, DC would make it difficult to isolate his conversation, Grant picked up the radiophone and dialed Houston. He had a short conversation with Georgia; he told her everything was all right and asked her to keep the office together until Monday.

Georgia reported that Dr. Sanchez's office, in McAllen, had forwarded copies of Lane's blood-profile which had been duplicated from the local medical laboratory. Agent Delaney instructed they be cross-referenced to the mysterious blood supply at M. D. Anderson. There was no definitive confirmation yet, but the samples were of the same blood type.

Grant thought about how lucky he was to have a staff that was quick, finding clues where there weren't any.

He remarked to himself, "Good for Eve."

From the remainder of his conversation with Georgia, it appeared everything was holding together. The organization was trained to run in his absence, even though he never admitted it.

*Good thing*, he rationalized facetiously. *They don't need me.*

Seriously, he admitted that it could have been him in that Philadelphia operating room, instead of Ranson. If so, the organization was a team that could continue. Delegation was a good management skill because of organizational continuity, and better than this, it prevented him from having to do the jobs he didn't want to do anyway.

He reached David Lasorta.

The showdown on the Mexican border had transformed into an ambush at the lake, and the show was now destined for a finale in the pines. Lasorta had spoken with Eve. At last contact, the women had reported an ETA in Houston any time, expecting it to be a little after five thirty. She and Shelly were going to pick up some items from the FBI stockroom before departing for the Alabama-Coushatta Reservation.

Grant knew the destination, Livingston. He told Lasorta to tell Eve and Shelly to expect him to arrive between nine and nine thirty. He requested Lasorta's assistance in taking care of some other much-needed business—making sure that the Lane family was shielded from danger until this was over. Grant also asked him to contact Sherman and James, two Texas Rangers with whom he had worked previously. The three had maintained a friendship over the years, and Grant trusted them. He called them Stonewall Sherman and Jesse James.

Texas Rangers. They were dependable…and good. One time in the 1930s, there was a major riot outside a police facility in Pharr, Texas, which was only about four miles from McAllen where Grant had been. The local law enforcement officials sent for the Rangers, and one Texas Ranger showed up on the scene. The official said, "They only sent *one* Ranger?"

The Ranger replied, "They said there's only *one* riot."

The riot was dispersed by *one* Texas Ranger, and this story was given to be the truth, at least that's the way the newspaper reported it. At any rate, Grant had a respected opinion of Rangers, which was similar to the opinion Delaney and Shelly now had for SEALS—and SACs, as it appeared.

When Grant completed his business with Lasorta, they agreed to reconnect after Grant departed Fairfax. Then Grant called the FBO and spoke to his pilot, Jerry Longren. They would file the flight plan for Houston and divert while airborne.

If anyone was inspecting FAA flight plans, this should sidetrack them from the true path. The helicopter would be landing at Fairfax in about ten minutes.

*A lot of progress since Monday*, Grant thought. *Maybe those guys would just come and surrender.*

He smiled to himself and decided not to waste his time considering that possibility. With the attempted murder of federal officers on the plate, the culprits were looking at some very lengthy jail time. It was becoming evident they would rather kill people so that no one could testify to anything. Of course, Grant had another option; he could give in to their demands and quit. *Sure*, he thought. *When pigs fly.*

The Gulfstream was ready when the helicopter landed. The pilots transferred his new bag and the armory bag into the jet. Jerry Longren reported that there wasn't any unusual activity around the airport.

As they prepared for departure, Grant boarded and reclined in the high-back captain's chair. He found himself relaxing for the first time since he left Eve in the early-morning hours.

He had been shot at and practically blown up. He had been in the FBI for more than twenty years and had never been this close to death, or even anything like it.

*Twice. What a day. What a week.*

After they were airborne and at cruising altitude, Grant asked the pilots to get a weather forecast for East Texas for tonight and tomorrow. As he laid his head back and closed his eyes for a moment, all he could see was the look on Veronica Lane's face when he had met her at the Lane home.

*Let's see*, he thought. *Two days ago, and a couple of lifetimes.*

Longren reported that the forecast was clear for precipitation; the overnight temperature would be cold, in the mid-forties, and tomorrow would be sunny and cool, in the mid-fifties.

He wondered how it was for Lane at the reservation, whether he was in some wigwam or huddled around a campfire trying to stay warm. Grant had to admit that Lane had done a good job, surviving some awkward circumstances for almost thirty years and escaping an intelligence manhunt for a week. He might continue to be safe, unless the FBI screwed up and found itself as the bait; that scenario would make Lane the meal.

They were all gambling, not only with Lane but with the lives of Bearing-Haas and Jackson as well, if they had not already compromised themselves. It was an important possibility. He pressured himself to keep those things in mind. They may be leading the hounds to the fox, or in this case, the wolf.

He knew from this point on that there wouldn't be any room for error. The conclusion was coming like liquid through a funnel, and the FBI's next move had to be well considered. To Lane, every hour was becoming a lifetime. Grant knew he needed a very strategic plan—a plan for the rapid and silent rescue of Benjamin Wells Lane.

# CHAPTER EIGHTEEN

Sometime later Grant found himself in Eve's arms with a burning desire she had resurrected within him, but he pulled away when he recognized the light static of a radio—the voice of air traffic control—and realized he had dozed off.

He did not like waking up and finding that Eve wasn't there.

What a bummer.

Not only was the interruption of the dream a bummer, but also his knees and the palms of his hands were aching from his early-morning dive into the concrete. His muscles were sore from the Mirror Lake excursion and Ranson's rescue.

He looked at his watch. It was six forty-five p.m. Central time. If Eve and Shelly were on time, they should be reasonably close to their objective and his, Livingston.

Grant decided to call his female associates, but first he would chance the office. He found that Lasorta was still there. He'd stayed until after the traffic cleared before he headed for Bellaire on the west end.

Lasorta recounted the afternoon activities and reported that Shelly and Eve had been to the Houston office. They stopped first at Eve's townhouse on the way into downtown and picked up some warmer clothes. At the Bureau repository, they picked up the additional supplies which Shelly had requested. The two left a little after six o'clock, and with the turtle-paced traffic, they should be somewhere on 59 north.

Both made it a point not to discuss the specifics, or the ETA, because they were afraid of disclosing any key elements of their plan over the phone. By this time, everyone in the FBI lineup was aware not to underestimate the capabilities of the opponent.

On this call, Grant had time to give Lasorta a full account of the afternoon occurrences at Mirror Lake and the bunker. He didn't know how much information the DC office had acquired this quickly, but he suggested that Lasorta set up a communication channel through Vicki, Lois Van Camp's Assistant. This way they could coordinate the pool of information between the two offices. This would be important in the event they needed to negotiate anything regarding Bearing-Haas or Jackson. Grant also wanted to find out about Ranson's condition following surgery.

After completing the conversation with Lasorta, Grant filed the new details in the extremities of his brain; it was becoming overcrowded. He added another possibility, a fifty-fifty chance, or maybe a little higher, that Defense Intelligence, the DSD boys or their assassins, would find his trail by morning.

Grant considered it might not be such a bad thing if it happened. Without Bearing-Haas, there was no hard evidence of the crimes. In some fashion, the FBI needed to trap and implicate the renegade faction in the commission of whichever crime, be it was attempted murder, kidnapping, interfering with a federal investigation, or some other treasonous behavior.

*Maybe I should just kill them*, Grant thought, *without a reason.*

He stopped in the tracks of the thought and wouldn't allow himself to even think of singing that song. Unjustifiable murder was on their level, not his. Besides, he would be justified; he'd have a reason.

To improve his attitude, he contacted E.J. Thursday and the Cowgirl Hacker of the Texas Airways. The sound of Eve's voice was enough to make his heart skip back to yesterday, back to the thoughts that had memorized her voice, her eyes, and the taste of her lips. He wanted to talk to her passionately, but again, the timing wasn't right. He wondered if it ever would be.

Eve and Shelly were only a few miles outside of Houston, but Grant knew the distance didn't matter as far as schedule was concerned. They only had about seventy-five miles to go to reach Livingston anyway.

The plan was to rendezvous at the airport.

Eve asked, "Is it safe to be talking about this now?"

Rather than explain the emerging 'bait-and-trap' tactics that were taking shape in his mind, Grant elected to wait until they were together and discuss it privately.

"It's OK. We'll talk about it in two hours or so. Just keep moving." He continued his instruction, "Drive around and find a place to spend the night, get familiar with the town, and learn your way…and, Evee, keep an eye on your rearview mirror."

Grant told her about the near miss for all of them, as well as Ranson's injuries, which had resulted from the explosion. He explained how it made sense that Jackson might be the one who had organized the scheme, located Lane through Bret's contact on the Internet, and blew the whistle on the Federal involvement. Jackson's discovery certainly put the heat on the entire intelligence community and the World Health Organization, but he couldn't get any help until he brought in the FBI. It was unfortunate he couldn't trust the press enough to let them take the story and run with it. In any regard, it was probably the right call.

Grant asked if the jeep was being followed, but Eve said she didn't think so.

"Are you missing me yet?" Eve asked him lightly.

"Every minute, all day. How about you?"

"We've been listening to Bret's music, and I've been thinking about you."

She talked to him about the music, and the conversation was a welcome detour. The tunes were mostly light country, pop, some from the sixties, and even a song by The Seekers that had become a favorite. Right after the brief mezzanine encounter months before, she had remembered the song and bought the album. It was a stroke of luck, or maybe fate, that Bret owned the song.

"Though the carnival is over, I will love you till I die." She didn't repeat the line, but there were other romantic words that seemed to echo the feelings in her heart. Eve responded, " 'I know I'll never find another you.' "

Grant responded, "Don't start looking."

Eve also told him she had been listening to Judy Collins; a familiar name, but someone she'd never listened to before. She attempted to add some humor to the conversation, joking that the biggest problem at the outset was the time required for Shelly to learn how to work the CD player.

"Grant, I've been listening to the words, and you're in all of them."

She couldn't wait to share the special words from those songs when they were together tonight in the pines.

Grant said, "Speaking of words, Miss Thursday, what was the name you kept secret from me last night?"

"Maybe I'll tell you tomorrow."

"How about tonight?"

"Tomorrow…maybe."

The conversation concluded for the unspoiled lovers as they remained separated by portions of three states and another short existence.

After signing off, Grant reviewed his own expectations regarding a plan. He told Longren it was time to change the landing site to Livingston and also change the destination flight plan when they were about thirty minutes out, assuming the flight was being monitored. This way the plane would arrive in Livingston well before the enemy could adjust.

One favorable situation of being the only passenger on the 'company' plane was that a person could change clothes without using the private curtain. Grant did. After taking off his bloodstained clothes, he put on the new pair of casual pants and a long-sleeved denim shirt and placed the lined hunting jacket on the bench seat.

Hoping he wouldn't need the jacket to keep warm, Grant held more favored thoughts of Eve, who was becoming much more than a friend.

He thought about one of Lane's songs. "My thoughts are not a good cold-night companion, but memories hold me until I hold you again."

Lane was a pretty good songwriter for a guy who never made any money at it.

Smiling, Grant realized this would be the first time Eve would see him without a tie. It would be a growth step in their relationship, an opportunity to be together in a less-formal situation, an opportunity for her to learn the different parts of him…with the hope, of course, that she kept the same attraction.

For a moment, Grant imagined, in his next life or in the remaining part of this one, becoming a poet or a songwriter. He wanted to write things like Lane wrote, learn to express himself properly, even if the poems weren't published and the songs weren't sung. Well, perhaps the songs would be sung, but they'd be for an audience of one.

There was a part of him that, with the passion created by these few days with Eve, had revived his youth. She had taught him to let go, to think about merry-go-rounds and walks on the beach.

He recollected earlier times when things were less complicated, when he would sit quietly with his friends and listen to folk music and talk about the words. There was a place that someone referred to as 'the poet's corner.' This type of place could exist anywhere, because it is in anyone's mind.

As he held those cherished thoughts, his sight drifted toward what was left of the lavender sunset on the painted winter sky. *Soon*, he thought, *I won't have time to think 'easy.'*

Grant called Lois Van Camp's mobile phone to find out whether there was any progress on the bunker at Mirror Lake. She told him they had outlined the bunker, and it included a series of rooms and tunnels that covered an underground area of at least twenty-five thousand square feet. They were unsure whether it was built on more than one level.

The FBI staff in DC had traced ownership of the property to Defense, and it was listed as a safe haven for foreign dignitaries if there was a war or civil unrest while they were in the US. As far as anyone knew, it had never been used. She told Grant she hoped to have the original plans by the following morning.

They discussed trying to force an entry into the bunker because they had been unable to find access, but opted to wait for the plans and see if they could locate a tunnel opening somewhere on the property.

Van Camp was interrupted in the middle of the conversation. While Grant was on hold for a moment, he tried to adjust the details in his mind. *How will this end?* He wondered.

Shortly, she returned her attention to his call. To Grant's sorrow, she reported that Ranson had died of heart failure while in surgery. There was too much internal damage and bleeding. They couldn't stop it fast enough, and he had gone into cardiac arrest.

Grant sat in silence, reflecting for a moment about the man...and the day. After praying for the safety of those remaining in harm's way, he and Van Camp continued the conversation. Since there was no word on Eldridge Jackson or Deborah Bearing-Haas, the two closed the conversation with the promise to keep each other apprised of further developments.

As Grant looked out the window, the sunlight had disappeared into darkness. He sat back in his seat in sorrow. The sun had set permanently for Bill Ranson. *Some people are plusses in the world, and some are minuses*, Grant thought. *Some people give more than they take, and Bill was one of those...a plus.* He vowed to make this death worth something.

* * *

Somewhere on the world below, the Jeep had found Livingston, the airport, and the bottomless CD stash of the Blue Retriever. The music filled the vehicle and the spirits of its passengers, as Judy Collins sang of love.

Eve listened and felt the emotions as the words reflected her life. "What we know and what we leave to chance..."

Shelly watched the intermittent traffic around the small town and felt a void for the lack of someone with whom to share the experience. She felt a small ache, perhaps a particle of envy, for the serene countenance of her new friend.

"The heart will teach us what we need to learn..."

Eve was falling in love with the song and the title, "Trust Your Heart." She trusted hers.

The music continued, and so did the ride around town until the phone buzzed at 8:52 announcing that the *Dixie Express* was on a crosswind leg for a final approach to Runway 34. The Jeep made a casual turn back toward the airport. As they continued west toward the edge of town, Shelly and Eve inspected the skies for lights of the welcome night bird.

They entered the small airport and located the best place to view the approach, which was from the parking area near the main hangar and office. The airport was small and almost abandoned except for a security guard outside the FBO office. They waited and watched the lights descend from the heavens, presenting Grant at the 'piney woods' playing field in time to prepare for the big game.

This time he was awake when he embraced Eve. As he held her, she could tell it was with a different purpose—more longing than passion. She knew he was in the midst of some deep emotion but elected to wait for a discussion later. It had been a very long day.

Shelly and Eve collected his bags and barely found a place to stack them. The Renegade was a great utility vehicle, but it didn't have much storage space, particularly if someone needed to ride in the rear seat. So with some FBI ingenuity, they stacked and rearranged Grant's additional baggage all the way to the canvas top and left scarcely enough room for a very cramped Anne Shelly in the rear seat...with a large weapons bag in her lap.

Grant questioned them about the large odd-shaped contraption that crowded the floor and shotgun-side seat. Shelly reported it was a cellular uplink scanning-and-recording device, to allow them to intercept and record the intelligence guys in their communications—turnabout, of course, being fair play.

Grant was proud of his associates, the way they had brought everything into focus in his absence. He couldn't be everywhere thinking everything. Everyone needs backup, and he hoped it would be an interesting evening, debriefing, planning and...whatever else.

A quick drive took them to the Lost Pines Inn, just a short distance back on Highway 190 from the main street through Livingston. They checked into three rooms and unloaded all the peripheral equipment in Shelly's room, including the new cellular uplink device.

When Eve had an uninterrupted opportunity, she explained the passphrase she had received in order to contact Three Owls and eventually Lane.

"Endeavor to persevere." Grant recalled that the phrase was spoken by Chief Dan George in a Clint Eastwood movie. Eve continued with a question. "Do you think we can get Lane tonight?"

Grant responded, "I wish it would be that easy, but I don't think so."

Allowing a short silence, Eve reiterated the other message for Lane—the one from Bret—that related to J.J. Then Shelly showed Grant the report on James W. Jackson Jr., which she had maintained in the memory of her laptop computer.

After the rather short reunion, it was decided the sooner they made the contact with Three Owls, the better. Shelly had confirmed that a small tourist post at the Alabama-Coushatta Reservation was closed between November and February, but there was a secure entrance on the south side of 190 that the reservation residents maintained for their private use.

Agent Shelly stayed in her room to set up her new equipment. She also thought about logging on to the Internet to see if Bret had made his plans for contacting them about his Jeep.

In response to a prior discussion, Shelly established duplication of the communications link to the Washington Bureau, as had been arranged with Lasorta. This way, everyone would be on the same page with the Mirror Lake investigation and the reservation trip.

Although Shelly conveyed these activities as reasons to stay in her room, Eve knew her young friend was giving her some private time.

* * *

On the short ride, ten miles or so, east to the reservation, Eve and Grant continued to exchange reports of the day.

Grant was silent for a while then reached for her hand. "Ranson, the Washington Agent who was hurt in the explosion, died during surgery."

Eve glanced at him in silence and squeezed his hand.

"I guess there was nothing else we could have done," Grant said. "We got him to the hospital as fast as we could. His internal injuries were too severe."

"I know it hurts, Grant, to be so close to it."

"What bothers me is that it could have been you." He held her hand up to his lips and kissed it. "It was Ranson, but it could have been any of us… you, me, Shelly, Van Camp. They're taking out the good guys. It's not supposed to be that way. The good guys are supposed to win."

"We will."

Grant thought out loud, "I hope we're not jumping the shark."

They crossed two more hills and another few thousand pine trees, and Grant seemed to perk up.

"Tell me about your run-in with them at Audie Murphy," he said.

Eve was proud to recount losing the intelligence tail, with the help of the SEALs of the VA, and she explained about the exchange for Bret's Jeep.

"I think I'm going to keep it," she told him. "It's fun to drive."

"What's Bret going to say about that?"

"He said he'd come tomorrow and get it back…and he'll probably tell me to get my own."

"Did he give you any details about coming here?"

"No, we didn't have any time. He just said he'd find us."

Grant considered her response and wondered, *how much does Bret know?*

After a pause, he went on, "The director of Central Intelligence contacted Spires and said there were three teams working on the case. If he was telling the truth, which is unlikely, we've only come across two— the men in McAllen, the same ones that tailed you, and the second group in San Antonio. There are more around somewhere."

"How about the guys who shot at you at the airport?"

"Assassins. Hired help, I imagine. But I think some of these guys must be DIA or DSD, or maybe they're just driving the bus." He felt accurate in his analysis; it was a renegade group, but the IC still had contact, even if they didn't have the lead.

"Well, at least we know to expect them," Eve said.

Grant continued with a more thorough account of his near miss at the airport and also related the conversation with Lois Van Camp about the bunker's history, specifically its function as a safe house for foreign dignitaries. Additionally, it was his guess that it might be where all the research was taking place.

About five minutes later they saw a rustic sign for the reservation. They pulled up to the entry gate, and there was a young Native American man waiting in a small shack next to it. Grant showed his credentials and told him he was supposed to obtain some information from Three Owls.

When the guard hesitated, Grant said, "Endeavor to persevere."

After a short conversation on the telephone, the young man asked Grant, "Can you ride a horse?"

Grant quickly answered, "Yes."

The young man asked them to wait for a few minutes. Three Owls was expecting them and would come to meet them shortly.

Grant backed the Jeep out of the gate and into a small parking area. Since the night was becoming colder, he left the Jeep running.

As they waited, he had a chance to take in the beauty of his companion. She had changed from her early-morning proper dress into a perfectly fitted pair of jeans with a white turtleneck sweater and a leather jacket. Her dark hair was fluffed up around the collar and outlined her perfect face. She looked prettier than a New York model.

A definite ten.

"You're beautiful tonight." Grant hesitated and questioned how the statement sounded. "Actually, you're beautiful all the time, but tonight I'm telling you."

"Why?"

He didn't answer.

"Why tonight?"

He responded carefully. "Because I got shot at, and because Bill Ranson is dead, and because I don't express feelings like this, and because it's true…you're beautiful."

Eve received the compliment in silence and smiled at him through the tenderness of her penetrating eyes. She didn't offer an immediate verbal response. She merely devoured him with her gaze, and the silence seemed like torture to Grant, who realized he was falling in love.

In time, Eve broke the silence. "Know what I think? I think you've been hunting Lane for four days…and finding yourself."

Grant leaned toward her and said, "Kiss me, Evee Thursday, or release me from your spell."

She selected the first option, and the temperature of the night increased by a few degrees.

All too soon, Three Owls appeared at the gate. He was riding a horse and leading two.

Grant thought, *I didn't know he meant now.* He asked Eve, "Do you know how to ride?"

Eve smiled and couldn't pass up the opportunity to ask, "Why? Do you like bowlegged women?"

Grant laughed. "You know what I mean."

Eve's eyes glistened as she laughed at him. "Just kidding…and the answer is yes, if the horse likes me. They say it's like riding a bike, right? You never forget."

They got out of the Jeep and introduced themselves to Three Owls. He was about the same age and height as Grant and wearing jeans and a wool-lined buckskin jacket. He had on a black cowboy hat with a feathered band, and his look matched his name. He appeared to be a chief or an elder; in any regard, he exuded a commanding presence.

They mounted the horses.

Three Owls said, "Wolf is up there." He made a head gesture into the forest of darkness to the north. "You may not be prepared to ride tonight, but we're not going far. I just need to show you the direction you'll go in the morning…to meet Wolf."

They crossed over the main highway and headed for a trail that led off the road where the highway crossed a bridge over a small river. Grant made a mental note of the bridge and the trail as they descended a slope; the horses plodded carefully near the riverbank.

As Three Owls led them, with the help of his floodlight, he occasionally questioned how they were doing. Actually Eve and Grant were having a good time on the adventure. Although the temperature was dropping, the wind was calm, and both were somewhat prepared for the cold.

They continued up the river for about ten minutes—Grant guessed it to be about a half-mile—until the river made a junction with a stream flowing in from the west. Three Owls crossed the very shallow rocky creek, and they followed. He dismounted, and Grant did as well, but Three Owls told Eve to stay on her horse.

"Wait here. We'll just be a minute."

They walked about ten paces farther up an embankment, and Three Owls pointed a floodlight back deeper through the trees. "You'll continue up this trail until you come to a small meadow. This creek will meet you as you enter it. There's a big oak tree about fifty yards farther across a field, at the creek's edge. Wolf will meet you there, at the oak tree."

Grant studied the trail. There was a fallen tree on the left and two boulders near the base. He knew he could find it in the morning.

"Thanks. I have it."

They passed back down the incline and remounted the horses. Grant timed the return trip, and they were back at the Jeep in less than fifteen minutes.

After they dismounted, Grant asked Three Owls, "Do you know anything about this?" Three Owls answered the question with a quiet stare, so Grant finished with, "What time is Wolf expecting me?"

"He didn't say—only that he would be waiting at the tree after the sun finds the meadow. I'll bring your horse here in the morning if that's what you want."

"That would be nice of you, Three Owls."

"I would go with you, but Wolf said you should come alone."

Grant anticipated this response because Lane didn't trust many people. "I expected that," he said.

Three Owls continued, "He doesn't tell me much."

Grant responded, "He doesn't tell anybody much. Thanks for your help. I'll see you in the morning."

Three Owls handed Grant a piece of folded notepaper. "He said to make sure you read this."

Grant took it and tried to read it, but the night was too dark and the light too dim. He folded it carefully and tucked it into his shirt pocket. With final thanks, he and Eve climbed into the Jeep and reined its nose back to Livingston.

Eve said, "Are you going to read the note?"

Grant shifted gears and replied, "I think it can wait a few minutes until we get back to the motel. It may be something I need to think about and I'd rather spend a little more quiet time with you before I put any more info in my overcrowded brain." With Eve's silence, he continued, "If it was something critical, Three Owls would have said so."

In the darkness of the night and the tranquility of the moment, Eve turned on the CD and punched up number seven on the auxiliary button.

"I heard this, and I thought about you."

As "Trust Your Heart" began to play and the words painted the emotions in her heart, the tranquility on Eve's face appeared to become a permanent expression.

"We have dreams… We hold them to the light like diamonds…to light the dark nights of our journey…and shine beyond the days when we have won."

Eve spoke to him in a still voice as the music played. "This is our song, Grant, and tomorrow will be one of those days, *"after our dark night's journey, and a day that we have won.'"*

The song continued, "The heart can see beyond our prayers… beyond our fondest schemes, and tell us…which are made for fools… and which are wise men's dreams… Trust your heart."

Looking at his new love, Grant asked, "Fools' or wise men's dreams?"

Eve smiled as she watched him drive on. Then she responded, "I don't know, but I guess we'll find out."

As the Jeep traveled back toward Livingston, the emotions of their night ride and reunion didn't rescue them from the facts. Grant thought about being back in Houston, and he was looking forward to the opportunity to be with Eve under less tense circumstances. However, as they arrived back at the motel, his thoughts collided head-on with the realities. He was in Livingston, Texas, and the game was still on.

When they pulled into the parking lot, Grant hesitantly released Eve's hand, and the two headed to Agent Shelly's room at the inn. She had finished the adjustments on her high-tech communications setup, and they sat down as she explained the theories of intercepting a signal, whether it was wave, analog, or digital.

Grant appreciated the education. However, most of the information was more technical and involved than he had the capacity to deal with. He wanted to look at the note in his pocket, and at the same time, his thoughts kept presenting a tormenting conflict.

The mental struggle centered between getting Lane out of harm's way…and admitting truthfully…it wasn't going to happen. With Ranson's death came an admission—ensuring Lane's safety may be impossible.

*Even if we stop the activities of DSD, the intelligence community, and WHO—right now, in a Livingston, Texas, showdown—what are Lane's chances?* Grant thought. *What's the bottom line? Does it ever stop for him, for any of us? Does the world still lose?*

Amidst Shelly's tutoring and his wandering thoughts, Grant stopped. He knew he wasn't giving his agent the proper attention and didn't want to appear discourteous. He studied his watch; it was just after ten p.m. He excused himself to make a call to locate Rangers Sherman and James. As he departed to his room, Grant told them he would return after he made the call.

In his absence, Shelly and Eve continued to discuss the use of the equipment.

Grant sat on the bed in his room and called David Lasorta at home. Lasorta told him he had contacted Sherman. The Rangers were coming from Huntsville and should be in Livingston by eleven or so. Lasorta had given the Rangers an update, and they were glad have a chance to work with Grant and the FBI again. Sherman would give Grant a call at the room when they arrived.

As Grant listened to Lasorta, he reached into his pocket and retrieved Lane's note, which Three Owls had delivered. When he unfolded the paper, he pondered the significance. This was the first time over the past four days that he'd had any type of direct contact with the subject of his pursuit.

As he started to read the note, he said, "Hold on a minute, David. Let me read this."

The note was printed with a very legible hand.

> *Agent Harris, they're already here, so expect them. There are more threats, beyond those you know about. If I'm getting out of here, I may need a new identity. Stay on the trail Three Owls showed you. There will be danger everywhere else, and wear the magic jacket of Mambrino. —Lane.*

Grant read the note to Lasorta.

"That's curious," David said. "I wonder what other threats would cause him to need a new identity."

"Maybe the antibodies in his blood have a higher value to somebody else. What do you think?"

"The black market's a bottomless pit." Lasorta kept his analysis alive. "Is it really possible? Our government has a cure for something, and they won't let the public use it?"

"Oh, it's being used…only selectively." Grant responded. "Bearing-Haas all but convicted the entire DSD with that webpage. That's the problem. The cure is being sold for such a high price, it's making somebody a hell of a lot of money."

"Or maybe the drug companies don't want a cure," Lasorta said. "There's a lot of money in the illness."

Grant quietly responded, "What do you call a conspiracy theory after you find out that its true?"

After a short silence, he cut the conversation short and closed by telling Lasorta he'd call later, sometime within the hour. During that time, Lasorta would assign four field agents for backup in Livingston in the morning. He also would coordinate with the Department of Public Safety so they could supply backup troopers if the Texas Rangers or FBI needed them. He would also need to bring the local police 'up to speed' on the situation.

* * *

The pace of the past week, the incidents at McAllen airport and Mirror Lake, and lack of sleep were catching up with Grant. He wondered whether he could seize a nap before he was needed with either his presence or his plan. The latter hadn't yet presented itself, but Miss Peacock was in the parlor with a rope. He hoped she didn't have a wrench as well.

Grant sighed, lay down on the bed, closed his eyes, and began to wonder how Lane could die. He wondered how Veronica Lane would feel if she knew what he was doing now…planning her husband's death.

Maybe she knew more than she had told Grant. Lane had been contacting her. Wade knew the worldwide Web pretty well. Rob knew more than he said. Bret was involved, and so was Jackson.

*The magic jacket of Mambrino.*

He was glad he had a bulletproof vest in the armory bag. He and Lane were thinking the same thing again. Grant thought about *The Man of La Mancha,* and the magic helmet of Mambrino, which, when worn by a knight of true courage, rendered him invincible.

As Grant drifted off to some location between planning and dreaming, he eventually was roused by a light knock at the door. He sat up and rubbed his eyes. It was almost ten thirty. He had dozed for about ten minutes. It felt good. He opened the door.

It was Eve in the gorgeous sweater with perfect hair, like a diamond setting sustaining a perfect face. She was alone.

He welcomed her inside and pulled her into his arms.

"Long day," was all he could say as she locked in his embrace.

"I know," she responded, delicately pulling back from him. "Shelly wants us to go down the road so she can call us on the phone and record us with the dish."

Eve looked into his eyes and inched her hand up over his shoulder and behind his neck. She pulled herself to him, her lips gently covering his. It wasn't a long kiss, but it was very deliberate, and it had a voice— a voice that said, "Soon this will be over." Eventually the importance of their relationship would extend beyond the competition, which was: the disappearance of Lone Wolf Lane.

# CHAPTER NINETEEN

Grant picked up his coat and joined Eve as she collected her jacket from Shelly's room. As they prepared to leave and become stand-in doubles for their intelligence adversaries, Shelly mentioned something about hunger pangs and a greasy burger.

Everyone needed to eat, but eating appeared more important to computer people. Grant noticed she had managed to locate and consume at least three Cokes during the short stay at the Lost Pines, but nonetheless Eve had agreed to find a suitable amount of grease while she and Grant were driving around for the recording test.

On this drive with Eve, there was a difficulty with words. An uncomfortable silence prevailed as she respected his space…and it allowed him time to deal with the passions of the day.

Grant didn't know whether to tell her about Lane's warning to wear the bulletproof vest; he didn't want her to worry unnecessarily.

Eve, however, had a gift of understanding, and whether it was a premonition or confident intuition, she knew something was overcoming him. She sensed he was preoccupied, but she couldn't pinpoint the reason.

Traveling to the East Coast and back, maintaining a high level of consciousness, trying to sort out the specifics of the case, being shot at and almost blown up by operatives of the 'third kind', losing an agent… Monday morning until Thursday night; a difficult course…at impossible speed.

Grant felt like Maverick in *Top Gun*—"Mach two with his hair on fire"—as he tried to conceive a plan for Lane's rescue.

*Where is Jackson?* He wondered. *And does the DSD or DIA really have Bearing-Haas?*

Then, in the middle of his unspoken thoughts, was E. Justine Thursday. He reached for her hand and told her about Lane's note. "The bad guys are already here, and Lane thinks he has more enemies than those the FBI has already identified." He recounted Lane's note that he might need a new identity. Then he became very solemn. "When Ranson was on the floor of the Ranger on the way to the hospital, he told Carl Watts, 'Tell Sara I love her.' I thought Sara was his wife."

Eve listened in silence.

"Later, in the elevator, Carl was being really quiet, and I asked him about Sara. I said, 'He asked you to tell his wife…' and he interrupted me. 'Oh, his wife knows he loves her, Grant,' he said. 'Sara's his little girl.' Then he broke down. Have you ever seen a big man, about the size of a mountain, cry? Something happened to me, Eve. We're FBI. We're tough. We don't have any emotion. But Carl did."

Eve squeezed his hand. "It's OK, Grant. We all have feelings; it's too bad we don't show them very often."

"This has been the longest day of my life. I'm feeling like a jigsaw puzzle. Now I need to get myself together."

"I'll help."

Eve's mobile phone buzzed.

It was an excited Anne Shelly, who exclaimed, "It works!"

"How do you know?" Eve responded. "We haven't used the phone yet."

"I intercepted some other calls and recorded them. I think one of them is the intelligence guys. You and Grant need to come back and hear this."

Grant had driven only a few blocks from the inn, so the drive back was slightly more than instantaneous. After a quick evaluation of the tape, he was glad they had the equipment and someone who could use it.

The enemy, most probably one of the DSD operatives who had been tailing them, was talking about stations for 'recovery red.' Grant knew about 'red.' He had seen it all over Ranson earlier in the day.

"Sorry bastards," he said. "I know what the red's for."

The message explained that Panther would be on 190, and Cubs 1, 2, and 3 would be at positions two-Alpha-six, four-Alpha-six, and one-Delta-three. These sectors were evidently outlined by maps in their possession.

Grant thought aloud as he listened to the tape again. "I'd kill for one of those maps. Off 190? Well, sounds like the location puts them close to where we're going to be. How are these guys getting their information?" He asked Shelly, "Can we get a directional fix on them?"

"Not exactly, with this equipment, but when they're actually talking, I can tell you where the strongest signal is at one end. I guess it'll point us in their direction, pretty close. We just won't know how far."

Grant considered this for a minute. "OK. Keep listening for now, and see if they say anything else. We'll work on getting a fix on them in the morning when everybody gets here. At least we know the Panther will be on 190. We have to catch them in the act of interfering with a federal investigation, and we need some proof." He turned to Eve. "Do we need to get a court order to use a cellular phone or shortwave recording?"

"No, because we're not doing anything illegal by listening to the radio. If we hear it, we hear it."

Shelly said, "You know, maybe I should turn this off, because if they have a scanner around here, they can find us and jam us. Then we won't be able to get anything."

"Good idea," Grant told her. "I didn't know they could do that."

Grant was increasingly more comfortable with his team as the game continued to play out. With Shelly's explanation, he knew she was wise to wait and not lose the opportunity of locating the enemy at first light. At least the FBI would have a better chance than if they alerted the IC now and ended up losing a stealthy advantage the next day.

Grant prepared to excuse himself in order to call the motel office and check on the rooms for Stonewall and Jesse, but he stopped for moment as other plans appeared in the offing.

Eve mentioned leaving to get some carryout food, but Grant objected. He was nervous and said so.

"Eve, I don't want you out there with these jerks with guns and explosives all over the place. I'll go get something in a few minutes."

"I'll go with her," Shelly suggested. "I need a break, anyway. My stomach thinks my throat's been cut. Bret hasn't returned my e-mail, and I'm nervous sitting here."

Eve turned to Grant. "Well, Chief? It can't be that bad."

He maintained a stiff composure while silently considering a response.

"We'll go right up the street to the drive-in and get some burgers and shakes or something. OK?"

Shelly joined the conversation, "It's OK, Mr. Harris. I'll take my weapon. Ask Eve. She'll tell you it's a big one."

He smiled as he surrendered to their request. "Please, Anne. Call me Grant. We've got history now." As they exited, he added, "Watch for a tail."

As they departed, Grant returned to his room and arranged with the motel office for another room at about eleven or after. It was no problem; they had plenty of vacancies on Thursdays.

Then he called Lasorta. The two needed to discuss how to arrange an "accident" for Lane, or how to lose him after they found him. One thing was for certain—things were going to happen fast. Since the FBI wouldn't be able to eliminate the threat of the entire intelligence community, they needed to set everything in motion, with some understandable specifics, before the adversaries could regroup. There was no guarantee that the enemy wasn't continuing with other forces and plans.

They needed a medical examiner or doctor to confirm Lane's death, and some rapid transportation. The FBI helicopter was bringing the backup agents and also would handle recovery. Lasorta verified all the final arrangements and confirmed that he would be on the chopper in the morning with whatever identity he could gather in the interim. Then they would have to 'wing' the final plans after calculating how and when the IC was going to move in.

The issue—which Grant continued to remind himself —was that Lane must have his own plan or why would he be forcing all of this to play out in the woods?

Lane's plan, however, was just that…Lane's plan, and since they didn't know what it was, he and Lasorta continued their preparations. The chopper would carry four additional FBI agents and a medic, as well as the pilots and Lasorta.

For preliminary planning purposes, they concluded two additional agents would be stationed east of the reservation turnoff on 190, but close enough for a hurried backup for Grant. Of the two remaining, one would be at the Lost Pines Inn with Shelly, and the other would be on 190, west of the location. The DPS Troopers would be standing by on east and west 190 and would set up roadblocks if required.

The Rangers would take on the Panther and capture him—that is, if Shelly could find him. The best opportunity for this outcome would be to locate him from the first directional signal and move in quickly. This strategy would allow the Rangers to make the arrests and keep the case in the state's jurisdiction at the outset.

A state lead in this operation would keep the Feds away from the Feds, so to speak. Prosecution in Texas might mean the witnesses would maintain better health and a longer life span while awaiting trial. Given the history associated with witnesses against 'the company,' it seemed like a good plan.

Grant's mind continued to project outcomes at redline 103—meaning, he was doing some very fast thinking. *More of the puzzle,* Grant thought. *If this...then what...outcome? Pluses and minuses of each alternative. What if...? Then the other. Alternative...backup plan. Wrench in the machine...solution, alternative...backup plan. Diversion...yes. Every covert action needs surprise...and surprise starts with diverting attention away from the main subject.*

The FBI would ask the local police to set up a roadblock in the early morning, somewhere out of the way, say on 59 north and south. The IC would see it and maybe talk to each other. This might cause them to break silence, and Shelly could get a directional fix for the Panther. This would be another piece of the puzzle the Rangers could handle.

Grant wondered about Lane's plan and whether he had a weapon.

* * *

If Wednesday's name was *Fire in the Sky,* what was the name of today, Thursday?

For Eve it had been *High Noon,* much more poetic than 'High Midnight,' which it was soon becoming, but when Grant's thoughts skirted the subject and returned to Eve, the only thing he could think of was his brush with death—not the name of it. The day's reality made all the details much more vivid and important. Fear could make you see more clearly, and the day had conferred this opportunity—it was almost crystal clear.

He forced himself to remember the sand in Lane's hourglass had to be draining low.

*God, how I wish this was over*, he thought.

Grant was exhausted, and it was evident there wouldn't be much time for sleep. Morning was already on the way somewhere on the planet, and it was almost eleven in Livingston, Texas.

Quickly, Eve and Anne returned with Chinese take-out from a local 'squat-and-gobble'--what fast food places are called in Lubbock, Texas, or so said Shelly. As it turned out, Eve had talked her into eating something a little healthier than grease—which was OK, as long as she didn't have to give up the Coke.

They opened the bags and placed the containers of Chinese food on the coffee table, and then positioned themselves on the floor. When Grant asked for a fork, Eve gave him a pair of chopsticks. After much chiding about the need to diversify, the women persuaded Grant to eat with the tools they had provided. As the old saying goes, "When in Livingston, do as the Chinese do."

Whether it was unintended or contrived, Grant continued to bungle the enterprise, which resulted in Eve feeding him bites with her chopsticks. Maybe it had to do with putting the pieces back together, but it was another romantic encounter and neither seemed to mind.

They joked about the dinner and were able to laugh, which relieved some of the pressure of the day. Grant liked the attention. The last four days had been a continuing burden, but as he looked at his new love he gave thought to something he wanted to write—about "discovering Eve Delaney," a book…or a poem. He already had started the research.

The Rangers showed up a little after eleven o'clock and checked into their room. Then all the parties met in Grant's room for a strategy discussion.

It was evident that the most important part of the day would be Grant's getting Lane safely in. Of similar importance, however, would be locating the Panther so that Shelly could tape a transmission; this would nail the culprits on an obstruction charge or more and provide some undeniable proof. The primary danger lay with Cubs, 1, 2, and 3...and their locations. If Grant and Lane were lucky, the guys could be isolated and captured. Hopefully, there would be enough evidence to cause one of them to 'roll over' on the rest of his comrades. That was the best case scenario.

In relating the locations of the FBI and DPS backups—east and west of the location on 190—Grant drew a map. Eve would be waiting at the reservation entrance with the Jeep. Shelly and a backup would be at the motel. After a few minutes' delay, Sherman and James would follow Grant and Eve and hang around the edge of town until Shelly got a directional fix from a Panther communication. The assumption was that Panther would be somewhere on 190, but they would stand alert for alternatives. Under any circumstance, they would continue after Panther.

Grant didn't say it, but he knew someone would say something, and out of the mouths of babes, Shelly did.

"Chief Harris, it's just going to be you and Lane up there, alone... with three of them."

Having already considered this, Grant didn't want to consider it anymore. He tried to pass over her remark gracefully.

"Anne, I don't think they are all going to be in the same place. Remember, they were talking about sectors, and the numbers had some distance between them. They don't know exactly where we're going to be. It's a forest up there. If I'm right, you'll get something recorded quickly, and you can send us some backup. Besides, Lane must have a plan of his own."

The explanation seemed to be what Agent Shelly needed to hear. *It's all up to me*, she thought.

Considering the importance of her computer skills and the complexities of the case, in many ways, this had been the truth all along.

Since they were dealing with the IC, they covered the need to change channel frequencies often, getting additional backup, using code names and the like, and what would happen after backup arrived...until it was becoming fuzzy as far as Grant was concerned.

Everyone was wound up like tight springs, but Grant needed to get a few hours' sleep, so he suggested his associates retire to another room if they needed to continue planning. He knew his part, what he had to do. He was in a struggle with time—to save Lane and finalize his own search for the truth.

The US government had a hand in developing some kind of disease that killed millions of people. No one blew the whistle, not a soul… unless, maybe they did and ended up like J.J. Now the information would vanish, and life would go on; theories regarding the origin of AIDS, or other viruses, would disappear with the passing of time.

Grant's team had an obligation to try to save some people, the ones who had stood up to the government and said, "This isn't right." Someone on the inside had to stand with them.

*Whether you live a good life or a bad one, each person must consider that there is a judgment day*, Grant thought. *Where you go after that is how you lived before you got there.* Ranson made the trip and made it well. Additionally, Grant knew one thing for sure—no one could un-ring the bell.

Grant had thought about it long enough. In summary, it seemed simple, and he didn't want to think it to death.

The others retired to the Rangers' room, except Eve, who delayed to say goodnight. Grant was still in deep thought, and Eve was silent for a moment until she felt he wanted her to say something.

She looked deeply into his eyes and complied. "Are your thoughts unkind?"

Grant smiled. "Yes, I guess they are. I was trying to get a picture in my mind, and I can't."

"What does it look like? The picture…"

"Confusing. It may be like you said. I've been looking for him… and finding me."

Eve nodded. "What did you find?"

"Different things matter to different people, but everything is important to somebody." Grant admitted this understanding from trying to understand Lane. "I didn't tell you, Eve, but Wade told me Lane really did have a dog named E-99, that shook his head 'yes' and 'no.' From reading the screenplay, I didn't know it was real. I thought Lane made this stuff up, but most of his fiction…was real."

Eve smiled while accepting the explanation.

He continued, "So when Lane said, 'You don't lose if you never quit,' I know he believed that too."

Eve reassured him, "You figured this all the way through, didn't you?"

"It's different," Grant said. "It's like I'm paying attention to *every* thing, *every* clue, *every* emotion I have…and it's complicated, but I think I'm seeing it."

"What are you going to do?"

"All I can do. Play it out." He ran his fingers through her hair. "You ever play chess?"

Eve nodded.

"One time I played with a chess master, a guy who lived across the street from me. It was fun. He won the first game in about five minutes." Grant hesitated, remembering, then spoke a bit more seriously. "Then we played again, and I played him to a draw."

Eve smiled and touched his hand. "How did you do it?"

"I knew he had me if I let him play his game, so I went at him where he didn't expect it and kept taking his men out. I just stayed after him… and ran right over him. The game was simpler for me when I got rid of a lot of his players and interrupted his plan. I think Lane must be thinking the same thing, or he wouldn't have set this up this way, with his being so isolated. But I won't know until I get in there. I hope we can dodge those Cubs until we get some help."

He stopped talking for a minute and embraced her. Then he rubbed her shoulders.

"I'm glad you've been here on this one, Eve. Since you showed up, my life sure seems to have taken on some interesting changes. At least my attitude has."

Eve kissed him tenderly. Then she drew away, looked into his eyes, held his face in her hands, memorized his expression, and matched it with the picture in her mind—a picture she wanted to keep forever.

From some distant mood, Grant voiced his thoughts. "What if I walk out there and take it like Ranson did? I mean…I can, and I will, if that's what's meant to be, but who's going to tell my kids I love them?"

"You tell them."

"I do, but who's going to tell them if something happens to me?"

Eve held him closely, then pulled away and looked in his eyes. "I'll tell them."

They held each other for another few sighs, and after a final kiss, Eve returned to her room.

Grant lay down on the bed, scrutinized the pattern of ceiling shadows created by the lamp, and reassembled the shadows of his fading day. He selected the parts he wanted to treasure, the elements that would become an integral part of his life, from this experience on—that is, if he still had a life from this experience on.

As he dozed off, his dreams centered on Eve, and although he didn't realize how long he had slept, a light knocking on the motel room door awakened him.

He saw his dream awaken to reality as Eve rejoined him.

"I don't want to be alone," she said.

Without speaking, he gathered her in his arms and embraced her, this time with unrestrained passion. He had been holding back a flood of emotion and for too long.

Their bodies met, and this time his caress had its own language. Eve returned his embrace with equal desire. She kissed him with an untamed rage as she guided his hands longingly over her body.

Holding her head in his hands, Grant kissed her face and neck, then moved back to her eyes and lips. As his hands moved about, familiarizing himself with her body, a passing thought brushed through his mind.

*Is this right?* He knew it was. *Love's not wrong—untimely maybe and improper sometimes, but not wrong.*

Loving *Evangeline Thursday* was not wrong.

This time he realized his desire as she unbuttoned his shirt. He felt her hands. He caressed her. They touched and explored…

Their bodies molded, and he thought, *our hearts are only inches apart.* In the undisturbed interval, they were as joined in their eyes and minds as in their bodies, and from that moment Grant felt complete.

He knew what he wanted. He wanted this to be more than a page, a chapter, or even a book. His relationship with Eve had to be everything, the whole library. He wanted the two of them to be as one.

As the minutes passed, their desires were temporarily satisfied, yet the affection continued. This time as Eve lay gracefully in his arms, her eyes looked at him differently—through a lens of love.

She smiled at him and recited softly, " 'We die... rich with lovers and tribes, tastes we have swallowed, bodies we have entered and swum up like rivers.' " She kissed him again and smiled beautifully. " 'The heart is an organ of fire.'"

Drowning in her eyes, Grant said, "Beautiful. Did you write it?"

She ran her fingers through his hair and looked at him longingly. "I wish...but no. They were Katharine's words in *The English Patient*." She held the thought as if she were watching the movie in her mind. "It was romantic. A second chance to love."

Grant proposed, "I love you. I don't ever want to be away from you."

Eve kissed him again. "OK with me."

They laughed, and he embraced her as his fingers moved gently through her hair, then on to a refined exploration of her beautiful body.

She became more serious. "You know me. Life is passion...and I don't want it to change. The world must be cold and lonely for people who don't allow themselves to let go and feel life, like we're doing right now. We didn't pick this place...or this time." She hesitated, sighed, and then continued, "Maybe, because I loved you, tonight picked us."

While drawing a small invisible heart on his chest with her finger, she continued, "I'm not being unrealistic. I know there'll be sunshine, and rain, but we can handle it. I just want to be with you for both of those and never ever give it up."

She looked deeply into his eyes to make sure she had his complete attention.

"I want all of you, Grant Harris." Eve framed those emotional words where they seemed to paint a picture that would last forever. As he gazed affectionately into her captivating eyes, Grant owned peace and a serenity he had always wished for. He had recovered "the recipe."

The late-night conversation never found a conclusion as the lovers drifted off to sleep in each other's arms, completing the day with elements of love—and within sight of the secrets that guarded the disappearance of Benjamin Wells Lane.

# CHAPTER TWENTY

Morning found them all too early as Grant awakened to the sound of shuffling feet in the parking lot of the Lost Pines Inn. He realized Eve had left his room at some point, but the night had been so short that he had slept soundly through her departure.

He heard the whisper of voices and a car door open and close. He raised himself up and looked at his watch. It was four fifty a.m.

Looking out the window and through the morning darkness, he saw the Rangers readying their Ram for the day's activity. Sherman was on the radio. Grant supposed he was talking to the local police about timing the diversion.

Grant showered and dressed quickly. As he prepared to go outside, Evangeline Justine Friday knocked on the door. She smiled and presented him with a cup of hot coffee. She seemed very professional and much more serious than usual in the forty-degree chill of the early-morning air, but she was dressed in another turtleneck sweater and the leather jacket that outlined the same perfect face.

"Hi," she said. "Everybody's here."

"When did you leave?"

"This morning, before anyone was up. I wanted to avoid the rumor mill."

Grant placed the coffee cup on the table and pushed the door closed, and again he held Eve in his arms. After the brief but seductive embrace, he cradled her face in his hands and kissed her gently.

"Marry me," he said.

Eve looked devotedly into his eyes and hesitated before she replied very seriously, "I did."

As his heart felt the impact of her statement, Grant smiled, held her closely, and kissed her again.

She held his hand as they went outside into the parking lot.

The senior FBI Agents, Brenda Hazling and Barry Davis, were already discussing the arrangements for backup. To Grant, the situation felt right. Even if this was going to be the last day for somebody, all the best people were there. Although he didn't know how it would end, it felt good.

Eve assisted with a morning Coke fix for Shelly, who had activated the interceptor dish. At last report, she was staying on without jamming interference.

About the time Grant finished talking to Hazling, Shelly came out of her room with an e-mail update regarding Mirror Lake. The bunker had blown up. The investigation team felt the ground shake like an 8.0 earthquake, and there was a significant escape of emissions and fumes within the forest. The thickness of the concrete structure contained the blast, but there were numerous cave-ins and large amounts of the smoke that escaped through the rubble.

Even with proper hazmat gear, it was too early for the bomb squad to determine much, and the unit reported only sketchy details from the original search. It was too soon to consider forensics because of the amount of debris that filled the cavern. There was no word from Bearing-Haas, but the worst news was that they had recovered one body from the rubble.

Grant shook his head. "So much for proof."

"What's that?" Davis asked.

Grant appeared dejected. "The bunker. My guess is that it was the lab. Now it's gone, and probably Bearing-Haas with it. Without her testimony, we're back to where we started."

Eve responded to Grant. "You know… On Monday we started out to find Lane. Well, I guess we've done that part. Now, we have to save him. Then he can tell the secret."

Grant winked at Eve. "I think we can handle that—try for a good ending to a bad song."

She smiled and nodded.

In a very deliberate tone, he continued, "All the evidence will disappear, you know?"

"Washington is one big cover-up, Grant, but at least we can try to *uncover* some of it."

Very seriously, Grant made a concluding remark. "I'll bet, right now, if someone walked into Langley and said the name Lane, or 'HIV,' they'd get shot."

\* \* \*

The group synchronized their watches and went over the frequency changes for the radio channels. They would be changing every ten minutes, and the series was set.

The plan was solid and established. Everyone knew a good plan wasn't the only thing they needed. The challenge which remained would be the quality of the execution. As the age-old saying goes, "The biggest slip is between the cup and the lip."

Grant knew today depended on his people. They were of his choosing, and they were the best.

After he exchanged final comments with his team and cleared notes with the Rangers, he and Eve climbed into Bret's Jeep and started toward the reservation on 190.

As they passed the sign that read WOODVILLE 30, Grant checked his watch. It was five fifty a.m. They were close on the schedule of being at the gate by six.

Over the next hill they passed an old, abandoned service station, and Eve had a funny feeling, as though someone were looking over her shoulder or staring at the back of her head. Her intuition paid off. She turned, and behind the station, she recognized what she thought to be the same dark sedan that had followed her the day before.

"There they are, Grant."

It was almost a relief to see them and to know instead of wonder.

"That's the car that followed us yesterday," she told him. "Maybe it's Panther?"

"Hope so. That'd be good."

Eve quickly radioed the location and target. It would be up to the Rangers and Shelly to take it from there, and they would. Everything was going to work out; it had to. Today, at some level, the truth would be revealed. It would be nice if someone paid attention.

Grant pulled the Jeep into the reservation entrance, and Three Owls was there with the horse Grant had ridden the night before.

Without emotion or a long farewell, Grant leaned over and gave Eve a firm but passionate kiss. "Just stay here until you get the message," he said, "and then come on in. Make sure you stay on the main trail, and be careful."

Eve prepared to say something that Grant interpreted as emotional. He shook his head and silenced her with his fingers on her lips. Those Evee eyes, the ones that could see through the cold morning air into the center of his life, saw a reflection—hers.

He whispered, "For the record, I'll love you 'til I die."

He quickly mounted the horse and rode across the road, then trailed down the embankment toward the river.

As she wiped a tear from her eye, Eve smiled at Three Owls. He too had eyes that could see until tomorrow and he returned her smile as they both listened to the horse carry Grant toward the distant danger.

* * *

The sounds filtered through the morning silence: the charger snorting, the crunch of the small sticks the horse's hooves were driving into the dirt. Grant tried to refine his perspective. It was important that he had considered everything properly and done his best, because more than one person would have to live with the results of the day. Whether the day was won or not, there were certain losses that could never be regained.

Like Ranson.

He wondered about Jackson and Bearing-Haas. He asked himself if truth and justice had lost their meaning; evidently it had for some.

*How can these things happen? How can government become this corrupt? Can anyone stop it?*

There were many questions but few answers.

So he told himself, *the conclusion is a horseback ride at daybreak, and 'the way things are' being chased by 'the way things ought to be.'*

Grant had a clear vision of what he stood for. He knew if government agencies had been compromised, if covert activities were disregarding truth and life, he had an obligation to move in there like a Rough Rider and do what was right…what had to be done. Teddy Roosevelt said patriotism means *standing by the country*, not *standing by the government*.

He recalled the novel *Don Quixote* again. Cervantes wrote, "I was born for him, and he for me… I give him to you."

Whether out of fear or nervousness, Grant thought, *Maybe I should have walked away from this one. I may be chasing a windmill.*

After arriving at the familiar embankment and walking up to the tree with the two small boulders, he tied the horse's bridle to a tree limb. Grant walked slowly beside the creek bank, then up the path and continued toward the clearing. As he reached the edge of the small meadow, he stopped, watched, and waited.

He saw the oak tree standing next to the creek that wound among the pines. He was sure it was the one Three Owls had mentioned, as it appeared to have a better size and character than the rest, and it stood more or less alone. He studied the area and the creek and judged the distance across the small meadow.

As he carefully walked on, he wondered how the meadow might look with spring flowers, maybe bluebonnets. He would have to come back again when this was over and bring Eve, possibly in the spring.

The forest was silent. Grant didn't see or hear anything. As he approached the tree, he knelt at the water's edge and picked up a small stone. He tossed it into the creek and watched the splash. Then he surveyed the forest across the stream as the ripples disappeared.

He was preparing to retrieve another pebble when a voice spoke softly from somewhere close behind him—probably behind the tree.

"Keep doing what you're doing, and don't let on that anyone's here but you. Keep looking like you're just killing time. There's a sniper in the trees about thirty yards from where you came into the clearing. Don't talk when you're looking that way, or he'll see your lips move. He's got a scope on that rifle about the size of a basketball."

Grant followed the instructions and tossed another pebble. Then he turned so that his back was toward the original direction and responded, "We intercepted one of their transmissions last night, and there are probably two more out there somewhere."

"One," came the answer. "One of my traps west of here got the other." After a short pause, the voice added, "I hoped I'd get them all."

Grant selected another stone, adjusted his position, and looked casually at his watch. "I don't know how these guys were able to track you so closely."

"I let them," Lane responded. "I knew you'd have to catch them committing a crime. Well, I think the sniper is going to try and commit one."

"Why did you set this up? Why now?"

After a moment of silence, he responded, "I didn't really set it up; it's been there. I started to go crazy not being able to remember anything. They tried to make me forget. They told me not to remember. My father-in-law said, "*adapt*"; it wouldn't be good to know. Guess he was right."

Grant adjusted his position as Lane kept talking. "I had nightmares, but there were no answers, so I snooped around. Then things started happening so fast that I barely had time to skip town. I got help from a few people who knew what was happening after I made the Internet contacts, but for me the whole thing had been going on too long."

Lane kept remembering and Grant kept listening. "To answer your question about 'Why now?' this is their time schedule, not mine."

Grant knew it. "Is that your blood in Houston?"

The voice from the tree explained, "Yes. I wanted to make sure someone on the outside had it, if something happened to me." There was a moment of silence before Lane continued, "I realized my whole life has been shaped by something they won't admit ever happened."

Grant responded with the passphrase from the previous evening. "Got tired of endeavoring to persevere?"

"Something like that."

As Grant pitched another ripple-maker, the voice asked, "Did you wear the magic jacket?"

Grant turned his head nonchalantly toward the tree to hide his lip movement. "Yes. How did you know I'd know what it was?"

"Wade said you'd been by the house, so I talked to Veronica. She said you'd know. I was just being clever."

Grant allowed a break for silence. In the light chill, he listened to the birds and wondered if Shelly and the Rangers had located the Panther.

Then he said, "We're sitting ducks up here, you know. Backup won't come until something happens."

Lane was silent for a moment. "Yeah, that's the plan. Hope this works."

Grant tossed another nugget. "What's next?"

"Well, since my traps only got one of them, I guess we'll just walk out there. I figure that bastard's probably going to take a shot at me. I plan to keep moving my head so he'll have to take a body shot. Then you can get some backup and try to keep 'em from killing me."

"Wish me luck," Grant said.

"Yeah, good luck, but if something happens, don't blame yourself. It was my idea."

Grant asked, "Are you ready?"

The chilled forest was silent except for the distant screech of a hawk in early-morning flight.

"Just a minute," Lane said, "…while I say my prayers."

Grant said his.

After a moment Lane said, "Why don't you stand up and look back behind the tree like you hear someone coming? I'll be out of his line of sight for a minute. Then I'll come around there, and we'll head toward the trail."

Grant looked around, glanced at his watch, and waited. He pulled his 9mm out of its holster and cocked it. The tension grew.

He felt his heart speed up as his new companion walked around the tree. Lane looked up at the treetops like Lord Jim before the natives. His gaze appeared to ask the pines for help, or for answers.

Grant took a step forward, as if to introduce himself, and as Lane started toward him, a loud crack echoed through the air. A bullet slammed into Lane. The heart shot knocked Lane about two feet backward, and he landed on his back at the edge of the creek bank.

No sooner had Grant turned with his pistol than a second shot caught him in the chest, knocking him into the light brush next to Lane.

The sound of rifle fire reverberated in the trees. The sniper moved down from his perch and surveyed the scene through his scope. Both Grant and Lane lay sprawled and lifeless.

The assassin smiled. "Damn, I'm good."

He pulled out his two-way radio and depressed the button. "Panther, Cub One here, mission accomplished. I took him out. Transfer the money…and, oh, yeah, I gave you the Fed for free."

A crackling voice came back over the radio. "Say again."

"I said I gave you the damned Fed for free."

"Uh…roger that, Cub One."

After the transmission, things happened at a lightning pace—and all at once. Special Agent Anne Shelly relayed a message to the Rangers, the FBI backups, Hazling, Davis, Spencer, and Allen; and Eve, who heard the shots and was bouncing the Jeep down the riverbank trail toward the location where she and Grant had ridden the night before. The message was short, but everyone knew what it meant.

"This is Shelly. *I got it!* Repeat… *I got it!* Go get 'em."

Probably the first thing that happened was when Stonewall Sherman and Jesse James, who had been staking out the Panther-mobile, walked casually up to the auto with drawn .45s. Stonewall was on the driver side, and Jesse on the passenger. They flashed their Texas Ranger badges.

Of the two in the car, the driver rolled down his window and said something about being federal intelligence.

Sherman stuck his gun in the guy's ear, "In Texas it's against the law to kill people. We don't care who you work for."

He told them they had the right to remain silent, but he wouldn't suggest it. What the Rangers really wanted was the location of the other Cubs.

The company man shut up tight as a clam.

About the same time, the sniper moved toward the clearing to check his kills. Anyone favoring justice would have loved to see his face when his foot touched a wire. Of course, no one was there to watch, but any-one could imagine what a person might think in the fraction of a second when he realized it was a trip wire and a well-constructed trap was spin-ning a row of nine spikes on three levels into his torso.

Four stakes found the target, or more properly, the target found another one of Lane's traps. The rifle fell to the ground as the marks skewered into the man's right eye, left arm, center chest, and left thigh, and impaled him backward into a tree. It was a good trap. Too bad he didn't have a chance to scream.

The thud of the trap as it hit the tree resounded into the clearing.

Hearing the noise, one of the 'lifeless' bodies shallowly gasped, "Ought to take care of that one."

Shortly after the trap was sprung, Eve had taken the Jeep into the brush about as far as it could go, which was near the creek junction where Three Owls and Grant had dismounted the night before. She scurried up the incline and slowed when she saw Grant's horse. She continued over the trail toward the clearing and stopped at the edge of the meadow, where she drew her .38.

About the time she saw the bodies of Grant and Lane near the tree, Grant moved. Eve hesitated and looked around for the shooter. She watched as Grant began to recover, but after deciding the shooting was over, she looked back to the south and realized it wasn't. She saw a commotion in the bushes. Remembering there were more Cubs, she hesitated and focused on the movement within the undergrowth.

Sure enough, she saw a rifle barrel come out of the brush and point toward Grant.

Eve jumped up shouting, "Drop your weapon!"

As the weapon turned toward her, she rapid-fired five shots at the target, and the body fell to the edge of the clearing.

Although she was shaking from the flow of adrenalin, she crouched back into the brush and called out, "Grant, stay down."

He yelled back, "I think you must have gotten the last one! We got the other two with traps."

Grant and Lane stayed down in the grass, and after a few minutes waiting, with no other signs of movement, Eve cautiously entered the clearing.

"Mmmm-hmmm... Wow." Grant was regaining his breath as Eve rushed to the scene and threw her arms around him.

"Are you OK?"

He hugged her. "Thanks to you."

Lane rolled over and groaned. "Whoa...oh... What a trip...almost felt like...that one made it through..."

Relieved they were all right, Eve leaned away from Grant and asked, "Mr. Lane, are you OK?"

He groaned and nodded. "Ribs aren't."

"I'm—"

"Eve Delaney," Lane moaned again, "Glad you showed up when you did."

He managed a smile as he checked out the hole in his buckskin jacket and stuck his finger in the dent in his body armor.

Although Grant wasn't absolutely sure this was a successful encounter, he was relieved, but unfortunately for the trio, another uninvited remaining Cub, most likely number four, appeared at the far back edge of the clearing. He was another one of those guys who could kill without a reason.

He didn't say, "Drop your weapons" or even give a warning.

Aware his associate gunman had failed with the body shot, he took aim at the back of Lane's head. It was too late—not for Lane but for the shooter.

Sometimes two things happen at once, and it was a good thing for Lane that this was one of those times. The gunman pulled off one round at exactly a half-second after three shots were rapid-fired and struck him in the face, neck, and heart. As he fell, his shot missed its mark, not completely, but enough to drop the trajectory into the back of Lane's magic jacket. It knocked him forward onto the grass floor near the water's edge.

Delaney instinctively turned with her .38, as did Grant with his 9mm, but the show was over.

They looked back, and there stood CIA Agent Eldridge Jackson and Bret, the Blue Retriever, about twenty-five yards away at the edge of the brush.

Jackson casually walked over to the corpse and looked down at him. "That's the last of this bunch."

Bret agreed. "Looks like it."

The two walked over to Grant and Eve, who were attending to Lane's second round of groaning and heavy breathing.

Lane moaned below his gasps for breath. "Sons of bitches. Supposed to have been three of 'em."

Grant, still recovering, tried for some humor. "I think they lied about that."

Lane shook his head. Between gasps for breath, he said, "A bulletproof jacket…is a great thing. Keeps you from getting…killed…but those bullets…can sure ding you anyway."

Grant looked up and said, "A little surprised to see you here, Jackson."

"Sorry, Harris. It had to be a secret until we blew their cover. Your people did a good job. You found all the pieces."

Eve spoke up. "And we found out about your brother."

Jackson was silent while considering Eve's comment, then he said, "Well, this is almost over. Maybe we can get the rest of them, and he can rest in peace. I'm not sure I ever will."

After a short silence, Bret joined the conversation. "I heard a transmission about your getting the two on the highway."

Bret explained about tracking through the woods and finding three traps, one with a Cub hanging upside down with a spear through his neck and two that were still active. Lane told him they heard the third trap take out the sniper, and four traps was the total.

Two of the backup agents arrived from the primary trail, and Grant told everyone they needed to clean up the mess. Jackson was requested to lead Agents Davis and Allen to recover the four bodies to get them in the middle of the clearing. At the same time, Bret and Lane withdrew to the forest to disarm the remaining traps.

Grant sent up a flare, and Eve used her radio to call Shelly.

"Shell, send the chopper in."

All of this took place in less than fifteen minutes after Lane had walked out from behind that tree.

When the helicopter landed, Lasorta got off and ran over to Grant. "Good to see you, Chief," he said.

The agents started to load body bags, and Grant pointed to the one on the left, the one who had received Jackson's face shot.

"Call that one Benjamin Lane." He smiled at Lasorta, and they shared the moment of truth. Grant continued, "Jackson shot his face off. You can get the coroner to sign off on the death certificate, then send the body somewhere for immediate cremation. Make sure you get a blood sample and prints from Lane, so you can use it to confirm the identity. The other three are hit men too, so we'll need to trace their identities."

Grant looked over and pointed at the one Eve had shot.

"By the way, Davis, how many times did Delaney hit that one?"

"Looks like five."

Grant looked back at Eve and smiled. "Damn. I'll buy lunch."

Returning to Lane, Grant questioned, "How do you want to handle your 'death'? Does your whole family need to get out with you?"

Lane responded, "I wish it were that easy, but I think it'll be better if I'm just gone." Grant listened as Lane continued, "Veronica…well, she'll do better with having the insurance money…and a life she likes. The kids are almost grown, and, well, you just sneak Wade a clue, and the kids and I will be good to deal with it later."

Lane had many questions regarding the chase and the tactics of the day, but he didn't have time to ask them. Grant shook his hand and escorted him to David Lasorta.

"David, notify Lois Van Camp that we made a clean sweep. Tell her we have two in custody, and four of them paid the max price."

The helicopter took off with the four bodies, the medic, Lasorta, and a no-name civilian hitchhiker with a buckskin jacket that had two nasty tears in it—one in the front and one in the back. This was the beginning of the end.

* * *

A memorial service was held for Benjamin Lane back in McAllen. Veronica was distraught about the government corruption that had caused the disappearance and eventual death of her husband. However, she was able to collect the insurance money, liquidate the assets, and retain enough money to retire comfortably after her husband's departure.

Grant and Eve went back down the reservation hill with the idea of sharing their lives with one another…on a day they had won. They discussed the fact that they hadn't given it much time, but as Grant put it, it was the perfect recipe.

When they were alone and Grant captured the opportunity, he asked her, "What name do you want to be called today?"

Eve hugged him and held him like she was never going to let go. "How about Evangeline Justine Always Harris?"

"Good answer."

That was all it took. Their courtship included a couple of dinners on the Mexican border, a chase across the country, a late-night horseback ride, learning to eat Chinese food with chopsticks, removing a brick wall, engaging in a gun battle, spending a passionate evening in the pines, and listening to a couple of songs. They were engaged and then married…again…in a church, as fast as anyone can plan a wedding.

After Grant and Eve celebrated their honeymoon in the Bahamas, they flew to Australia on a very well deserved holiday. As an interesting highlight, when vacationing they made a 'new' acquaintance, a song-writer-poet named Grant Harrison.

After all, Lasorta didn't have much time to create the new identity. In addition, Lane and Grant did seem a lot alike, so in the continuing relationship, they had a lot in common, like birthdates and places—much more than just the circumstances that brought them together: the facts behind the disappearance of B.W. Lane.

* * *

*After 1998 the Defense Security Division was defunded and eliminated as an active branch of the US intelligence community. Since then, government records that were once available have continued to vanish. It is now difficult to prove the DSD ever existed. Although no information was publicly released regarding medical cures for certain diseases, in the mid-nineteen nineties new anti-retroviral therapies were released to the public. Subsequently, the virus responsible for AIDS began to surrender its reputation as an uncontrollable global plague. The media has never reported on research into the origin of the virus, nor has it fully disclosed the foundations for the cure.*

www.ingramcontent.com/pod-product-compliance
Lightning Source LLC
Chambersburg PA
CBHW070604130626

46556CB00001B/265